Smells Like Pirates

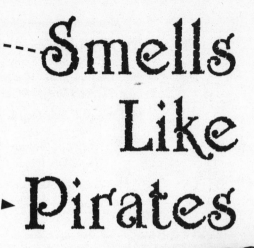

WOO Discard

by
Suzanne Selfors

LITTLE, BROWN AND COMPANY
New York Boston

Also by Suzanne Selfors:

The Imaginary Veterinary Series
The Sasquatch Escape
The Lonely Lake Monster
The Rain Dragon Rescue

The Smells Like Dog Series
Smells Like Dog
Smells Like Treasure
Smells Like Pirates

To Catch a Mermaid
Fortune's Magic Farm

Copyright © 2012 by Suzanne Selfors

Little, Brown and Company

Hachette Book Group
237 Park Avenue, New York, NY 10017
Visit our website at www.lb-kids.com

Little, Brown and Company is a division of Hachette Book Group, Inc.
The Little, Brown name and logo are trademarks of Hachette Book Group, Inc.

The publisher is not responsible for websites (or their content) that are not owned by the publisher.

First Paperback Edition: September 2013
First published in hardcover in November 2012 by Little, Brown and Company

Library of Congress Cataloging-in-Publication Data

Selfors, Suzanne.
Smells like pirates / Suzanne Selfors.
p. cm.—(Smells like dog)
Summary: "Homer thought membership in L.O.S.T., the mysterious Society of Legends, Objects, Secrets, and Treasures, would help him find pirate Rumpold Smeller's missing treasure. But when Homer's enemy Lorelei forms an evil organization called FOUND, Homer and Dog face an impossible decision: Work with Lorelei to find the prize once and for all, or abandon their lifelong quest to locate the treasure."—Provided by publisher.
ISBN 978-0-316-20596-2 (hc) / ISBN 978-0-316-20595-5 (pb)
[1. Adventure and adventurers—Fiction. 2. Dogs—Fiction. 3. Pirates—Fiction.
4. Secret societies—Fiction. 5. Mystery and detective stories.] I. Title.
PZ7.S456922Smp 2012
[Fic]—dc23
2012028738

10 9 8 7 6 5 4 3 2 1

RRD-C

Printed in the United States of America

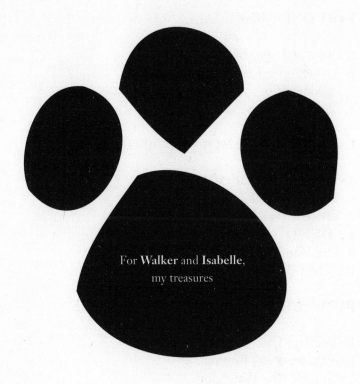

For **Walker** and **Isabelle**,
my treasures

CONTENTS

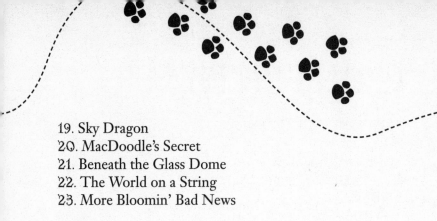

"Keep yer hands off me booty!"

—Rumpold Smeller the Pirate

Dear Reader,

Welcome to another Homer and Dog story. If you've read their other two adventures, then you know I always make a promise at the beginning of each book. But if this is your first Homer and Dog story, then I assume you've been living on a deserted island with only coconut bowling and sand sculpting for entertainment and I feel very sorry for you. Allow me to fill you in. The promise I make is that no dogs will die in this story, which is a huge relief for dog-lovers everywhere.

There is, however, a great deal of danger in this story. Because you'll probably scream out loud during the spine-tingling moments, you might consider reading this in a private place so people won't think you're crazy. As you near the end, there is a good chance you will faint from the thrill of it all, so I recommend wearing a helmet to protect your cranium. If you are a nail-biter, bite-proof gloves are in order.

Writing Homer and Dog's third adventure shook me to my very core, for never have I encountered so much excitement. When I finished, I took a long vacation to recover. After you've read this book, I highly recommend that you also take a vacation to clear your mind and settle your nerves. While you sit beside the hotel pool, be sure to read something very light, perhaps a story about rainbows or butterflies. But stay away from those horrid dead-dog stories. Never read those.

Happy reading,

L.O.S.T.

OFFICIAL CERTIFICATE OF MEMBERSHIP

It is hereby proclaimed that Mister Homer Winslow Pudding has been granted lifetime membership in the Society of Legends, Objects, Secrets, and Treasures and thusly reaps all of the society's questing benefits, which include access to the L.O.S.T. library, guidance and assistance from other members, and financial support.

If at any time or under any circumstances Mister Homer Winslow Pudding breaks his oath of secrecy, he shall be forever banned from the society.

Furthermore, if at any time or under any circumstances Mister Homer Winslow Pudding chooses to ignore L.O.S.T.'s purpose, which is to recover the world's treasures for the benefit and greater good of humankind, he shall be forever banned from the society.

Signed,

The Honorable Lord Mockingbird XVIII

President of L.O.S.T.

DISCLAIMER: L.O.S.T. IS NOT RESPONSIBLE FOR FAILED TREASURE QUESTS OR FOR ANY UNTIMELY OR TIMELY DEATHS DURING THE PURSUIT OF TREASURE.

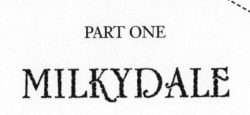

PART ONE

MILKYDALE

1

Sweet and Sour Sixteen

It was a nearly perfect morning on the Pudding Goat Farm.

The sun rose with the rooster's crowing, then gently shone through Homer Pudding's bedroom window, tickling Homer's cheeks with its long, warm fingers. A songbird settled on the windowsill, the notes of its sweet melody dancing through the air. The scents of huckleberry pancakes and sizzling bacon wafted up the stairs, filling the bedroom with deliciousness. And a loving voice called—

"Get out of bed, you big dork!"

Okay, so it wasn't a loving voice. It was a moody, bossy voice, and it belonged to Homer's sister, Gwendolyn Maybel Pudding.

If she knew my secrets, Homer thought, *she wouldn't call me a dork*. He yawned and rubbed crust from his eyes, then stared up at his sister's scowling face. "What time is it?"

"Do I look like your personal alarm clock?" she snarled. "Mom told me to tell you to get out of bed. So *get out of bed*." She stomped out the door, her white lab coat billowing behind her.

Gwendolyn's foul personality was, according to Mrs. Pudding, a direct result of her age. Fifteen years, three hundred and fifty-nine days, to be exact, which made her a teenager. "Just because you've got pimples is no reason to be so rude," Homer mumbled as the lab coat disappeared around the corner.

"Urrrr," agreed the dog lying beside him.

Although he looked like an ordinary basset hound, the dog lying next to Homer was not one bit ordinary. An ordinary basset hound has a highly tuned sense of smell. Because the world tends to be a smelly place, an ordinary basset hound spends a great deal of time being led around by its nose. Homer's dog, however, had been born with a nose that didn't work quite right. Dog's nose

4

didn't smell rotting garbage or frisky rabbits or grandma's pot roast. Dog's nose smelled only one thing—treasure. And that was Homer's most treasured secret.

Dog rolled onto his extra-long back and stuck his extra-short legs straight up in the air, presenting his white belly for a morning scratch. Homer obliged. Dog had arrived at the Pudding farm earlier that year, and since then, he'd spent almost every night sleeping next to Homer. Some of those nights had been filled with danger and excitement as Homer pursued his dream of becoming a famous treasure hunter. The month of August, however, had proven to be a bore—day after day of the same blue-sky weather, day after day of the same old farm chores, and day after day of wondering when adventure would come knocking.

"Urrrr?" Dog complained when Homer stopped scratching.

"We'd better get downstairs," Homer said, "or Gwendolyn might eat our pancakes."

While many kids got to sleep in during the summer months, dreaming of bike riding, swimming, and kite flying, the Pudding kids always got up early. This was the reality of life on a goat farm.

After dressing in his work clothes, a pair of jeans and a plaid shirt, Homer did what he did most mornings—he checked under his bed. Lying on his belly, he pushed aside a pair of dirty socks, then pried free a loose floor-board. He peered into the hole and counted. His secret items were all in attendance: his L.O.S.T. membership certificate, his professional treasure-hunting clothes, and a book called *Rare Reptiles I Caught and Stuffed*, which contained the most famous pirate treasure map in the world. Why was it the most famous pirate treasure map in the world? Because it had been drawn by Rumpold Smeller, a pirate who spent most of his life traveling the world, amassing a treasure said to be greater than any-one could imagine. And Homer secretly owned this map.

With a smile, he returned the floorboard to its place. All was well beneath his bed.

Homer led Dog down the hallway, down the stairs, and into the kitchen. The swirling scents of breakfast pulled Homer like a leash. The Pudding kitchen was a charming place. Checkered curtains framed a window that overlooked a vegetable garden. Farm-animal mag-nets covered the refrigerator, and a blue pitcher of field flowers sat on the counter.

Mrs. Pudding bustled around the stove, her brown curls bouncing. Mr. Pudding sat at the end of the kitchen table reading the Sunday *City Paper*, his overall straps hanging at his waist. Gwendolyn sat slumped in her chair, slurping her orange juice. Across from her on a bench sat Squeak, Homer's little brother. He stopped pushing his toy truck around the table and smiled. "Hi, Homer."

"Hi, Squeak."

Dog waddled to his dish, his tail wagging. Because Dog couldn't smell anything but treasure, he wasn't a picky eater. In fact, he'd been known to eat shoes, wood, worms, and toenail clippings. Mrs. Pudding often filled his bowl with leftovers, but sometimes Squeak tried to sneak in weird things—which is why Homer always stopped at the dog bowl first. "Squeak," he scolded as he picked out a snail, "please don't feed gastropods to Dog."

Squeak snickered.

As Dog inhaled his meal, Homer sat in his usual chair at the table's end, opposite Mr. Pudding. He sighed and stared at his empty plate. He sighed and stared out the window. He tapped his fingers on the tablecloth. Another long, hot, boring, totally routine August day.

To an outsider, this scene in the Pudding kitchen would appear normal—an ordinary family sitting down to an ordinary breakfast. But this was no ordinary family. Although Homer looked like a regular kind of kid, at twelve years of age, he was the youngest member of the Society of Legends, Objects, Secrets, and Treasures—a secret organization dedicated to treasure hunting. Although Homer's family knew Homer wanted, more than anything in the world, to be a treasure hunter, they did not know that he actually *was* a treasure hunter, for Homer had sworn an oath of secrecy. It made him kind of sad that he couldn't tell his family about how he and Dog had jumped out of an airplane, or how they'd found a cave of harmonic crystals, or how they'd defeated the evil Madame la Directeur. But Homer knew that an oath of secrecy was nothing to mess around with.

"I've been thinking about a theme," Mrs. Pudding said as she slid pancakes and bacon onto her family's plates.

"A what?" Mr. Pudding said, turning a page of his newspaper.

"A theme for Gwendolyn's sweet-sixteen party."

Sweet sixteen? Homer thought as he poured syrup onto his pancakes. *More like sour sixteen.*

"I was thinking a butterfly theme, or a pony theme." Mrs. Pudding smiled lovingly, the gold flecks in her brown eyes sparkling. She sat next to Gwendolyn. "How about a teddy bear theme?"

"Mom," Gwendolyn groaned, sinking lower in her chair. "I'm not a baby. Those themes are creepy."

"I like teddy bears," Squeak said, syrup dripping down his chin. Dog moseyed across the room and stood right under Squeak's feet. Since nearly half of Squeak's food ended up on the floor, this was a rewarding place to stand.

Mrs. Pudding stirred her coffee. "If you don't like my suggestions, then what theme would you like, Gwendolyn dear?"

"Roadkill," Gwendolyn replied.

Mrs. Pudding gasped. Squeak giggled. Mr. Pudding closed the newspaper and scowled. But Homer didn't flinch. It made perfect sense that his sister suggested a roadkill theme. She wanted, with all her heart, to become a Royal Taxidermist for the Museum of Natural History. She had her own laboratory out in the shed, where she practiced the art of stuffing dead animals.

"And it's got to be fresh roadkill," Gwendolyn said. "No maggots."

"Now, sweetie," Mrs. Pudding said, "you can't expect me to decorate with roadkill."

"Why not? It's my birthday."

"Forget it," Mr. Pudding said, slapping his hand on the table. "No daughter of mine is going to have a roadkill party. You'll choose one of those nice themes your mother suggested."

Gwendolyn darted to her feet and uttered the same statement she'd uttered yesterday, and the day before, and the day before that. "You are totally! Ruining! My life!"

"No one is ruining your life," Mrs. Pudding said. "We want you to have a special sweet-sixteen party. In fact, your father and I bought you a very nice present. And Homer went to town last week to shop for you, didn't you, Homer?"

This time, Homer flinched. He'd gone to town to buy Gwendolyn's birthday present—that much was true. But he'd taken his shovel and metal detector with him and, well, because the detector kept beeping and because Homer kept digging, he forgot all about Gwendolyn. The search for a birthday present wasn't as interesting as the search for treasure, even though that day's treasure had turned out to be nothing but a bunch of rusty tin cans.

"Uh, yeah, I got a present," Homer lied. He'd go shopping that afternoon, as soon as he'd finished his chores.

Gwendolyn peered at Homer through her long brown bangs. "You got me a present?"

"Yep." He stuffed a whole pancake into his mouth, just in case she asked any more questions.

Gwendolyn smiled wickedly. "If you bought my present, then it's hidden somewhere in the house, isn't it? I bet I can find it."

"Gwendolyn Maybel Pudding," Mrs. Pudding said. "You'll have to wait for your party to open your presents. Now sit down and eat your breakfast."

Huckleberries burst in Homer's mouth as he chewed.

His mind raced. What kind of present do you get a moody sister who spends her summer days stuffing dead squirrels and gophers? A gift certificate to Ice Cream World didn't seem quite right.

Just then, barking arose in the yard. Max, Gus, and Lulu, the farm dogs, were upset about something. Dog, who'd been licking syrup from Squeak's fingers, scurried to the kitchen door and joined in the barking. "What's all the ruckus?" Mr. Pudding asked.

A knock sounded on the kitchen door. Mr. Pudding pulled his overall straps over his shoulders and went to answer it. "Well, hello there," he said. "What are you doing here?"

The rest of the Pudding family turned and looked toward the open doorway, but Mr. Pudding was blocking their view. *It wouldn't be the mail lady*, Homer thought, *not on a Sunday. Maybe it's one of the neighbors.*

"Good morning," a voice said. "I say, is Homer up and about? I have rather important news."

Homer's heart skipped a beat. He knew that voice.

2

A Once-in-
a-Lifetime
Opportunity

A man stepped into the kitchen. He tucked his long black hair behind his ears and looked around. His gaze landed on Homer.

Homer scrambled out of his chair. "Hi, Ajitabh."

Ajitabh (pronounced AAAH-jih-tahb) did not return Homer's smile. He narrowed his dark eyes and ran his hand over his thin mustache and pointy beard. A doctor of inventology, Ajitabh was a fellow member of L.O.S.T. He'd been a trusted friend of Homer's treasure-hunting uncle, who'd died earlier that year, and he was now Homer's trusted mentor. The rest of the Pudding family knew Ajitabh from the Milkydale County Fair, where Dog had led a wild chase that resulted in the destruction of the beloved gunnysack slide. Ajitabh, inventor extraordinaire, built a new and improved slide, to everyone's approval.

"Hello, Homer." His tone was serious. He leaned over to pet Dog. "Hello, Dog." Dog *thwapp*ed his tail against Ajitabh's leg.

Mrs. Pudding hurried over to the cupboard and grabbed a plate. "You'll join us for breakfast?" She set it on the table, but Ajitabh shook his head.

"That would be delightful, but time is of the essence," he said.

"What's your important news?" Mr. Pudding asked.

"Quite right." Ajitabh rolled up the sleeves of his white shirt, then reached into the back pocket of his khaki pants and handed an envelope to Homer. "It's an invitation."

Homer half expected the envelope to be secured with a L.O.S.T. seal, but that wasn't the case. The envelope was as plain as could be—no seal, no return address, nothing. He opened it and pulled out a piece of paper.

"What is it?" Mrs. Pudding asked.

Homer read the letter aloud.

To: Homer W. Pudding
Pudding Goat Farm
Grinning Goat Road
Milkydale

From: Lewis Dimknob, Royal Cartographer
Map of the Month Club Headquarters
Boulevard of Destinations
The City

Congratulations, Mr. Pudding.

Your name has been drawn at random from our list of subscribers. I am pleased to inform you that you have been awarded a VIP tour of our headquarters. This tour is a once-in-a-lifetime opportunity that will not be offered again.

We eagerly await your arrival on Monday, August 20, at noon precisely.

Signed,
Lewis Dimknob, Royal Cartographer

"Wow," Homer said. "This is really cool. I love the Map of the Month Club."

"VIP?" Gwendolyn grumbled. "How come Homer keeps getting these VIP invitations, huh? What's up with that?"

This was, in fact, Homer's second VIP invitation. *VIP* stands for "very important person." The first invitation had come from the Museum of Natural History and had led Homer to the discovery of Madame la Directeur's lair and a near-death escape from a man-eating tortoise. This invitation sounded a bit safer. "Can I go?" Homer asked. "I'd really like to go."

"August twentieth is tomorrow," Mrs. Pudding said worriedly. "That's not much notice."

"Sincerest apologies," Ajitabh said in his lilting accent. "As a board member of the Map Club, I was asked to deliver the invitation last week but was waylaid by circumstances beyond my control." He shot a serious glance at Homer. "We need to leave immediately, old chap."

Homer looked yearningly at his father. Was the boredom of August about to end?

"How long will he be gone?" Mr. Pudding asked.

"A bit of uncertainty there," Ajitabh said. "The Map of the Month Club's library alone covers three floors. I have reserved a room for us at a very nice City hotel. I'll act as Homer's guardian. You needn't worry about a thing."

"It sounds like a wonderful opportunity," Mrs. Pudding said to Ajitabh. "Homer loves maps. He's always loved maps. But he'll need to be back for his sister's sweet-sixteen party. It's next Saturday."

"Righteo. That shouldn't be a problem."

"I can go?" Homer beamed, the corners of his smile nearly reaching his ears. But Ajitabh didn't smile. His eyebrows knotted as if twisted by troubling thoughts. Why wasn't he happy? Homer stepped closer to Ajitabh. And why didn't he smell like cloud cover? Homer glanced out the kitchen window. Instead of a cloudcopter, Ajitabh's usual method of transportation, a black limousine waited in the driveway.

"You can go," Mr. Pudding said. "But Gwendolyn will have to cover your chores."

"No way!" Gwendolyn blurted, her cheeks turning red. "Homer gets to go on another vacation and I'm stuck here doing his chores? I'm too busy to do Homer's chores."

"I'll do Homer's chores," Squeak offered.

"I'll make it up to you when I get back," Homer told his sister. "I'll do your chores for a whole extra week."

Gwendolyn chewed on her lower lip, her eyes narrowed in thought. "You really want to go?"

"Yes."

"Then tell me where you hid my present."

"Gwendolyn Maybel Pudding," Mrs. Pudding said. "You will wait until your birthday to open your presents, and that is final."

"Fine!" Gwendolyn pointed at Homer. "But he's doing my chores for an entire month."

"Agreed," Homer said. He held back a sigh of relief. He'd expected to do his sister's chores for an entire year.

"I'll help you pack," Mrs. Pudding said.

If Homer had packed on his own, he would have reached into one of his drawers, grabbed some random clothes, then stuffed them into a backpack as fast as he could. But Mrs. Pudding didn't want her son going anywhere without clean underwear and socks. "Wait," she said as he grabbed the backpack. "You almost forgot your toothbrush." She slid it into one of the pockets. "You'll get cavities if you don't brush."

Homer didn't care if moss grew on his teeth. He just wanted to jump into that limo with Ajitabh and get off the farm.

"I had dreams of becoming a cartographer," Mr. Pudding was telling Ajitabh when Homer hurried back into the kitchen. "Homer gets his love of maps from me."

"Let's go," Homer said, grabbing Dog's blue leash.

After hugging everyone good-bye, except for Gwendolyn, who'd disappeared, Homer flew down the front porch steps. With a grunt and a heave, he pushed Dog into the limousine. Then he climbed in and settled on the soft leather seat. Ajitabh climbed in next to him. "Drive on," Ajitabh said. The driver's outline was blurry through the dark glass panel that separated the front and back seats. The engine started.

"Did you bring your coin?" Ajitabh asked.

Homer reached under his shirt, where a coin hung from a chain. It was his official membership coin with the letters *L.O.S.T.* engraved on one side and a treasure chest engraved on the other side. "Yeah, I've got it."

The goats watched as the limousine headed down the Pudding driveway and onto Grinning Goat Road. Homer looked back at the house. Mrs. Pudding and Squeak waved from the front porch. Mr. Pudding headed toward the barn. But why was Gwendolyn standing in Homer's bedroom, staring out the window? She didn't wave or smile. Was it because he got to go on a little vacation and she didn't? He'd be sure to bring her back a nice birthday present.

"Hey, Ajitabh," Homer said as Dog settled at his feet. "Why do I need my membership coin if we're going to the Map of the Month Club?"

"We aren't going to the Map of the Month Club, old chap. The invitation is fake. I lied to your parents."

"You lied?" An eerie tickle crept up Homer's spine. "Then where are we going?"

Ajitabh frowned. "Homer, I'm afraid I'm the bearer of bad news."

3

Prisoner #90

The prisoner sat behind a security window made of extra-thick glass. She wore no makeup or jewelry, and her short black hair was slicked back behind her ears. The blue stripes of her prison pajamas matched her serious eyes. When she spoke, her voice slithered through a speaker.

"The map is hidden in a book called *Rare Reptiles I Caught and Stuffed*," she said.

The visitor rustled nervously in the chair on the other

side of the window. The room's cold air had awakened goose pimples on the visitor's arms. "The map?"

"Yes, the map," the prisoner said. "The *only* map anyone cares about. Rumpold Smeller's map, of course. Are you stupid or something?"

"You're calling *me* stupid?" The visitor frowned. "I'm not the one in jail."

A frustrated growl vibrated through the speaker as the prisoner's face turned red. "I wouldn't be in here if that overfed Pudding kid and his mangy dog hadn't interfered with my plans."

"You wouldn't be in here, Madame, if you hadn't stolen all the gemstones from the Museum of Natural History."

"Well, you do have a point." The prisoner, whose full name was Madame la Directeur, patted a rebellious lock of hair back into place.

"Some people think you should be convicted of murder," the visitor said. "Some people think you turned your turtle into a man-eating monster on purpose."

"Tortoise," Madame corrected. "Edith is a tortoise, not a turtle." Her tone turned sad, as if she missed the carnivorous beast.

"Whatever. The fact is, that monster ate Homer's uncle, and some people think you planned it."

"Mean-spirited people can say what they like. There's no proof."

The visitor's eyes narrowed. "Let's stop wasting time. Why did you call me here?"

Madame looked over her shoulder. A guard sat, reading a magazine, in a chair in the far corner of the room. Two other prisoners had finished their conversations and were heading back to their cells. Madame leaned closer to the microphone, lowering her voice to a whisper. "I thought the book was gone. But I've had a lot of time in solitary confinement to think about it. Edith did not digest the book." The visitor leaned closer to the speaker, trying to catch every secret word. "Edith swallowed the book that contains Rumpold's map. I saw her swallow it, and I thought the map was gone forever. But I'd forgotten that Edith can't digest paper. She can digest radioactive nuclear waste and people, but paper always disagrees with her. It comes back up. So that means she ate the book, but she *didn't* digest it."

"Two minutes left," the guard announced.

"So where is it?" the visitor asked. "Hurry. There's not much time."

Madame scowled. "The fat kid has it."

"How do you know he has it?"

"Intuition. I can feel it in my bones." She clenched her

trembling fingers into fists. "He's a Pudding. The map always finds its way back to a Pudding."

"Why are you telling me this?" the visitor asked. "What good does it do you? You're stuck in here. Even if you are correct and Homer has the map, you can't get it. You can't search for treasure from a jail cell."

"I'm telling you this because I don't want that meddling kid to find Rumpold's treasure."

"You'd rather I found it?"

Madame la Directeur pressed her palms against the window. She breathed rapidly, anger seeping from every inch of her being. "Of course I don't want you to find it," she snarled. "I'm the one who deserves that treasure. But those Puddings are the bane of my existence. I'll do whatever it takes to keep another Pudding from outmaneuvering me, even if it means hiring you."

The guard cleared his throat. "Visiting hours are over."

Madame removed her hands from the glass and stood. She took a long breath, then smoothed out her crumpled prison pajamas. Before turning to leave, she said one last thing to the visitor. "Do not double-cross me again."

The visitor shivered, for the look on Madame's face was as cold as the air-conditioned room.

4

Bloomin'
Bad News

W hat kind of bad news?" Homer asked as
the limousine turned down Peashoot Lane
and crossed the bridge over Milky Creek.
"Bloomin' bad news," Ajitabh said.

Homer gripped his membership coin. "Are they going
to kick me out of L.O.S.T.?" he asked. "Did they decide
I'm too young?"

"No."

What else could it be? Homer remembered the morning when he'd learned his uncle Drake had died. His

chest tightened at the possibility that someone else he loved was gone. "Has someone died?" Ajitabh nodded. "Not Zelda," Homer whispered. He reached down until he felt Dog's warm back. "Please not Zelda."

"Zelda is fine." Ajitabh folded his hands on his lap and stared out the window as the limo passed through the little village of Milkydale. A group of kids sat on the mercantile porch, eating ice cream bars. Carpenters pounded nails into the framework of the new Milkydale library. Firefighters washed one of the Milkydale Volunteer Fire Brigade trucks. "Lord Mockingbird has died."

"Oh." Homer stopped petting Dog and sank into the depths of the leather seat. It was sad news, definitely, but not totally unexpected. The Honorable Lord Mockingbird XVIII, the president of L.O.S.T., must have been a hundred years old, at least. "He told me he was very sick."

"Quite right. There's no reason to suspect foul play. It was his time."

Homer looked around the limo. The silhouette of a small bird was painted on each window. The letters L. M. XVIII were painted in gold on the ceiling. "Is this his car?" Homer asked.

"Yes." Ajitabh stroked one side of his mustache. "The thing is, His Lordship's death leaves us in a bit of a pickle."

"What do you mean?"

"Lord Mockingbird's been a steady presence in our organization. He's upheld the traditions of L.O.S.T. But his death forces us to elect a new president. If the wrong person is elected, I daresay the very fabric of L.O.S.T. could be torn."

Homer cringed. He knew exactly what Ajitabh meant. The purpose of L.O.S.T. was to share the treasures of the world with the public, rather than using them for private gain. But there were some in the group who, even though they'd taken an oath to follow this rule, yearned to change it so they could become rich.

"There are dark personalities in our organization," Ajitabh said. "Lord Mockingbird kept them in their places, but I worry they will see this as an opportunity to rise and try to sway the rest. Greed is a condition of being human—we all can suffer from it."

Homer swallowed. Sometimes he dreamed of bringing jewels home to his mother. Was that greed?

"L.O.S.T., as we know it, could cease to exist," Ajitabh said.

"Cease to exist?" Homer nearly teared up. Just when he'd become a member? He hadn't even had the chance to go on a L.O.S.T.-sponsored treasure quest. How could he find Rumpold's treasure on his own? He needed

L.O.S.T.—museums and universities everywhere needed L.O.S.T.

But then he smiled as a brilliant idea popped into his head. He scooted closer to Ajitabh. "You should be the next president. And then everything will stay the same. You'd be a great president. Everyone would vote for you."

For the first time since their morning reunion, Ajitabh smiled. "By Jove, that's kind of you, Homer, but I've no desire to get caught up in the paperwork and all that administrative rubbish. I'm not an office sort of fellow. Besides, I'm busy inventing a robotic gold detector."

"Then who will it be?" Homer asked.

"There's no bloomin' way to tell. The funeral is tonight. Most of the membership will attend. There will be much to discuss."

"Is that where we're going? To His Lordship's funeral?"

Ajitabh nodded. Then he placed his hand on Homer's shoulder and squeezed. "I know you want L.O.S.T. to assist you in your quest for Rumpold's treasure, but that will not happen if the wrong person is elected."

A knot formed in Homer's stomach. He'd promised his uncle that he'd continue the search for Rumpold's treasure. He owned the map. It was his inheritance—his destiny—to find that treasure. No one would take that away from him. "Then we'll have to make sure the right person is elected," he said.

Ajitabh stretched out his legs and closed his eyes. "It's a long trek to The City, Homer. I suggest you take a nap. And your hound, too. We've got a devil of a night ahead of us."

Dog was already snoring.

PART TWO

THE MOCKINGBIRD HOTEL

5

The Cleaning Lady's Warning

The limousine drove down a wide boulevard, skyscrapers looming on either side. As twilight descended, lampposts flickered, then glowed yellow.

They'd arrived in The City, a place as different from Milkydale as cigar ashes are from goat milk. There were no rolling hills dappled with daisies and clover. The only dappling came from the dark shadows that lurked between buildings. There were no quaint farmhouses. People lived in tall apartment buildings. There were no brooks that bubbled beneath covered bridges. If any bubbling was heard, it came from the sewer grates that sat in the middle of the busy intersections. To Homer, The City was a concrete labyrinth, which is a fancy word for *maze*. Each street led to another, each crowded with cars, taxis, and buses. Pedestrians, with important places to go, moved in a constant stream along the sidewalks. Even with the day near its end, the hustle and bustle continued.

Dog stood on Homer's lap, his nose pressed against the limousine window. *Does he remember this place?* Homer wondered. A few months back, they'd come to The City looking for answers. Did Dog remember meeting the evil Madame la Directeur? Did he remember the nearly deadly ride in the Snootys' elevator or how he almost got eaten by the same tortoise that had eaten Homer's uncle?

But as Dog looked out the window, he didn't tremble or whine. Rather, he wagged his tail. Maybe he was remembering the good stuff that had happened in The City. A bowl of tomato soup served by a girl with pink hair. A tour of The City Public Library. And best of all, the moment when Edith the tortoise upchucked the book that contained Rumpold Smeller's map.

The limousine pulled up to the front of a stone building. Four flags, each with a white background and the black silhouette of a bird, hung above the building's entry. A bellhop dressed in a red uniform with a red pillbox hat and white gloves opened the limo door. A black band wound around his forearm. "Welcome to the Mockingbird Hotel," he said as Ajitabh and Homer got out.

Homer set his backpack on the curb, then reached back in. After he tugged the leash a few times, Dog plopped onto the sidewalk. As Dog peered up at the building, his tail began to wag. "Lord Mockingbird owned this hotel?" Homer asked.

"It's been in his family for generations," Ajitabh said.

Lord Mockingbird had been one of Dog's previous owners. *Dog must have lived here*, Homer realized.

As the limo drove away, the bellhop took Homer's backpack and carried it through a revolving glass door and into the hotel.

"We'd best hurry," Ajitabh said. With precise timing, he stepped into the revolving door and disappeared. Homer grabbed the end of Dog's leash and started to follow.

"Urrrr." Dog stiffened his back legs.

"Come on," Homer urged, tugging on Dog's leash.

Dog froze. He stared at Homer with sad, red-rimmed eyes, his ears seeming droopier than ever. This was his "I'm-not-budging-and-you-can't-make-me" stance.

Homer was well familiar with this posture. Begging never helped, but he tried anyway. "Come on, *please*. We need to go inside."

Dog groaned and lay on his belly, transforming his sausagelike body into something like a bag of cement. So Homer tried a technique that had always worked for his mother. When the Pudding kids acted up in public—arguing in the movie theater about who got to hold the popcorn bucket or riding the cart down the grocery-store aisles—Mrs. Pudding would simply say, "You're embarrassing me," and the kids would feel bad and stop acting like primates.

So Homer crouched next to Dog and whispered, "You're embarrassing me."

Dog turned his face away.

"Basset hounds don't like revolving doors," the bell-hop said as he stepped back outside. "I know that because a basset used to live here. He always had to be carried through the door."

"Homer," Ajitabh called, "get a move on, old chap. They're waiting."

"Why do you have to be so stubborn?" Homer slid his hands under Dog's belly. Lifting a full-grown basset hound is best left to a muscle-builder or a giant. It's a tricky maneuver because if you grab the back end, the front end droops. And if you grab the front end, the back

34

end droops. With a groan and a grunt, Homer managed to get Dog's rump about a foot off the ground. "You need to go on a diet," he grumbled.

Taking a deep breath, he heaved Dog higher and stumbled toward the door. A few steps forward, a step back, then forward again. Dog's ears swayed with Homer's uneven steps. Homer missed the door's first opening, then missed the second and third openings. He managed to dart into the fourth opening. Once inside, he hurried to match the door's rotation but missed the exit into the hotel. Dog moaned as they went around again. And again. "What are you complaining about? You don't have to carry *me*." Just when his arms felt like they might fall off, Homer lunged out of the revolving door and into the hotel lobby.

After they landed in a heap on the floor, Dog wiggled from Homer's arms and waddled over to a potted plant, where he raised his leg for a little piddle. Fortunately, the lobby was empty, so no one noticed. Homer got to his feet, wiped sweat from his brow, then looked around. A brass bell sat on the check-in counter. Comfy chairs were tucked into the lobby's corners. A bank of elevators lined the wall. But where was Ajitabh?

Footsteps approached.

Just as Dog raised his leg for a second piddle, a cleaning lady hurried around the corner. An assortment of stains covered her gray dress and white apron. Athletic socks reached to her knees. In one hand she carried a mop, in the other a bucket of sudsy water. She stopped next to the potted plant and glared at Dog.

"Sorry," Homer said, stepping away from the little puddle.

The cleaning lady made a *tsk-tsk* sound. She adjusted the plastic shower cap that covered her gray hair, then stuck the mop into the bucket. She glared at Dog again. Dog scratched at a flea.

"I'm really sorry," Homer said. "He usually doesn't do that inside."

After swirling the mop, she pulled it from the bucket and began to clean up Dog's mess.

The scent of bleach filled the lobby. Homer wasn't sure what to do. He'd apologized twice. And Ajitabh was waiting. So he took the end of Dog's leash and began to walk away.

"Not so fast," the cleaning lady said sternly.

"Do you want me to clean it up?" Homer asked. He glanced at her name tag. It was blank.

She stopped mopping and crooked her finger. "Come closer."

Homer gulped. He didn't like the way she'd narrowed her eyes. And that blueberry-sized mole on the end of her nose was gruesome. He took a hesitant step toward her. "I said I was sorry."

Then she said something under her breath.

"What was that?" Homer asked, stepping closer. The cleaning lady's face was level with his. Her gaze was fierce.

"Beware the lost and found," she said quietly.

Homer frowned. What did that mean? "Uh, okay." He tried not to stare at the mole. "Well, I need to be going." Dog stuck his nose into the bucket, attempting to drink the sudsy water, but Homer pulled him away.

"Beware the lost and found," the cleaning woman repeated, louder this time. Did she think that by saying it louder, it would suddenly make sense?

Homer shrugged. "Okay," he said. "Good to know."

With a grumble, the cleaning woman collected her mop and bucket and hurried from the lobby. As she disappeared around the corner, a *ding* sounded.

Dog barked, his tail wagging madly, as a boy with wiry black hair stepped out of one of the elevators.

6

A Graveyard of Mockingbirds

Hercules!" Homer called, a smile bursting forth. Dog pulled the leash from Homer's grip as he bounded toward the elevator. The boy, whose name was Hercules Simple, entered the lobby. He set three boxes on the floor, then knelt and scratched Dog's rump. "Hi, Dog. How've you been?" Dog's back legs did their little happy dance.

Homer was surprised to see his friend, even though they were both members of L.O.S.T. "I didn't know if you'd be here," Homer said. "Lofty Spires is a long way away."

"I just got here this afternoon." Hercules stood and stuck his hands in his pockets. He wore his usual attire—jeans and a long-sleeved rugby shirt. This one had red and white stripes. "Ajitabh said the membership would be electing a new president so they'd need me for the paperwork. Being L.O.S.T.'s records keeper means I have to be at all these important events. I hope this doesn't take long. I've got to get home to study for the World's Spelling Bee. It's in one month."

"I hope you win again."

"Me, too." Hercules scratched his wide nose, which was dotted with pimples. Then his expression turned serious. "I wish I didn't have to be here. I hate funerals."

"I've never been to one," Homer said.

"Well, they're always sad. And they're always long." Hercules's gaze settled on the spot where the cleaning lady had been mopping. "Better not walk over there. You could slip and break your neck."

Same old Hercules, always worried about everything. Despite the fact that a funeral was about to take place, a warm feeling filled Homer's chest. Even though he and Hercules were different in many ways, they'd become the best of friends. The boys had known each other for only a few months, but they had faced near death in a coliseum, had jumped out of an airplane, and had almost been killed by a bear. Those are the kinds of experiences that bond people. Plus, Hercules had saved Dog's life. And that was a huge plus.

The truth was, Homer had no real friends back in Milkydale. All his classmates thought he was a weirdo. But so what if he used to wear a compass to school? So what if he preferred digging holes to playing dodgeball? So what if he knew the names of every great treasure hunter but didn't know who had won the World Series or who had the best batting average? He had a treasure-sniffing dog!

"What's in the boxes?" Homer asked.

"Oh, right." Hercules handed one to Homer. It had his name written on it. "Ajitabh said we're supposed to change into these new clothes. There's one for Dog, too."

They headed to the gentlemen's lavatory—a huge room of polished marble and gleaming mirrors. The boys set the boxes next to a row of sinks with mocking-bird faucets. Homer opened his. Inside, a note card lay on perfectly folded tissue paper.

Traditional Mourning Attire
Designed and Fabricated by Victor Tuffletop,
Official Tailor of L.O.S.T.
For Mr. Homer W. Pudding

The two large boxes contained identical clothing—a pair of black pants, a white button-down shirt, a black vest, a black suit coat with long coattails, a black tie, a pair of white gloves, and a black top hat. Hercules showed Homer how to tie the tie. "Never make the knot too tight or you could suffocate." Then they pulled on the gloves and set the top hats on their heads.

"This wool is going to make me hot and itchy," Hercules said, running his hand over the suit coat. "I'm sure to get a rash."

Homer inspected his reflection. "We look like we're in a movie or something." He glanced at his sneakers. They didn't match the fancy outfit, but since no shoes were included, they'd have to do.

He opened the third, smaller box.

Traditional Canine Mourning Attire
Designed and Fabricated by Victor Tuffletop,
Official Tailor of L.O.S.T.
For Dog

A black vest was the only garment in the box. It fit perfectly around Dog's tummy.

"They're waiting for us in the graveyard," Hercules said.

The lobby was still empty. They stuffed their day

clothes into the boxes and stored them behind the reception counter along with Homer's backpack. Then Homer and Dog followed Hercules down a hallway. Sweat prickled the back of Homer's neck. Hercules was right about the wool being hot and itchy. "How far away is the graveyard?"

"It's behind the hotel."

"That's a weird place for a graveyard." Homer scratched his neck. "Hey, you want to hear something else that's kinda weird?" He didn't wait for a reply, because of course Hercules wanted to hear something weird. "The cleaning lady told me to beware the lost and found."

"That is weird. Maybe there's something dangerous in the hotel lost and found. I wonder what it could be." Hercules fiddled with his top hat. "I wish I had my helmet. If we have to look at Lord Mockingbird's dead body, I might faint. If I faint, I might hit my head on a tombstone."

Homer wasn't worried. He'd seen lots of dead things, thanks to his sister's gruesome hobby. Her laboratory was like a convention for dead things. But he remembered how Hercules had passed out when they'd come face-to-face with a grizzly bear on Mushroom Island. "Stand close to me. I'll try to catch you if you faint."

"Thanks."

A pair of glass doors stood at the end of the hallway. Dog and the boys pushed through and stepped into a walled-in cemetery that had been built behind the Mockingbird Hotel. "This place is creepy," Hercules whispered.

"Real creepy," Homer agreed.

"Urrrr."

The night air had turned brisk. Streetlamps towered above the wall, casting a glow over the cemetery. Most of the headstones were ancient, worn down by wind, rain, and time, their edges crumbling away. The stones were tilted, as if each grave's occupant had vertigo. Moldy flowers lay on a few graves. A lifeless tree reached with gnarled, leafless arms. A hawk sat on one of the branches, preening its feathers.

Homer read the headstones as he passed by. A silhouette of a mockingbird had been carved into each one, along with the occupant's name: *Lord Mockingbird the X*, *Lady Mockingbird the VII*, *Little Lord Mockingbird the III*. A tiny headstone read: *Baby Mockingbird*. Homer held tight to Dog's leash. Thankfully, Dog had already piddled.

A group of people stood in a cluster at the far end of the cemetery. The women all wore black veils. The men wore the same outfits as Homer and Hercules. Their top hats bobbed as they turned to look at the boys. No one spoke. Ajitabh stepped away from the group and motioned for the boys to approach.

Homer immediately recognized his friend Zelda. At eight feet two inches tall, she stood out in any crowd. Her long hair cascaded down her black cape like molten silver. Wearing her usual sad expression, she nodded at Homer. He was about to wave at her when the leash tightened. Dog pushed his way past black pants and coattails with the urgency of a sled dog. Homer stumbled forward. "Excuse me," he said. People stepped aside as Dog pulled Homer through the crowd.

Dog stopped at the edge of a deep hole. Homer caught his breath and looked down into the newly dug grave. A casket rested at the bottom. Homer's face, reflected in the casket's shiny surface, peered back up at him. Dog lay on his stomach and pointed his nose into the hole. He whimpered. Did he know that Lord Mockingbird, his previous owner, had died? How could he possibly know that? That would be amazing. But then again, Dog *was* amazing.

Ajitabh cleared his throat. "I believe we are all gathered," he said. People mumbled and nodded. "Righteo. Let us commence." Ajitabh walked around the perimeter of the grave. A stone pedestal stood on the other side, directly across from Homer. A television set, the old-fashioned kind with knobs and a bulging oval screen, sat atop. Ajitabh removed one of his white gloves and turned a knob.

A crackling sound filled the graveyard. Black-and-white lines rolled across the screen. Then a voice said, "Gather round, you blithering numbskulls."

A shiver ran up Homer's spine. He knew that ancient voice. Dog got to his feet, his tail wagging as he stared at the screen.

A face slowly appeared on the screen—a white-haired old man with prunelike skin. Lord Mockingbird XVIII stared from the television, waiting, as if he knew it would take a while for his image to focus. Once it had focused, and once everyone in the crowd had stopped gasping with surprise, His Lordship smiled wickedly.

"If you are hearing this, then I must be dead," he said. "And if I am dead, then you are all in for a big kerfuffle."

7

Advice from a Dead Man

W hat's he saying?" someone asked.

"What's a kerfuffle?"

Hercules cleared his throat. "The word *kerfuffle* is Scottish in origin. It means 'a commotion or disturbance.'"

"Would someone tell that giant woman to move out of the way?" someone else said. "We can't see the television screen."

People pushed against Homer as they tried to get a better view. Homer stiffened his legs and held tight to the leash, afraid he and Dog might fall into the grave. Hercules and Homer shared a confused look.

"Quiet down," Ajitabh said with a wave of his hand.

Lord Mockingbird XVIII hadn't bothered to put in his fake teeth for his televised appearance. His lips folded over his gums like crinkled candy-bar wrappers. He sat hunched, as if his spine had gone all floppy. Although he looked weak and a bit stupid, Homer knew this was an act. His Lordship, in life, had pretended to be senile, but all the while he'd been sharp as a tack.

"Firstly, I shall address those to whom I am most unfortunately related—the Mockingbird clan."

"Here it comes," someone whispered. "We're going to be rich."

His Lordship wagged a gnarled finger. "You're a bunch of greedy, rotten, bloodsucking malcontents, and I despise you all. The only reason you hauled your lazy, worthless, rotund bottoms to my funeral is because you want to know what I'm going to do with all my money." He broke into a fit of coughing. Then he wagged his finger again, his voice weak and shaky. "Well, the joke's on you. There is no money. I flushed it down the toilet. Every last cent. So good riddance to the parasitic lot of you." Then His Lordship left the screen. But the tape continued to run.

"Flushed it down the toilet?" someone said. "He's crazy!"

"What a horrid old man!"

"How dare he treat us this way!"

"This has been a total waste of time!"

There was much complaining and name-calling. In a flurry of black, most of the crowd hurriedly exited the cemetery—leaving just eight people and a dog standing around the grave, watching the television.

After a long pause, Lord Mockingbird returned to the screen, a muffin in hand. He said nothing, just gummed the muffin and stared into space. *Was that the end of the show?* Homer wondered. Were they supposed to stand around and watch him eat? It was kinda boring. There wasn't even a sound track. "Is this what funerals are usually like?" he whispered to Hercules.

"No." Hercules peered down. "I sure hope I don't fall in."

Homer recognized the remaining people, all members of L.O.S.T. "Are we supposed to stand here all day?" a large woman asked as she pushed her veil from her face. Diamonds hung from her pale earlobes. "I have better things to do."

"Hold your horses, Gertrude," a man said, adjusting his black cowboy hat. His name was Jeremiah Carson, and he lived out west with cattle and prairie dogs. He was the only man in the crowd who hadn't worn a top hat. "I reckon he's got more to say."

"I don't care what he has to say," Dr. Gertrude Magnum

said. "I had to listen to him ramble on and on when he was alive. I don't see why I have to listen to him now that he's dead. He was a senile old buffoon."

As if he could hear everything, His Lordship stopped eating. "You all thought I was a senile old buffoon, didn't you?"

Gertrude gasped. Homer dropped Dog's leash. Was this some kind of joke? Was he listening to them? How was that possible?

The television crackled, and black-and-white lines rolled down the screen, disrupting the image. The hawk, which had been sitting in the tree this whole time, flew down and landed on top of the television. After another crackle, the screen cleared and Lord Mockingbird's image returned. He tossed the remaining muffin over his shoulder and slid his fake teeth into his mouth. Then he sat up straight. His weary red eyes widened, and his voice bellowed with strength. "That's better. I assume my money-grubbing relations have left. Now we can get down to business."

Dog, probably bored with the whole thing, wandered off to investigate the cemetery, his black vest snug around his belly, his blue leash dragging behind. Homer knew he should probably go after Dog, who was sure to dig holes and eat moldy flowers, but he couldn't peel his eyes from the screen.

"While I was alive, I pretended to be senile so I could find out the truth about each and every one of you," Lord Mockingbird said. He tapped the side of his head, indicating the source of his brilliant plan. "That's right. The truth."

"I'm confused," a man said. This was Professor Thaddius Thick. He rubbed his gray beard. "Is he saying he's been...been...been spying on us?"

"That's exactly what he's saying," snarled a young woman as she tore off her veil and let it fall to the ground. This was Torch, the owner of the hawk.

"Well, I'll be hog-tied," Jeremiah Carson said.

"That's right," His Lordship said. "I wanted to find out the truth, and the truth is this—some of you are not as you seem. Some of you are hiding secrets."

Homer gasped. Would His Lordship tell everyone about Dog? Because Lord Mockingbird had previously owned Dog, he knew Dog's treasure-hunting secret. *Oh, please don't tell them about Dog*, Homer thought. He wanted to grab the television and toss it over the graveyard wall. *Please don't tell them.*

"Turn that thing off," Gertrude said. Her jeweled bracelets clinked as she lunged at the television, but Ajitabh blocked her. "He's a crazy old man. He'll tell you a bunch of lies."

"Yeah," Homer blurted. "Turn it off."

"Why do you want to turn it off?" Torch asked Homer, her black eyes piercing him. Her hawk possessed an equally chilling gaze. "You got something to hide?"

Homer's face went all hot. It suddenly felt like a million degrees under that wool suit coat.

"I say, quiet down," Ajitabh said. "His Lordship is speaking."

"Because I am dead, you will be choosing my replacement." His Lordship fiddled with his membership coin. "I may no longer have a vote in L.O.S.T., but I have an opinion on who should be elected. An opinion based on information gathered while pretending to be a blithering idiot." He scowled. His gaze scanned the gathered membership, as if he could actually see them. "Do not elect Gertrude Magnum. She cares only about wealth. As president, she would use L.O.S.T. to fund her opulent lifestyle."

"I don't know what he's talking about," Gertrude said, tucking her emerald necklace beneath her black collar.

"Do not elect Jeremiah Carson. He is in love with Gertrude and thus could easily fall prey to her greedy plans."

Jeremiah pulled his cowboy hat so the brim hid his eyes. "What can I say?" he said. "It gets lonely way out there in Montana."

"Do not elect Torch," His Lordship continued. "She cares only about fame. As president, she would claim all discoveries as her own."

Torch narrowed her dark eyes. The snake tattoo that wound around her neck moved slightly as she clenched her jaw. "It don't matter what he says. He's dead."

"Do not elect Professor Thick. He cares only about Egyptian mummies. As president, he would turn L.O.S.T. into a mummy-only operation."

"It's . . . it's . . . it's true," Professor Thick stammered. "I love mummies."

Homer cringed. *Please don't tell them about Dog.*

Lord Mockingbird took a long breath. "As for the rest of the membership, Ajitabh is too busy with his inventions. Zelda's gloominess does not bode well for a leadership position. Sir Titus Edmund is missing. Angus MacDoodle is a hermit. Hercules is needed in his role as records keeper, and The Unpolluter is out of the question, since we've never met her. So that leaves us with one remaining member."

Everyone turned to look at Homer. That's when Dog waddled up to the grave. He'd found a bone of some sort and dropped it in. It landed on the casket with a loud *thunk*. Then Dog turned around and began kicking dirt into the grave, grunting with each kick. "Ur, ur, ur, ur."

Homer might have wondered what kind of bone it

was. He might have scolded Dog for digging in the graveyard. But like everyone else, Homer waited to hear what Lord Mockingbird had to say next.

His Lordship raised his gray eyebrows and smiled. "That's right. It is my opinion that the best person to replace me as president of L.O.S.T. is Homer W. Pudding."

8

FOUND

Even in a comfortable room at the Mockingbird Hotel, a good night's sleep is hardly possible in The City because of the constant flow of traffic and street ruckus.

Room 15 was a smallish room with twin beds. Images of mockingbirds decorated the quilts and wallpaper. Late last night, the boys had piled the traditional mourning attire in the corner and had changed into their pajamas. Stretched out on a bed, Homer had stared at the hotel ceiling. Had it really happened? Had His Lordship announced that he should be the next president of L.O.S.T.? No one had warned or prepared him. No one had asked if he wanted to do it. It was all very sudden and a bit unsettling.

Now, being the president of the Society of Legends, Objects, Secrets, and Treasures isn't exactly like being president of a country or something equally large and important. But it did come with a fair amount of responsibility. Homer had never been president of anything, unless you counted the mapmaking club at his school, of which he was the only member and thus listed as president/vice president/secretary/treasurer in the school yearbook.

Lord Mockingbird's recommendation hadn't gone over well. It was as if His Lordship had recommended that a baboon become the next president. (Baboons, by the way, are highly intelligent creatures that might actually do well in leadership roles if given the opportunity.) There'd been a huge argument among the membership. "I'm not voting for a child!" Gertrude had exclaimed.

"I don't thi-thi-think it would be a wise choice," Professor Thick had stammered.

"Dang right," Jeremiah Carson had agreed. "I'm fond of Homer, but a boy can't handle the duties of the presidency."

"That is not necessarily true," Zelda had said. "It's

important that we consider His Lordship's recommendation. We need time to think about this."

"Let's discuss it in the morning," Ajitabh had advised. "We could all use a good night's sleep."

But for Homer, the night dragged on and on like a boring geometry lesson. Had he slept at all? Dog, who was stretched out alongside him, snored blissfully. The City's noise didn't seem to bother him. And what worries did he have? No one wanted him to lead a secret organization.

As the gentle hues of sunrise tickled the window, Homer punched his pillow, then rolled onto his side. Hercules was sleeping across the room, a lightproof mask covering his eyes. *The Complete Dictionary of the English Language* was tucked under his arm, and his first-aid kit sat next to his bed.

"Psst," Homer spat. The night was finally over, and he needed to talk. Hercules didn't flinch. Homer grabbed a mint off the nightstand and tossed it at Hercules's chest.

"What's going on?" Hercules asked as he sat upright, ripping the mask off his face. "What's happening?"

"I don't know," Homer said innocently. He also sat up. "But since you're awake, what do you think I should do?"

Hercules rubbed his eyes. His wiry hair stuck straight out, and a line from his mask ran across his face. "Huh?"

"What should I do? Should I tell them I don't want to be the president of L.O.S.T.?"

"Oh, that." Hercules scratched his head. "I'm not sure you'll get enough votes anyway. But if you do get enough votes, I don't think anyone would force you to do it if you don't want to do it." He yawned. "Come to think of it, why wouldn't you want to be president? It's a huge honor."

"How could I run the organization?" Homer asked. "I live on a goat farm. What would I tell my parents?"

"That could be problematic," Hercules said.

A knock sounded on the door. Dog shot to his paws, a growl vibrating his lower lip. Homer pushed back the covers. After putting on his red bathrobe, he hurried to the door. Ajitabh entered, pushing a wheeled cart. "Brought you some breakfast," he said. His golden silk pajamas matched his robe. Dog stopped growling and wagged his tail.

Zelda followed in a long cotton nightgown, her black cape thrown over her shoulders. Her silver hair was tied back with a ribbon. She ducked to avoid bumping into the ceiling light fixture. Even though Homer had known Zelda for a few months, he was still amazed by her stature. She sat on the end of his bed, her expression as sorrowful as ever. "Funerals make me feel so weary," she said in her low, rumbly voice.

Ajitabh passed around the breakfast plates, including one for Dog. Everyone but Hercules had scrambled eggs, sausage links, cinnamon toast, and orange juice. Because Hercules worried about food allergies and digestive issues, he ate a plain egg-white omelet and dry toast. Dog gulped his meal the way all dogs do and then stared up at everyone as if he hadn't been fed in ages.

Hercules carried his plate across the room and turned the knob on the room's old-fashioned television set. "I hope you don't mind," he said, "but the European Spelling Bee finals are supposed to be televised today. I want to see who my competition is going to be."

"Ah," Zelda said. "You will compete again?"

"Yes. I want to be the first person in the world to win the World's Spelling Bee two years in a row."

While Hercules searched for the right channel, Homer ate a few bites of egg, but his fork felt like it weighed a ton. "Why would Lord Mockingbird want me to be president?" he asked. "He barely even knew me."

Ajitabh settled on the end of Hercules's bed, across from Homer. "Clearly, His Lordship admired you, and rightly so. You've proven yourself to be an intelligent, passionate, and honest chap. We couldn't ask for higher qualities." His thin mustache twitched as he smiled.

"You're pure of heart," Zelda said as she delicately nibbled her toast. "That is refreshing, especially in a world riddled with corruption and greed."

"What about my age?" Homer asked. "I'm only twelve."

Ajitabh's smile faded. "What's the matter, Homer?"

Homer looked away. "I don't want to do it. I don't know how to be a president. I'm just getting started."

Ajitabh reached out and patted Homer's shoulder. "Then put the whole matter out of your head. When you've grown up and finished your schooling, then you will follow in your uncle's footsteps and search for Rumpold Smeller's treasure. By Jove, you may well become our president one day, but in the meantime, the membership can choose someone else."

Homer nodded, and his shoulders relaxed. One day, but not this day. What a relief.

Dog barked. He stood in front of the television set, his tail wagging madly.

"Hey," Hercules said, pointing to the screen. "It's that girl Lorelei. The one with the pink hair."

As Homer whipped around, his plate tumbled to the floor. There, in the middle of the television screen, a girl with spiky pink hair smiled and petted a large gray rat perching on her shoulder. A brief sparkle of happiness lit in Homer's eyes. It was always this way when he saw Lorelei and remembered how they'd been friends. She was the first person to welcome Homer and Dog to The City. They'd explored The City and defeated Madame la Directeur together. But those were the good times. Lorelei had revealed a darker side when she kidnapped

Dog. Twice! She shared Homer's desire to find treasure, but, unlike Homer, she was willing to ruin friendships in the process.

Homer darted to his feet, eager to see why Lorelei was on television. The smile on her face was one he'd seen before. It held wicked plans between its upturned corners. Lorelei was up to something.

"Homer, you shouldn't stand so close to the television," Hercules warned. "The radiation isn't good for you."

But Homer didn't care about radiation. And he certainly didn't care that Dog was now eating his spilled breakfast off the carpet. His heartbeat doubled as the television camera widened its shot. Lorelei stood at a microphone. She wore a pink jumpsuit, the kind that zipped right up the center. Two people stood behind her, dressed in identical pink jumpsuits. One of the people was rather fat, and the other had a hawk on her shoulder. Each held a little Jolly Roger flag.

"Oh dear," Zelda said. "It's Gertrude and Torch. What are they doing?"

"And what does it say on their jumpsuits?" Ajitabh asked.

Homer nearly pressed his face against the screen, trying to read the tiny word. "I think it says *FOUND*."

"Hush," Zelda said. "She's talking." She pulled Homer away so everyone could get a good view.

A banner ran along the bottom of the screen: MYSTE-RIOUS GIRL TO MAKE TREASURE-HUNTING ANNOUNCE-MENT. Lorelei tapped the microphone. "Is this working? Can you hear me?" The rat sniffed the air.

The camera widened further to reveal a throng of reporters. "Yes," the reporters said. "We can hear you."

At the sound of Lorelei's voice, Dog raised his head and looked up at the television screen. His tail wagged twice, then he went back to eating.

"My name is Lorelei. Don't bother asking about my last name, because Lorelei is my whole name. L-O-R-E-L-E-I," she spelled. "And this is my sidekick, Daisy." She stroked the rat's head. "I am the president of a treasure-hunting organization called FOUND."

Homer sank onto the bed next to Ajitabh. He almost forgot to breathe as he listened.

"What does *FOUND* stand for?" a reporter asked.

Lorelei pursed her lips. "I'm still working on that," she said. "So for right now, it doesn't stand for anything. It means what it means. FOUND. Our mission is to find the world's most important treasures."

"Houston," Hercules said, "we've got a problem."

Torch and Gertrude waved their Jolly Roger flags, all the while glancing at a plain brown grocery bag that hung from Lorelei's left hand. She swung the bag as she continued talking. "Some people think that all the great

61

stuff has already been found, but I'm here to tell you that it's not true. One great treasure remains."

"What treasure?" a reporter asked.

"The treasure of Rumpold Smeller the Pirate."

Confusion spread among the reporters. "Who?" "What's she talking about?" "Did she say something about smelly pirates?" "That's ridiculous."

Torch stepped forward. "Hey!" she hollered. "Listen up and you'll learn something." Getting yelled at by a person with a snake tattoo around her neck and a beady-eyed hawk on her shoulder is a bit intimidating. The reporters quieted.

Lorelei continued. "Rumpold Smeller was the most fearsome pirate to sail the seas, and he took everything he could find. Then he hid all of it in one place. As the president of FOUND, I am about to lead my crew on the most exciting quest of this century, one that will be written about in history books. I will find Rumpold Smeller's treasure."

Everyone in room 15 of the Mockingbird Hotel shared a confused look. Except for Dog, who was licking the breakfast plate clean.

"You're just a little girl," a reporter said.

Another reporter snickered. "How can you, a mere child, be so sure you will find the treasure? Haven't others looked for it? Haven't *adults* looked for it?"

Lorelei flared her nostrils. "Many people have looked for it, including a secret organization that is made up of losers, and they better not try to stop me or I will tell the world all about them."

Ajitabh leaped to his feet. "She wouldn't dare."

"She's wicked," Zelda said.

"I will find the treasure!" Lorelei cried. Daisy the rat flicked her tail and rubbed her front paws together.

"You mean *we*," Gertrude Magnum corrected as she leaned close to Lorelei. Diamond barrettes sparkled amid her short blond curls. "*We* will find the treasure."

Lorelei scowled at her. "I am the president. Not you. And I have the map. So that makes me the boss."

Gertrude's gaze darted to the grocery bag again. "Fine," she said through clenched teeth. "You're the boss. For now."

"Map?" Homer's stomach clenched. "What's she talking about?"

"Homer?" Ajitabh said, running a hand over his beard. "When was the last time you saw your map?"

Hercules was the only person in the room who didn't know that Homer was in possession of the real Rumpold Smeller map. But he was soon to find out.

"I saw it yesterday when I got out of bed," Homer said. "I checked it before I went down to breakfast. I always check on it in the morning. It was right where it always is." He stepped close to the television screen. As Lorelei stuck her hand into the grocery bag, a dreadful silence fell over room 15 of the Mockingbird Hotel.

"I am here to announce that I have in my possession the most coveted pirate map in history—the map of Rumpold Smeller the Pirate." She pulled a book from the grocery bag and held it up. It was the same book that had been hidden beneath Homer's bed, *Rare Reptiles I Caught and Stuffed.* His uncle Drake had cut apart Rumpold's map and had pasted the individual pieces into that very same book. And now Lorelei had it!

"It can't be," Homer whispered, his legs beginning to tremble. "How did she...?"

Then he remembered a face peering at him from his bedroom window as the limousine had driven away.

Homer nearly burst into tears.

9

The Map Thief

Homer lunged for the telephone. It was the old-fashioned kind that plugged into the wall. And instead of buttons, it had a round dial with finger holes. Gripping the receiver, he stuck his finger into one of the holes and dialed the first digit. It spun slowly. He dialed the second digit—this was going to take forever!

"Lord Mockingbird was spot on about those two," Ajitabh said. He stormed over to the television, his golden robe billowing with his angry steps. "They are traitors to the cause. They should be ejected, rejected, expelled, banished, cast out forever from L.O.S.T."

"I think I have the document for that," Hercules said.

"By Jove, then do it!"

Hercules hurried to the closet and took out a briefcase. While he rummaged through its contents, Homer dialed the last digit of his home number. The dial spun. He wound his fingers in the twisted cord, waiting as the phone rang. On the television screen, Lorelei was still holding the book high for all reporters to see.

"Hello?" a voice answered.

"Mom," Homer said. "Where's Gwendolyn? Get Gwendolyn."

"Why, hello, Homer," Mrs. Pudding said chipperly. "Just a minute, sweetie. I have a pie in the oven."

"Mom?" A clink sounded as she set down the phone and walked away. "*Mom!*" he yelled. "*I need to talk to Gwendolyn!*"

On the television, Lorelei was putting the book back into the grocery bag. "One week from today," she told reporters, "I will return to this place to prove to the world that FOUND is the best treasure-hunting organization on the planet." Then Lorelei made one final statement. She looked right into the camera lens. "If you want your map, Homer, you know where to find me. I'm saving a place for you in FOUND." And with that, she turned and walked off through the throng of reporters, followed by Gertrude and Torch.

Homer wanted to yell at Lorelei, but yelling at a television screen seemed like a useless thing to do. So instead, he yelled into the phone. *"Mom! I need to—"*

"Homer W. Pudding, why ever are you hollering like that?" Mrs. Pudding asked as she picked up the receiver.

"Sorry," Homer said. He took a long breath, trying to calm down. "It's just that—"

"How are things at the Map of the Month Club? Are you having fun?"

"Fun?" Homer gritted his teeth. He hated lying, but unless the vow of secrecy was lifted to include parents and loved ones, he had no choice. "It's really fun. Can I talk to Gwendolyn?"

"You want to talk to your sister?" She sounded surprised, as if he'd asked to talk to the refrigerator or the laundry hamper.

"Yeah." He twisted the cord tighter. "Can you get her? Please?"

While Hercules continued to shuffle through his briefcase, Ajitabh, Zelda, and Dog watched Homer.

"She's in her laboratory," Mrs. Pudding said. "She told me not to disturb her until dinnertime. She's doing a delicate stuffing."

"Mom, I need to ask her something. It's *very* important,"

Homer said. He shook the receiver, as if that might get her attention.

"Homer, you sound very cranky. Did you get enough sleep last night? Have you eaten a wholesome breakfast? Did you put on clean underwear this morning? Oh dear, now your father's hollering about something from the yard." She paused. "Oh no, the goats are in the vegetable garden. I need to go. Call again tomorrow."

"But—" The dial tone filled Homer's ear. With a groan, he hung up.

"Homer, dear boy, what's happened?" Ajitabh asked. "Are we to assume that Lorelei does indeed have Rumpold Smeller's map?"

"I don't know," Homer said.

"Gertrude and Torch wouldn't have defected unless they had good reason," Zelda said. "They must truly believe that the girl has the map. Did you give it to her?"

"What?" Homer couldn't believe the question. "No way. I'd never do that."

Zelda raised her thick eyebrows. "Homer, you can tell us if you gave it to her. She is a cute girl. Boys do stupid things when they are in love. I have done many stupid things in the name of love."

"What? I'm not in love. She's not my girlfriend. I would never give her the map. Never!"

"Then why did she say you knew where to find her?" Ajitabh asked.

Homer looked away. He couldn't answer that question. After he and Lorelei had defeated the evil Madame la Directeur in her lair, Lorelei had decided to claim the lair as her own. So she and Homer had made a gentleman's agreement—Homer would keep the secret of the lair if Lorelei kept the secret of Dog's treasure-smelling talent. With Madame la Directeur locked away in prison, Homer was the only one who knew where to find Lorelei.

"Here it is," Hercules said, breaking the uncomfortable silence. He held up a piece of paper and read. "Bylaw Number Forty-Two-A, the Issue of Defection. If a sworn member of L.O.S.T. should choose to defect to a competing treasure-hunting organization, that member will be immediately banished from L.O.S.T. and under no circumstances be allowed to return. Form Seven-D, Official Banishment Form, must be filled out and filed in triplicate."

"Then fill it out," Ajitabh said, grabbing a pen off the nightstand. "Fill it out and banish those two collaborators." Hercules took the pen and began to work on the forms.

"I didn't give her the map," Homer said. "She's either

lying or someone else gave it to her." He grabbed the phone and dialed again. The phone rang and rang. Just when he was about to give up, someone answered. "Squeak, is that you?"

"Hi, Homer."

"Squeak, go to Gwendolyn's laboratory. Tell her I need to talk to her. Please."

"Uh-uh," Squeak said. "It's scary out there." Homer couldn't argue with that. Squeak was only five years old. Gwendolyn's laboratory was like something from a Frankenstein movie, complete with skulls hanging from the ceiling and eyeballs in glass jars.

"Squeak," Homer said, "did anyone come to the house yesterday? Anyone . . . *weird*?"

"Mom says I can't have a pet rat," Squeak said. "I want a pet rat."

Homer took a deep breath and squeezed the receiver. "Did you meet a girl with a pet rat? Did she come to the house?"

"The rat climbed up my arm," Squeak said. "It tickled." Then Squeak started to hum the theme song from his favorite cartoon.

"Did the girl with the rat talk to Gwendolyn? Squeak, stop singing and listen to me. Did the girl talk to Gwendolyn?"

But Squeak wasn't listening anymore. He muttered

something about a butterfly on the windowsill, then hung up. Homer groaned. His brother's attention span was about as long as a bee's stinger. Homer turned to face the others, who were waiting with expectant expressions. "She was there," he said. "Lorelei came to my house."

"But how the devil did she get the map?" Ajitabh asked. "Surely you hid it in a secure location."

"Uh, yeah, it was in a good place." Homer pushed his bangs from his eyes. Looking back, he realized that a loose floorboard beneath his bed probably wasn't the most *secure* location. But he didn't own a safe or a vault. And he'd wanted to keep it close. "Gwendolyn was looking for her birthday present. She must have found the reptile book, and then she gave it to Lorelei." He clenched his fists. "Gwendolyn had no right to do that! That book belonged to me! If she thinks I'm getting her a sweet-sixteen present after what she's done—"

"Hey!" Hercules interrupted. He pulled a piece of paper from Dog's mouth. Then he wagged a finger at Dog. "Do not eat the official documents." He held the paper by its corner. "There's dog slobber all over this. I'll have to do it again."

Ajitabh paced the room, his hands behind his back. "It is evident that Lorelei filched the map. But a piece of this puzzle doesn't quite fit. How did she know you had the map? I thought only Zelda and I knew."

"I don't know how she found out," Homer said.

Ajitabh stopped pacing and stared out the window. "I know what you're thinking, Homer. You want to recover the map. You want to go after her."

"Yes," Homer said.

"As your mentor and your friend, I forbid it," Ajitabh said sternly. Hercules looked up from his scribbling, a stunned expression on his face. Dog took the opportunity to snatch another piece of paper. "I absolutely forbid it."

Homer sank onto the bed. "But it's mine."

"She told us not to interfere," Zelda said. She wrapped her cape tightly around her shoulders, her head a mere inch from the ceiling. "She threatened to reveal L.O.S.T."

"But she also said for me to come find her."

Ajitabh folded his arms. "The reason we've kept L.O.S.T. a secret is to protect our quests so that those with unsavory motives don't get wind of them, so that we can uncover treasures and get them to their proper places without the risk of others stealing them. If our identities were to be revealed, then there would be no L.O.S.T."

"But if Lorelei finds the treasure, she'll keep everything for herself."

"The map is gone, Homer. You must accept that and move on."

Homer darted to his feet. "I can't accept that! I promised my uncle I would find Rumpold's treasure." It was the last promise he'd made to his beloved uncle Drake. And he'd made it during Drake's final visit to the goat farm. Now Drake was gone. All Homer had were memories and that promise. "My uncle died because of Rumpold's map!"

Once again, silence descended. Homer's whole body felt shaky. Zelda reached out and touched his arm. "I know your heart is breaking," she said. "Heartbreak so early in the morning is a tragedy indeed. But do not despair. You will learn to live with it. My heart has been broken countless times."

"This is a dark day for L.O.S.T.," Ajitabh said as he headed toward the door. "I will change into my travel clothes and pack my bag. It's best to get you back to Milkydale as soon as possible." And with that, he opened the door and left.

"We must stand united," Zelda told Homer. "Your uncle would have wanted it that way." Then she also left the room, closing the door behind her.

Homer frowned. Sure, his uncle would have wanted the members of L.O.S.T. to stand united. But what about the promise he'd made to his uncle?

Dog sat at Homer's feet, whining for attention. Homer slid to the floor and wrapped his arms around Dog's neck. Everything had fallen apart. The map that held his dreams and aspirations was gone. The girl who had once been his friend had deceived him again. Having lost its president, two other members, and a famous treasure map, L.O.S.T. stood on the verge of collapse.

10

The Unpolluter

I'm sorry about your map," Hercules said. He collected all the documents and returned them to the briefcase. "You must be pretty mad."

"That's the understatement of the year," Homer grumbled.

"Do you think she'll find the treasure?"

Homer's stomach clenched. Lorelei was brilliant. She didn't let anything stand in her way. "Probably."

"Then we have to stop her!" Hercules exclaimed with a burst of courage. Despite his fearful disposition, he'd proven himself to be courageous in times of need—like when he'd jumped out of an airplane to save Dog's life. "We can't let her get away with this. You defeated her before. You can do it again." He grabbed an inhaler and took a hit.

"Dog defeated her, not me," Homer reminded him. "Dog ate the membership coin. That's the only reason why Lorelei lost on Mushroom Island."

"The point is, you were victorious. And you'll be victorious again. I'll help you."

"How can you help me? Don't you have to get ready for the World's Spelling Bee?"

Hercules frowned. "Oh, right. Well, I can help you for a while, but I will need to get home so I can officially register. I have to get my parents' signatures."

Homer tapped his fingers against his thigh as he thought about the situation. It would definitely be nice to have another person by his side. Lorelei was a formidable competitor, and while Dog could sniff treasure over garbage, he wasn't so good at figuring out who was friend and who was foe. But then Homer remembered something. "Ajitabh *ordered* me not to go after Lorelei."

"I don't think he can do that." Hercules pulled a file from his briefcase and began to thumb through its contents. "You were given full membership, and with full membership come all the full rights of membership." He stopped on a document, read silently, then thumbed through more documents. "I don't think Ajitabh has the authority to tell you what to do." His finger stopped again. "Yes, here it is." And he read: "'Statement of Democratic Principles: Let it be known that L.O.S.T. is a working democracy, and therefore no one member holds authority over another. Exception made only if a majority vote is reached.'"

Homer stopped petting Dog's ear. Ajitabh and Zelda were not a majority. He didn't have to follow Ajitabh's orders. This was great news.

"Well?" Hercules asked. "Are we going to look for her?"

We? Homer turned away from his friend's eager gaze. He couldn't take Hercules along. Lorelei would be in her lair, and he had made a gentleman's agreement to keep the lair's location a secret.

"I think I should listen to Ajitabh," Homer lied. "We should both listen to him and go home."

"You sure?"

Homer tried to sound sincere. "Yes. I'm sure. I'm totally sure. I don't want to upset Ajitabh. And I don't want to upset my parents." He waited, hoping he'd been convincing.

"Yeah, okay. It sounds kinda dangerous anyway. Torch

scares me. And that hawk of hers could peck our eyes out." Hercules scratched behind his ear. "I was hoping we could hang out. Do you want to come and stay at my house? There's still a couple of weeks left before school starts."

Under normal circumstances, Homer would have jumped at the possibility of staying with Hercules at the Simple mansion. But under these circumstances, with his future crashing down around him like a demolished building, he didn't think anything would be fun. The world had turned dark and stormy.

After dragging Dog out of the bathroom, where he'd been drinking from the toilet, Hercules took a shower. As the water ran, Homer hurriedly dressed in his jeans and plaid shirt. He stuffed his pajamas, robe, and mourning attire into his backpack, along with Dog's vest. There was no room for the top hat, so he'd have to carry it. Then he attached Dog's leash. "You ready to go get our map?"

"Urrrr."

A receptionist stood behind the counter in the hotel's lobby. There was no sign of Zelda or Ajitabh. "Can I leave a message here?" Homer asked as he set the top hat on the counter. The receptionist handed him a piece of Mockingbird stationery and a fountain pen.

Dear Ajitabh and Zelda,

Don't worry and don't try to follow me. My parents said I didn't have to come back home until my sister's birthday, so that gives me five more days. I've decided to explore The City. I will meet you back here before Saturday, but if you can't wait for me, then Dog and I will take the train home. We've done it before.

Homer

He folded the paper and handed it to the receptionist. "Could you please make sure that Ajitabh gets this?" She nodded and tucked the note into the mail slot for Ajitabh's room.

"Ah-hem." Someone cleared her throat. The cleaning lady stood behind Homer, a whisk broom swinging from one hand, her other hand clutching a wheeled garbage can. "You shouldn't pollute," she told Homer. Then she whisked the top hat into the garbage.

"I didn't pollute," he said as the receptionist helped another guest. "That's my hat."

"You did pollute." She pointed into the can. "The evidence is right there."

"But—"

"Pollute," she said. "P.O.L.L.U.T.E. Proof of Lost

Leaves Us Totally Exposed." She took a spray bottle from her apron pocket and spritzed the counter. Then she wiped it dry with a rag.

"Proof of lost leaves us totally exposed," Homer repeated slowly. He narrowed his eyes. "You know about...?" He couldn't say it.

"Of course I know about L.O.S.T.," she said, lowering her voice. "I'm The Unpolluter."

No one had ever met The Unpolluter, the most mysterious member of the society. Could this be one of Lorelei's tricks? "I don't believe you," he said. "How much did Lorelei pay you to try to get information from me?"

"That's a very good response. Never admit to knowing about L.O.S.T." She set aside her cleaning supplies and rearranged her plastic shower cap. Its elastic band had left a red imprint across her forehead. "I hope you won't be like your uncle. He left messes everywhere. I was constantly cleaning up after that boy."

"What do you want?" Homer asked.

She scratched her mole. "I need your help."

"*My* help?"

"The girl is tricky. She's cunning. I'm not sure what she's got hidden up her sleeves. I suspect she's got plans the likes of which we can't even imagine. I may have to get rid of her."

Homer gulped. "Get rid of her?" Except for the

humongous mole, she looked like such a nice old cleaning lady. "Do you mean, get *rid* of her?"

"Yes." The Unpolluter looked over her shoulder, then leaned closer to Homer. "She knows too much for someone who is not a member."

"Wait a minute." The leash slipped from Homer's fingers. "You can't get rid of her."

"My sole job is to clean up messes so no one learns about L.O.S.T., and right now, that girl is a great big mess." She wiped her hands on her grimy apron. "Of course, if there's a way you can keep her from blabbing, you'll save me some work." Then she collected her supplies and began to wheel the garbage can back across the lobby. "Good luck," she called as she disappeared around the corner.

Before Homer could call after her, the revolving door spun and the bellhop stepped into the lobby. "I'll take your backpack, sir," the bellhop said with a tip of his red hat. "You're gonna need both arms to carry that dog of yours."

Dog stared at the door and whimpered. Homer wanted to whimper, too.

PART THREE

FOUND HEADQUARTERS

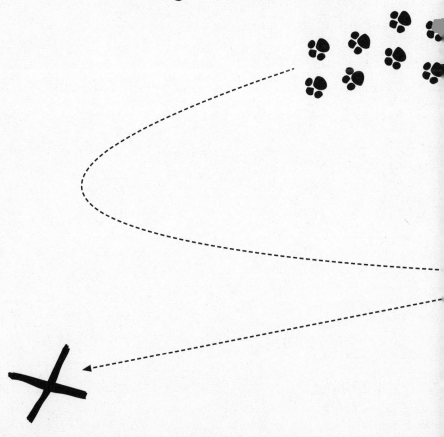

11

Lorelei's Lair

It is common knowledge that in order to be a serious villain, you must have a lair. But not just any old lair. It should be a really cool, state-of-the-art, storybook kind of lair. Only with that sort of lair can a villain expect to become feared *and* famous.

Now, I'm not suggesting that you become a villain. Au contraire—villainy is an expensive, time-consuming, and lonely lifestyle. It is not for the tenderhearted or sweet-tempered. If your goal is to be popular and get invited to lots of parties, do not become a villain. If you like to go out in public without people booing you, throwing rotten fruit at your head, or fleeing from you in terror, do not become a villain. However, if you relish the thought of being alone and you have a single goal in mind and are willing to do anything to reach that goal, whether it be ruling the universe or becoming the richest kid in the world, then villainy might be an option.

It appeared, to Homer, that Lorelei had chosen the villain lifestyle. She didn't care about having friends, which was why she'd stolen from Homer on three different occasions. She was willing to do anything to become the most famous treasure hunter in the world, including lying, stealing, and cheating. And she was the current owner of an amazing lair. He needed no more proof than that. Lorelei had gone to the dark side.

Lorelei's lair had once belonged to Madame la Directeur. It lay in the bowels of the Museum of Natural History, which happened to be a short walk from the Mockingbird Hotel. And so, leash in hand, backpack on back, Homer began the trek down the sidewalk. Dog was blissfully unaware of the destination. If he'd known they were about to revisit the place where he'd come face-to-face with a mutant, carnivorous tortoise, he most assuredly would have plopped onto his belly in his "I'm-not-budging-and-you-can't-make-me" stance. But since he was unaware, he practically pranced, his ears and jowls swinging in a carefree way. Homer, however, was filled with trepidation. How would he get the map? How would he keep Lorelei from blabbing about L.O.S.T.? And worse, if he failed, how would he face Ajitabh and Zelda?

After a few minutes of worried walking, during which Homer almost persuaded himself to turn back, the museum loomed into view. A pair of towering lion statues sat at the museum's entrance—noble guardians that greeted all visitors. Homer wiped the back of his neck. Was it the muggy August air that had made him all sweaty or was it fear? If only he'd had the time to come up with a plan. Even a half-baked plan was better than no plan. "What am I going to do?" he asked Dog.

Dog stared up at one of the lions and growled.

Tourists waited in line at the museum's ticket booth. A horse and carriage pulled up to the sidewalk and deposited more tourists, who ran up the steps, cameras in hand, sunglasses and sun hats bobbing. Homer wished he could be an ordinary tourist, off to explore the museum's exhibits, instead of a L.O.S.T. spy, off to stop a rival treasure-hunting organization. For a brief moment, he yearned for the good old days when he'd known nothing of danger except for the occasional slip in the mud or collision with a dodgeball.

"Grrrr," Dog growled at the other lion.

"Come on," Homer said with a tug of the leash.

There were two ways to get into the lair. One was by water, via City Lake. A channel opened at the edge of the lake, in an area accessible only by boat. This channel led directly into the depths of the lair, where it formed a pool. The channel, however, was blocked by a heavy gate, upon which hung a sign.

WARNING:
High levels of toxic waste. Off limits to people.
Loitering could cause brain damage.

This sign, put there by Madame la Directeur when she'd been the lair's owner, kept curious boaters from peering through the gate. The gate itself could be opened only by remote control—a special universal remote that Lorelei now owned.

The other way to get inside the lair was through a giant tortoise statue, which sat in the museum's basement. The easiest route to the basement was to walk through the museum's main entrance, then take the elevator. But this option was not available to Homer. First, the museum had security cameras posted throughout, and Homer didn't want Ajitabh or Zelda to be able to track his movements. Second, dogs weren't allowed inside the museum.

So, to get to the tortoise statue, Homer had to use the more difficult route, and that is why he and Dog followed the museum's north wall. This was the wild side of the building—no parking spaces or sidewalks, just a lot of shrubs and trees. Homer stopped at the wall's midpoint and kicked aside an ivy vine. A metal grate had been set into the ground. Dog's ears went limp, and he looked up at Homer with his sad eyes.

"I know you don't want to go in there, but we have to," Homer said. "Too bad I don't have your glow-in-the-dark vest." Too bad he didn't have a flashlight or his uncle's night-vision goggles, either. He'd been in such a hurry to pack for his VIP tour of the map club that he hadn't thought about bringing his treasure-hunting gear. After all, this was supposed to have been a fun-filled trip, not a clandestine quest to retrieve a stolen pirate map.

Homer knelt and, with a heave, pulled the grate free. Dog started to back away, but Homer grabbed his collar. "It'll be okay," he said gently. But would it? Dog stuck his nose into Homer's sleeve and whined. Homer patted his head. "The killer tortoise is gone. I promise."

It was a tricky operation. First Homer had to shove Dog into the dark tunnel. Of course, Dog went totally limp and made the whole thing more difficult than it had to be. Then, after tightening his backpack straps,

Homer climbed in. As his shoulders brushed the tunnel walls, he remembered Lorelei's warning from a few months ago. "It's a long crawl and there's lots of spiders," she'd said. Homer grimaced, hoping no spiders would jump onto his head or find their way into his ears.

Even though it was downhill, the going was slow. It's nearly impossible to gain momentum with a stubborn basset hound blocking the way. It turned out that the best technique to keep Dog moving was a headbutt to his plump rump.

"You're lucky you can't smell," Homer whispered, the dank moldy air filling his nostrils. Thanks to his sister's hobby, he recognized the sweet scent of decay. Maybe a mouse or two had died in there. Homer shuddered. Maybe twelve or a hundred.

Just as the light from one end of the tunnel faded, light drifted in from the other end. Ten headbutts later, they arrived at the tunnel's end, where another metal grate was set into a wall. Homer climbed over Dog and peered through the bars.

Everything looked the same. A hallway lit by sconces stretched to the left and to the right. He pushed on the grate, and it swung open. He slid out. As soon as his feet were firmly planted on the museum's basement floor, he reached back in and grabbed Dog.

Because this wasn't Homer's first visit, he didn't gasp

when he came face-to-face with the giant tortoise statue, its reptilian eyes reflecting the hallway light. He didn't tremble when, after standing on tiptoe and pressing the statue's left eyeball, a rumbling sounded and the mechanical statue opened its mouth. Wider and wider it opened until a gaping hole had formed in the wall. Homer slid his arms under Dog's belly, his stomach muscles aching from all the lifting. Once Dog was inside the tortoise mouth, Homer pulled himself in. As soon as his feet had passed through, the mouth began to close quickly, then snapped shut, leaving Homer and Dog in total darkness. But Homer knew what was next, so he was prepared this time. He pulled Dog onto his lap. "Don't worry," he whispered. "I'll hold on to you." He scooted forward until the ground gave way, and they slid around and around, down the corkscrew slide, and landed with a thud inside Lorelei's lair.

Homer cupped a hand over Dog's muzzle, listening for voices. He expected to hear wicked, satisfied laughter or evil plans being made. But he heard only his heart beating in his ears. "We need to be very quiet," he whispered as he checked to make sure the leash was securely fastened. "No barking. No howling. Okay?" Dog licked Homer's hand.

Together, they stepped onto the balcony. The lair's main room, a vast, cavelike fortress, lay beneath. Homer peeked over the railing. His gaze immediately rested on a head of pink hair. He took a sharp breath, then ducked below the railing. Pulling Dog close, Homer peered through the bars.

Lorelei sat in a red velvet chair that looked a bit like a throne. She still wore the pink FOUND jumpsuit, which perfectly matched her hair. Her rat, Daisy, slept curled in a ball on her lap. She picked up a remote control, then spun the chair around so that she was facing a huge flat-screen monitor on the wall. Her back to Homer, she pushed one of the remote's buttons. The screen lit up, and Torch and Gertrude Magnum appeared, seated side by side, wearing FOUND jumpsuits.

If there were a television show called *Totally Opposite People*, these two would have been the perfect guests. Torch was slender; Gertrude was, well, rather hefty. Thick black eyeliner circled Torch's black eyes. Blue glitter sparkled on Gertrude's eyelids. Torch's only accessory was the snake tattoo that wound around her neck. Gertrude dripped in jewels, including a diamond-studded anchor that adorned a doll-sized sailor hat. While everything about Torch spoke to the serious side of life, everything about Gertrude was silly. The way she sparkled, she might have been mistaken for someone's fairy godmother, but Homer knew better. She was a scorpion disguised as a butterfly.

A ship's railing could be seen behind the two women. Water shimmered in the background. They were probably on one of Gertrude's yachts, Homer guessed. He pulled Dog closer, ready to clasp a hand over his muzzle if he started to growl or whine.

"Hello, ladies," Lorelei said. "I think my little press conference went well."

Torch grunted and folded her arms. "Those reporters didn't believe you. And they didn't take us seriously." Her hawk flew into view and landed on her shoulder.

"It's because of the name," Gertrude said. The hawk sidestepped to the edge of Torch's shoulder and stared at a pearl that dangled from Gertrude's ear. "We need a better name."

"*FOUND* is a great name," Lorelei said. "And it makes total sense, since I'm trying to defeat L.O.S.T."

Gertrude leaned forward, her chins quivering. "Yes, but what does it stand for? What does *FOUND stand* for?"

Torch glared at Gertrude from the corner of her eye. "**F**at, **O**ld, **U**gly—"

"You are a rude young lady," Gertrude said as she pinched Torch's arm. "I've always wanted to tell you that, but I've always been too polite to do so." The hawk suddenly lunged at the earring. Gertrude squealed and pushed the bird away. "Keep that filthy creature away from me."

"So what's the plan?" Torch asked Lorelei. "I didn't leave L.O.S.T. so I could sit on this stupid boat with old Gertie here."

"It's not a *boat*," Gertrude said, scooting her chair away from the hawk. "It's a yacht. Yachts are much more expensive than boats."

"Whatever," Torch snarled. "What's our next move?"

"We need to cut all the original map pieces from the reptile book, then put them back together," Lorelei said.

"No problem. I'm good at jigsaw puzzles." Torch narrowed her eyes. "Where are you? It looks like you're in some kind of cave."

For a moment, Homer thought Torch might spot him and Dog seated up on the balcony.

"Never mind where I am," Lorelei said. "While I'm gathering supplies for the quest, you and Gertrude can piece the map together."

"Now that's a plan I can live with," Torch said with a satisfied smirk.

What? Homer sat up real straight. Lorelei was going to leave the reptile book with those two while she did errands? How could she do such a thing? They'd steal it. No doubt about it.

"I know," Gertrude said, pointing a painted fingernail in the air. "How about, **F**inders **O**f **UN**told **D**iscoveries?

No, that's not it. How about, **F**ortunes **O**pened and **U**nearthed... No, that's not it, either. **F**ollowers **O**f **Uni**fied... hmmm. **F**abulous **O**perators **U**nder**N**eath... This is very frustrating. Why did you choose such a difficult word?"

"We're all girls," Torch said. "*FOUND* could stand for **F**emales **O**f **UN**told **D**estiny."

"I'm not keen on that," Gertrude said, pursing her red lips.

"How about **F**abulous **O**verlords of **UN**believable **D**oom," Torch said.

"You are a very disturbed person," Gertrude said, patting her blond curls. "Very disturbed. I'm not sure I want to work with you."

"Well, I ain't happy about working with you, either," Torch said. Her hawk flew onto Gertrude's hat and began pecking at the jeweled anchor. Gertrude screamed and flapped her hands wildly. Torch snickered. Dog started to growl, but Homer clamped his hands around his muzzle just in time.

"Shhhh," Homer whispered in Dog's ear.

"I hate you," Gertrude said as the hawk flew off with her hat.

"I hate you more," Torch said.

Lorelei groaned. "Ladies, stop arguing. FOUND is

what it is. And once we bring back Rumpold Smeller's treasure, FOUND will forever be known as the winner, and L.O.S.T. will forever be known as the loser."

"Well, they are a bunch of losers," Torch said. "They let that stupid Homer Pudding kid join. And they won't give me money for my quest to find Atlantis."

"That's because it's your *seventh* Atlantis quest," Gertrude said, patting her hair again. "You should have found it by now."

Torch rolled her eyes. "Whatever."

Despite his worries about the map, Homer smiled. The arguing was a good sign. Lorelei's plan was off to a rocky start. It served her right to get stuck with those two. Maybe the remaining L.O.S.T. members should thank Lorelei for stealing Gertrude and Torch.

Beware the lost and found, Homer thought as The Unpolluter's words echoed in his mind.

"The reptile book will be delivered to your yacht in one hour," Lorelei said. "You'll need scissors and a couple of glue sticks to put the map together. I will join you when I'm done with my errands." Then she pushed a button on the remote, and the screen went black. She leaned back in her throne and sat in silence for a moment.

Then, without turning around, she said, "Hello, Homer. I've been expecting you."

12

Prisoner #90's Revenge

Madame la Directeur had spent most of her jail days sitting on her cot in her tiny concrete cell thinking about how much she hated Homer Pudding and about how much she wanted revenge. She imagined feeding him to her tortoise. She imagined pushing him into a hole filled with venomous cobras or dumping a bag of pinching scorpions into his bed. But these fantasies did not soothe her. Each day, her hatred grew. Each night, she screamed his name in her sleep.

"Homer Pudding, I'm going to get you!" This nocturnal meltdown, naturally, disturbed the other prisoners.

"I wish that Pudding kid had never been born," Prisoner #75 complained. "Then at least I'd be able to get some sleep."

Hatred is a strange and powerful thing. It does not exist in nature as air and water or people and trees do. It must be created. But because it can be created, it can also be destroyed. All it takes is a bit of positive thinking. Madame la Directeur didn't realize this, however, and so hatred filled her body like sand filling a vase, until there was no room for anything else. *"I hate you, Homer Pudding!"*

"That Homer Pudding kid sounds like a real brat," Prisoner #82 told Prisoner #83.

Prisoner #83 yawned. "It's so rude of him to keep waking us up."

In the mornings, when Madame put on her daytime prison pajamas, she remembered how she used to wear expensive designer suits made of silk and virgin wool. As she sat on a bench in the cold prison cafeteria, she remembered how she'd once owned a glorious lair. As she ate her lumpy prison porridge, she thought about how she used to eat Belgian chocolate mousse and pomegranate parfaits.

Things were supposed to be different. Fame and fortune had been so close. But the Pudding kid and that homeless girl had ruined everything. They'd turned her in to the police with proof that she'd been stealing gemstones from the Museum of Natural History.

The sands of hatred filled Madame to the brim.

And so it was that she decided to escape. She'd made sure that Homer's precious map was taken from him, but she wanted more. She wanted to be there to see the look on his face when the treasure was found—by someone else! She laughed wickedly as she imagined this moment. Then he'd know how it felt to have all his hopes and dreams ripped from his heart and shredded.

How can I get out of here? she thought as she stirred a particularly lumpy bowl of porridge. Soupwater Prison, her current address, was set deep in the swamps of Soupwater County, a region thick with alligators and water snakes. Tall concrete walls surrounded the prison, and the entrance was heavily guarded.

But Madame knew that escape was always possible. Rumpold Smeller had proven this when he'd been trapped in the Pit of Eternity. He fell in while exploring a deserted island. The tribe that once ruled the island had built the pit to capture intruders. The large pile of skeletons at the bottom would have dashed the hopes of most, but not Rumpold. He knew that whoever had dug the pit would have created a way to get himself out.

As Rumpold sat there, contemplating his escape, a

mouse scurried through a tiny hole in the wall. After clearing the hole of the mouse's nest, Rumpold found a release mechanism that opened one of the walls. He was free.

Escape is always possible, Madame told herself. Not even the Pit of Eternity. Not even Soupwater Prison.

I need to explore every room in this place, she thought. She took her porridge bowl to the dishwashing station. "How did you get this job?" Madame asked the prisoner who was washing dishes.

"I volunteered," Prisoner #41 replied.

"Volunteered?" Madame wasn't familiar with the term.

"Yeah. It means you work but you don't get paid."

"Why would anyone work and not get paid?" Madame asked.

"'Cause it's better than sitting on my cot all day," Prisoner #41 said with a shrug. "There's a list of jobs over there on the bulletin board."

Madame read the list: POTATO PEELER (KITCHEN), TOILET SCRUBBER (MAIN FLOOR), GARBAGE SORTER (BASEMENT), HALLWAY SWEEPER (SECOND FLOOR), and TOWEL WASHER (LAUNDRY ROOM). By volunteering, she'd be able to explore every inch of the prison. She grabbed the pen that hung from a chain and signed her name to each job: PRISONER #90. Surely one of these places would become her escape route.

Homer W. Pudding, I'm coming to get you.

13

Speckles the Watchdog

Lorelei swung the chair around and looked up at where Homer and Dog sat on the balcony. She smiled. It wasn't the evil smile of a villain. It wasn't the satisfied smile of someone who'd just won a game of hide-and-seek. She smiled as if she was looking at a long-lost friend.

Friend?

It's perfectly normal for friends to argue and have hurt feelings. Buddies disagree about all sorts of things and then apologize, and life goes back to normal. But even if Lorelei were to apologize for stealing the reptile book, Homer wasn't going to forgive her. He'd forgiven her for stealing Dog the first time. He'd forgiven her for taking his uncle's membership coin and lying to L.O.S.T. about it. He'd forgiven her for stealing Dog the second time. But there'd be no forgiveness this time. She was no friend of his.

He scrambled to his feet and stomped down the stairs. "I want my map," he said when he reached the bottom step. "And I won't leave until I get it."

Daisy the rat, who'd been sleeping on Lorelei's lap, stretched and yawned. She twitched her black nose at Homer, then slid off. Her stomach brushed along the floor as she waddled to a wall of vending machines. Daisy's normally sleek body looked totally different, like a stuffed gray sock. Standing on her hind legs, she reached up and pushed a button on one of the vending machines. A whirring noise sounded and then *plop*. She reached into the bin and removed a bag of chips. Then she tore the bag open and feasted. *She's been eating too much junk food*, Homer guessed.

"I changed a lot of stuff," Lorelei said as she clomped over to another vending machine. "Remember how Madame la Directeur kept mice in here?" Homer nodded. One of the machines used to spit out white mice—food for Madame's cobra. "I put in all my favorite snacks instead." She pressed a button, and a bag of Dinook-ies tumbled into the bin. "Want one?"

Homer glared at her. He wasn't about to accept treats from his mortal enemy, even if they were delicious dinosaur-shaped cookies. "I want my map."

Lorelei waved the bag at Dog, who was still sitting on the top step. Who could blame him for not wanting to venture into the lair? His last visit had been hair-raising. "Dog? You want some?" She shook the bag. The sound of tumbling cookies proved to be more powerful than terror-filled memories. A dog's stomach has a mind of its own. Lorelei shook the bag again.

"Urrrr." Dog's long body and short legs were not designed for stairs, so it took him a while to get down.

Homer eyed the bags of corn snacks, barbecue twists, and red licorice vines, but he had other things on his mind. "We're not eating your food," he said, blocking Dog's path.

"But it's polite to offer guests something to eat."

"This isn't a tea party," Homer snapped. "Give me the map!"

Lorelei frowned. "I'm sorry I had to take it."

"Sorry?" Homer's voice cracked. He clenched his fists and stomped toward her. "Sorry? I heard you talking to Gertrude and Torch. You're not one bit sorry. You're trying to ruin L.O.S.T."

"Homer," she said as she opened the bag of Dinookies and turned it upside down. Dog charged, slurping up each cookie as soon as it hit the floor. "There are some things you understand and some things you don't understand. Not everything is as it seems."

"Stop talking in riddles, Lorelei. Just give me the map."

She tossed the empty bag into a trash can. "You shouldn't be so mad at me," she said, flaring her nostrils. "Your sister gave me the map."

"Yeah, well, what were you doing at my house, anyway?"

Lorelei folded her arms. "I chartered a plane to Milkydale because... because... well, I wanted to say hi. Your sister was sitting on the porch reading *Rare Reptiles I Caught and Stuffed.*"

Homer clenched his jaw. "She wasn't supposed to have that book. I never gave it to her."

"I asked her where she got the book. She said she'd found it under your bed. Really, Homer? Under your bed? That's the most obvious hiding place in the world."

Her smirk was almost too much to bear. "Yeah, well, sometimes the most obvious hiding place is the best," Homer said. That wasn't the real reason he'd chosen the hiding place, but it sounded brilliant when he said it.

"I asked her if it was a good book, and she said that you'd ruined it by pasting bits of your maps on most of the pages." Lorelei raised her eyebrows. "I couldn't believe my luck. She had no idea she was holding the hiding place of Rumpold Smeller's map. So we traded. I gave her a harmonic crystal. Those crystals have come in superhandy. I sold a bunch of them to collectors. Want to see what I bought with all the money?" She spread her arms wide and smiled. "I got some real cool stuff."

Despite his anger at his sister, who'd had no right to trade away something that didn't belong to her, Homer was curious about some of the new things in the lair. A fountain that sprayed colored water caught his eye. Lorelei followed his gaze. "Do you like my soda fountain?" She took a paper cup from a dispenser and held it beneath a green stream. "This one is lime-flavored." She took a drink. "Are you thirsty?"

Homer was thirsty, and, after eating the bag of Dinookies, Dog was probably thirsty, too. So Homer took a paper cup and held it beneath a red stream, which turned out to be fruit punch. If Lorelei had been his friend, he would have told her he really like the soda fountain, but instead he said, "No big deal." Then he filled the cup again and gave it to Dog. As he knelt, he whispered in Dog's ear. "Smell the map, boy. Go find the map. The map is treasure." Dog was his greatest hope. He'd found the map before—he could find it again.

Lorelei took Homer on a tour of her lair. A trampoline,

a popcorn machine, and a purple golf cart were among her favorite purchases. "I set up a laser detection grid around the perimeter. That's how I knew you were on the balcony."

Lorelei, who'd once been homeless, had turned Madame's lair into a place any kid would love. When Homer first met her, she was living behind a utility closet in a soup warehouse. In those days, a few milk crates had held her meager belongings, but she'd been proud of her little hideout. Now she lived in Wonderland. A pang hit Homer as he remembered their friendship. He wanted to tell her how great the lair was. But that would be nice. *She doesn't deserve nice*, he reminded himself.

"Watch this," Lorelei said. She clapped her hands, and the lair went dark, but the stone ceiling twinkled like a star-filled sky. Homer hoped that during the blackout, Dog would take the opportunity to sniff out the map and seize it. But when Lorelei clapped again and the lights turned back on, Dog was lying on his belly, having some sort of staring contest with Daisy the rat. "The self-destruct button still doesn't work, but that's okay. Oh, and look what I found." She pointed across the pool to where some kind of vessel, partially submerged, was moored. "That's a seaweed-powered submarine. Pretty cool, huh?"

"Hey, that used to belong to my uncle," Homer said. "Ajitabh invented it."

"Well, it belongs to me now."

Homer watched Dog from the corner of his eye. Why wasn't he sniffing around? The book with its hidden treasure map was in here somewhere. "Pssst," Homer said while Lorelei walked over to a vending machine and punched a button. Dog ignored him. "Pssst. Dog. Pssst."

"He won't find it," Lorelei said. "Do you think I'm stupid or something? I know Dog's secret, remember? Do you think I'd leave the reptile book somewhere where he can smell it?"

Darn it!

Lorelei grabbed another snack bag from the vending machine's bin. "Want to see the very coolest thing I bought?" She walked to the edge of the pool and opened the bag. A ripple appeared next to the submarine. Dog growled. Homer's palms turned clammy. Something was in there.

Lorelei faced the pool and whistled. Dog ran to Homer's side, then pressed his head between Homer's shins, watching as the ripple moved. A red speedboat, which was tied to a mooring post, began to rock back and forth as the ripple passed by. Dog trembled. Who could blame him? The last ripple he'd seen in that water had belonged to a vicious monster. "What's in there?" Homer asked, grabbing Dog's leash just in case.

"Wait until you see," Lorelei said. She knelt at the edge and put her hand into the murky water. "I call him Speckles." The ripple moved straight for Lorelei, and just before it reached her, something surfaced—something black and covered in white polka dots. Whatever it was, it was huge! It lifted its smooth, flat head above the water and opened an enormous mouth. The mouth opened so wide it looked like a black hole. Lorelei dumped the snack bag's contents into the mouth, which then closed, and the creature disappeared below the water. "Freeze-dried plankton," she said as she crumpled the bag. "Speckles loves it."

"What was that thing?" Homer asked.

"He's a whale shark, the biggest fish in the ocean." She patted the shark's tail as he passed by. "You don't have to worry. He's my watchdog. He guards the place. He looks scary, but whale sharks are gentle. They aren't like other sharks. Speckles wouldn't hurt anyone. Sometimes I ride on his back. I bought him from a zoo. Poor thing lived there his whole life."

For a moment, Homer thought that shark-riding might be a fun thing to do, but then anger rushed over him. "I don't care about all this stuff, Lorelei. I want my map!"

"I won't give it back, but I'm glad you're here." She

flared her nostrils. "I need Dog and his treasure-sniffing nose."

Homer's cheeks burned red. "You can't have him." He gripped the leash so tightly his fingers ached. "I'll never give him to you. And you promised you'd never kidnap him again."

"I know that," she said. "That's why I want you both to become members of FOUND. Come on, Homer. Join me. Why not? You had the map in your possession and you did nothing with it. Why didn't you do something with it?"

"I was waiting...." he mumbled.

"Waiting for what?"

"Till I got older. Ajitabh and Zelda said I should finish school before I set out on the quest."

Lorelei laughed. "Why would you do a stupid thing like that? You're young and strong. This is the time, Homer Pudding. Right now. You should have gone after that treasure the minute you got the map instead of listening to those L.O.S.T. people. You're never going to get anywhere in life if you let other people tell you what to do all the time."

Some of the things she was saying made sense. Homer had promised his uncle that he'd continue the quest. But while he was busy growing up and finishing school, someone else might find Rumpold's treasure. Homer stared at the word on Lorelei's pocket. FOUND. She wasn't waiting around. She was making things happen.

But by helping her, he'd be a traitor to L.O.S.T.

"So what's it gonna be, Homer?" she asked. "Are you gonna go back to Milkydale and clean goat poop, or are you gonna come with me on the most important treasure quest the world has ever known?"

Goat poop or treasure quest? That seemed an unfair choice.

A buzzer sounded. Lorelei yanked the remote control from her pocket. Her face went pale as she stared at the yellow light that flashed on the remote's surface. "Someone just went down the tortoise slide," she whispered. Then she frowned at Homer. "I'm not expecting anyone. Are you?"

14

Lost and Found

Daisy the rat waddled down the stairs with an inhaler clenched between her sharp teeth. She dropped the inhaler at Lorelei's feet. Dog barked and wagged his tail as Hercules appeared on the top step.

"Someone needs to vacuum that tunnel," Hercules said. "I nearly choked on a spider. And there should be a mattress at the end of the slide. I think I bruised my tailbone. I'm going to need some anti-inflammatory medicine." He walked down the stairs and set his first-aid kit on the floor as if he'd been invited. Rummaging through it, he pulled out some nasal spray and spritzed both nostrils. "This dank air will aggravate my mucus membranes for sure."

Lorelei grabbed Homer's arm and pulled him aside. "What is *he* doing here?" The question shot out of her mouth with a fair amount of spit.

"I don't know," Homer replied with a shrug. Dog wagged his tail and poked Hercules with his nose until he was rewarded with a pat on the head.

"Hi, Dog," Hercules said. Then he recapped the nasal spray and looked around. "Hi, Lorelei. What is this place? Is this some kind of fort?"

"It's not a *fort*. Little kids make forts. This is my lair." Then Lorelei jabbed a finger into Homer's chest. "Did you tell him how to find me? We have a gentleman's agreement, remember? I keep your secret and you keep mine. Did you break our gentleman's agreement?"

"I didn't break it," Homer insisted. "I don't know how he found this place."

"I followed you," Hercules said. He closed his first-aid kit, then stuck his inhaler in his pocket.

"I don't believe you," Lorelei said. "I think Homer broke our gentleman's agreement. And if that's the case, then what's keeping me from breaking it?" It was a threat that shot right to Homer's heart. Dog would be in terrible danger if the world knew his secret. Every thief, from the lowly pickpocket to the glamorous international spy, would want Dog.

"You've got to believe me," Homer said. "I had no idea Hercules was following me."

"He's telling the truth," Hercules said. "Hey, do you have proper ventilation in this lair? All this dampness could lead to mold growth. My lungs are very sensitive to mold spores."

Lorelei folded her arms and stared suspiciously at Hercules. "Why did you follow Homer? Did you come here because you want to leave L.O.S.T.?"

"Of course not." Hercules picked a bit of spiderweb from his wiry hair. "I'm not a traitor like Gertrude and Torch."

"So why are you here?"

"Because I knew Homer wouldn't let you go on this quest without him. This is his dream. Just like it's my dream to win the World's Spelling Bee twice in a row. I wouldn't let anyone take that chance away from me." He smiled at Homer. "Also, I'm here to protect him."

Lorelei snorted. "Protect him? How can you protect Homer? You're afraid of everything. You fainted on Mushroom Island when we faced that bear."

"For your information, Lorelei, I'm not afraid of *everything*. I have certain phobias, I admit that. But I can help Homer because..." He glanced at Homer.

Homer grabbed Hercules by the arm. "Don't," he warned under his breath. "Don't tell her. You can't trust her."

"It's okay," Hercules whispered. "I want to help you. This is the only way I'll be able to persuade her to let me join you on the quest."

"But I'm not going on the quest."

"Of course you are. You can't let her get away with this." He turned and faced Lorelei. "I can protect Homer because I'm superstrong."

She laughed. "You? No way." Her doubt was understandable. Hercules possessed arms and legs so skinny they might have belonged to a stork. And his ever-present first-aid kit might as well have had the word *wimp* painted on it. "Superstrong?" She laughed again.

Hercules shrugged, then walked over to one of the vending machines. Without a grunt or a groan, he picked it up as if it were the family cat.

"*Whoa!*" Lorelei cried. "That's impressive." She looked around and pointed to the purple golf cart. "Can you lift that?" He did. Then he lifted the trampoline. Even though Homer already knew his friend's secret, he still smiled with amazement. "Holy smoke, you *are* superstrong," Lorelei said. "So that explains your name."

"Not exactly," Hercules said. "My father, Senator Simplisticus Simple, is a Romanophile—that's someone who loves all things Roman. He chose Roman names for everyone in the family—Tiberius, Caesar, Diana, Romulus, and Brutus the dog. It's just a weird coincidence that I'm strong like the original Hercules. But my parents don't know. Neither do my brothers and sister."

"So you've kept your strength a secret this whole time?" Lorelei said.

"If my parents knew, they'd make me play hockey or soccer or worse—they'd make me play football. Such a Neanderthal sport."

"You're strong and you don't play sports?" Lorelei's eyebrows knitted. "But you could be a champion."

"I am a champion," he said, throwing back his shoulders. "I won the World's Spelling Bee."

She narrowed her eyes and gave Hercules a long look. "The real Hercules didn't win spelling bees. The real Hercules had to complete twelve labors. He skinned a lion that was terrorizing a town. He slayed a nine-headed sea serpent. He even kidnapped a three-headed dog."

"I don't want to skin or slay or kidnap anything. I want to use my strength for good, not evil."

"I thought you said you wanted to protect Homer?"

"I do." Hercules shrugged. "I guess if we come face-to-face with a nine-headed sea serpent, I'll do my best to keep it from eating us."

Lorelei broke the stare with a smile. "Okay. You can come with us."

"Hey, wait a minute," Homer said. "I'm not going anywhere with you. I'm not helping you find Rumpold's treasure."

"Yes, you are," she said. "Because if you and Dog don't help me, then I'll tell the world about L.O.S.T."

They stood nose-to-nose, arms folded, faces red with stubborn pride, breathing like a pair of bulldogs. The happy tomato-soup days were long gone. The last dregs of friendship evaporated in the heat of their glares, like beads of water on a sizzling-hot sidewalk. Homer vowed to himself that he would never *ever* trust her again. "I'm not joining FOUND."

Hercules cleared his throat. "There's a simple solution to this, and I'm not just saying that because my last name is Simple." He pushed up his rugby sleeves. "If you two work together, then Homer can undertake the quest in the name of L.O.S.T. and Lorelei in the name of FOUND. The two of you can split the treasure fifty-fifty. In other words, you cooperate."

"Cooperate?" Lorelei asked.

"You work together. *Cooperation* comes from the Latin *co*, meaning 'together,' and *operatus*, meaning 'work.'"

"I know what cooperation means," Lorelei said. "It's just that I hadn't considered..." She nodded. "Yes, I think it's a good idea. We work together, we split the treasure. Why not? Rumpold's treasure is sure to be huge. There will be plenty for both of us."

Homer wasn't sure. It sounded good. But this was Lorelei.

"Think about it this way," she said. "I have the map, and I'm going after this treasure with or without you. But I have a better chance of success with you. You can give your half to some stupid museum so you won't be breaking any of L.O.S.T.'s rules. And I'll do what I want with my half. And everyone will be happy."

"And I'll keep a record of the event," Hercules said. "An official record for posterity."

"This time I need a definition," Lorelei said.

"*Posterity* means 'future generations.' It's from the Latin *posterus*, which means 'coming after.' Your biographers will need to know exactly what happened."

"Biographers?" Homer said with surprise. He'd often imagined that one day a book would be written about him, but he'd never discussed this with anyone. And no one had ever brought it up in casual conversation until now. He'd imagined *The Biography of Homer W. Pudding* as required reading for students all over the world. He'd be a role model for those who'd been called *fatso* or *weirdo* or *dork*.

"Let's make this clear," Homer said. "I'm not joining

FOUND. I'm doing this in the name of L.O.S.T. Hercules, Dog, and I are doing this for L.O.S.T."

Lorelei held out her hand. "We must make a second gentleman's agreement." She waited for Homer and Hercules to plop their hands on top of hers. Her voice grew very serious. "We three agree that we will search for Rumpold Smeller's treasure, and when we find it, we will split the booty fifty-fifty. Half going to FOUND, which is me, and half going to L.O.S.T., which is you guys."

"And we'll do it in a week," Homer said, " 'cause I have to get home for my sister's birthday."

"And I need to register for the spelling bee."

A buzzer sounded. A light flashed simultaneously on the universal remote. Lorelei ran over to the big screen. "It's Gertrude and Torch," she said. "They're calling."

"Don't give them the reptile book," Homer warned. "We can't trust them."

"I have it all figured out," Lorelei assured him. "You'd better hide over there, where they can't see you." She pointed to a beanbag chair that was tucked into a corner. Homer grabbed Dog. The plastic beans squeaked as the boys sat. Lorelei settled on her red throne and pushed a button. "What do you two want?" she asked.

The two traitors still sat on the deck of the yacht, the sails of other boats bobbing behind them. Gertrude's little sailor hat was back on her head. She held up *Rare Reptiles I Caught and Stuffed*, an enormous grin plastered on her pasty face. "I just wanted you to know that your delivery arrived safe and sound."

Homer leaped to his feet. Lorelei had delivered the map into their greedy hands? Wasn't she smarter than that? She was going to ruin everything.

"I'm glad to see you have the book," Lorelei said. "I paid that delivery boy a lot of money. We can't be too careful with the only known copy of Rumpold's map. Do you have the glue sticks and scissors so you can start putting the map together?"

"Oh, we have what we need," Gertrude said. "Believe me, we have everything we need."

Torch yanked the book from Gertrude's hands and started flipping through the pages. Her hawk watched from her shoulder as the pages flew. A snicker seeped from Torch's mouth. She leaned close to the camera. "Where are you?" she asked Lorelei.

"I'm at my... house, packing my suitcase for the quest. I'll be joining you soon."

Gertrude and Torch glanced at each other, then broke into a round of wicked belly laughing. Gertrude's chins jiggled. The hawk flapped its wings trying to keep its balance on Torch's rocking shoulder.

"You're so stupid," Torch said. "You think we're gonna

wait around for you to join us?" A rumble sounded, like a motor. The scenery behind the women began to move.

They were leaving! Homer ran to the screen. "Wait!" he cried. "That's my map!"

Torch stopped laughing. "Well, well," she said with a snort. "Look who's gone to the dark side. And to think His Lordship had so much confidence in you. When the membership finds out you're helping FOUND, you'll be cast out."

Gertrude grabbed the book from Torch and waved it at the camera. "This is my revenge, little girl. You stole all those harmonic crystals from me. Did you think I'd forgive you?"

"Give our regards to the losers at L.O.S.T.," Torch said. Then the screen went black.

Lorelei sat back in her throne and folded her arms behind her head. She was oddly quiet for someone who'd just been double-crossed. Homer, on the other hand, wanted to shake her for making such a huge mistake.

"Why aren't you freaking out?" he cried.

Lorelei sighed. "Homer, calm down."

But how could he calm down? His dream was sailing away. His promise to his uncle would never be fulfilled. "We've got to stop them." He grabbed Dog's leash and headed toward the stairs.

"But, Homer—"

"This is all your fault, Lorelei. That map was safe under my bed, and now Gertrude and Torch have it." With a grunt, he pushed Dog's rump up the first two steps. Hercules grabbed his first-aid kit and started toward the stairs.

"They don't have it," Lorelei called.

Dog grunted. "What do you mean, they don't have it? I saw it. They…" Homer stopped pushing and paused for a minute. Lorelei was many things, but she wasn't stupid. She'd proven her ability to outsmart people time and time again. He whipped around. "You gave them a fake book."

She nodded.

"Oh, it's a ruse," Hercules said. "That's quite brilliant."

"I can't believe you thought I'd hand over the map," Lorelei said. "How could you think I'd do something like that? It was so easy to fool them. I figured they've never read a copy of *Rare Reptiles I Caught and Stuffed*. I mean, who has? It's such a totally boring book. So I got a dusty copy from the library, and I took a map, cut it into bits, and pasted it inside."

"What map?" Homer asked.

"Something I found in Madame's things. A map to some place called the Lost Temple of the Reptile King."

"That's in the middle of the jungle," Homer said.

"Uh-huh. That should keep them busy for a while."

She frowned. "I do hate ruining library books, though. I'll be sure to replace it with a nice new book."

Homer was so relieved he wanted to hug Lorelei, but of course he didn't, because ex-friends don't get hugs.

Lorelei opened the seat to her throne and took out a metal box. The box was sealed in airtight plastic. As soon as she ripped off the plastic and opened the lid, Dog went nuts. He ran in a circle, sniffing the air as if a rabbit had appeared on the scene. He pressed his nose into the box, sniffed some more, his tail wagging. Lorelei set the box on the lair's floor. Dog flipped onto his back and rolled against the box, spreading its luscious scent all over himself. Thanks to Dog, Homer knew without a doubt that what Lorelei held was real.

"So, shall we put the map together and get started on our quest?"

"Yes!" Hercules and Homer said.

15

The Belly of a
Whale Shark

Some people are good at jigsaw puzzles. They buy those fat boxes, the ones with more than twenty thousand pieces. Days drift by, maybe weeks, as the puzzle takes shape. When it's done, they frame the puzzle and put it on the wall so whenever a guest comes over, they can say, "Look at that puzzle. It took two whole years. Aren't you impressed?"

Other people, however, prefer puzzles with, say, ten or twenty pieces at most, because after a few minutes of puzzling, boredom sets in and the swimming pool calls, or that shady spot beneath the willow tree, or the movie theater. Lorelei was that kind of person.

"Why is this taking so long?" she complained for the hundredth time. "This is soooo boring."

Homer, Hercules, and Lorelei lay on their stomachs on a pink carpet. They had cut out all the map pieces from the reptile book and had spread them out.

"Boring?" Homer held one of the squares. Like most of the other pieces, it was plain white with little black dots sprinkled in no apparent order. A bunch of pieces had words on them. Hercules was working on those. "This is Rumpold Smeller's map, the most important map in pirating history, and you say it's boring?"

"The map isn't boring. But putting it together is. Can't you go faster?"

"It's not that easy," Homer grumbled.

A spray of water hit Homer. Speckles the whale shark swam along the edge of the pool. Luckily the water hadn't hit the map pieces—though the map had already been inside the belly of a mutant tortoise, so a little water probably wouldn't hurt it.

"Hey!" Homer cried again as another spray of water hit his face. The whale shark's eye peeked over the pool's edge. "I think he's doing that on purpose."

"He wants to play," Lorelei explained. She stomped

over to a toy chest and grabbed a red beach ball. "Fetch," she called as she tossed the ball into the pool. Speckles swam after it and caught it in his enormous mouth. Then he swam back to the side of the pool and spat out the ball at Lorelei. Dog, who'd kept a cautious distance between himself and the lair's pool, took a few wary steps forward. "Fetch," Lorelei called again as she threw the ball. As the shark went after it, Dog wagged his tail.

While it was odd, indeed, that a whale shark wanted to play fetch, Homer had only one thing on his mind. "Lorelei, will you please stop making so much noise? We're trying to concentrate."

In truth, Lorelei wasn't the source of Homer's frustration. The map was proving to be very confusing. There were no lines indicating mountains or rivers or roads. But there was a date in the bottom corner and a little directional key in the upper corner. Other than the words, everything else was just black dots.

Hercules sat up. "I've pieced the words together."

"What does it say?" Lorelei asked as she ran over.

Hercules read:

> *Flammae geminate supra et infra*
> *Speculum infinitum inter eas*
> *In oculis caelestibus stellae lucent*
> *Post salivam quod quaeritis latet*

"Huh?" Lorelei and Homer said.

"It's Latin."

"Can you translate?" Homer asked.

"Sure. I'm the spelling bee champion of the world. But it might take a while." He began to scribble in a spiral notebook.

Lorelei sighed and stomped back to the side of the pool, where she grabbed the red ball and returned to her game of whale shark fetch. Homer furrowed his brow and glared at her. "We've got serious business over here, Lorelei. We could use your help figuring this out."

"You're the map reader," she said. A spray of water hit Homer's sleeve as Speckles spat out the ball.

I'm the map reader, Homer thought. And so he was. That's why it would be very difficult for him to admit that this map didn't make sense.

Hercules stared at the Latin words, deep in thought, mumbling to himself. Homer, on the other hand, was a bit worried about how close Dog was standing to the edge of the pool. "That shark's got a really big mouth," he said to Lorelei. "Aren't you afraid he might eat you?"

"Speckles would never eat me," Lorelei said. "He doesn't eat mammals. Fetch!"

As she threw the ball into the pool, Dog jumped in after it. He paddled up to the ball and sank his teeth into the red plastic. That's when Speckles opened his enormous mouth. Dog didn't stand a chance. Even if Dog had been an athletic sort of creature, even if he'd had flippers and a mermaid tail, he would not have been able to escape the suction of that mouth. In an instant, Dog and the red ball disappeared into the black hole. The whale shark's mouth snapped close.

"Bad Speckles!" Lorelei cried.

Homer's heart got confused for a moment and tripled its beat. No words came. Pure agony shot through his body like a bolt of lightning. What had just happened? Had his beloved dog been eaten by a shark? No survival training could have prepared Homer for this. The only word he managed to utter was "Dog?"

Lorelei, however, was quick to react. She leaped onto the whale shark's back. "Open up!" she ordered, kneeling on the creature. "Come on, open up!" She rapped her knuckles on his head.

Angry tears filled Homer's eyes. "He ate Dog!"

"He didn't eat him," Lorelei said. "He's playing hide-and-seek."

Homer ran to the side of the pool as Lorelei and the shark took a lap. "He ate Dog. I saw him eat Dog!"

"Homer, don't worry. I have an idea." Lorelei pointed to the vending machine. "Get a bag of brine shrimp. He can't resist."

Homer ran to the machine, got a bag, and ripped it

open. Then he knelt at the pool's edge and held out the bag with a trembling hand. The whale shark swam up and opened his mouth. A spray of spit coated Homer's face as Dog was ejected. Dog flew through the air, the red ball still in his mouth, and landed right next to Hercules. Hercules looked up from his word puzzle and said, "Oh, hi, Dog."

Homer tossed the bag of shrimp into the shark's mouth. Just before the shark submerged with his treat, Lorelei jumped back onto land. Homer threw his arms around Dog.

"Are you okay?"

"Urrrr." Dog shook shark spit from his ears.

Homer didn't know whether he should yell at Lorelei or thank her. But that was nothing new.

"Hey, you guys, I've got it. Do you want to hear the translation?" Hercules asked. And this is what he read:

Twins of flame above and below
An endless mirror between
In heavenly eyes the stars do shine
Behind saliva hides what you seek

"Saliva?" Lorelei said. "The treasure's hidden behind saliva? That's disgusting." She sat between Homer and

Hercules. "So? What does it mean? Where are we going?"

"I'm not sure," Homer said, his heart settling back to its normal rhythm.

"What do you mean, you're not sure?" She folded her arms. "You're supposed to be a map expert."

"The only thing I can figure out is that it's a celestial map. That makes sense, since Rumpold spent so much time at sea and he'd navigate using the stars."

"Can you read a celestial map?" Hercules asked.

This was no time to be embarrassed. He had to admit the truth. "No. I can't read it. We're going to need help. But I know just the place to go."

16

Prisoner #90's Escape

It was called Soupwater Prison for good reason. From a distance, the swamp that surrounded the concrete fortress looked like pea soup. Up close, the water had a thick, goopy consistency with mysterious lumps floating at the surface. Every so often, one of the lumps moved on its own accord.

"Disgusting," Madame la Directeur hissed between clenched teeth. Waist-deep in the swamp, she grabbed an overhanging tree branch for balance. A water snake slithered past, leaving a fleeting pattern in the muck. Madame took a deep breath and pushed forward.

That morning, while she was sitting in the prison cafeteria, there'd been a press conference on the prison television. A pink-haired girl had told the world that she possessed an important treasure map. And the girl had said, "If you want your map, Homer, you know where to find me." A malevolent laugh had risen in Madame's throat. The Pudding kid wouldn't be able to ignore the invitation. Revenge was close at hand.

The escape had been so easy. Whoever had designed the prison's security system had ignored an obvious fact—that the best way to hide is to simply blend in.

Rumpold Smeller the Pirate often used this technique, which is known as camouflage. While searching foreign ports for treasure, he would leave his pirate clothing on his ship and wear whatever the locals wore, even if that meant donning a grass skirt and coconut-husk shirt. When traversing a forest, he'd stick branches into his hat. And while his competitors preferred to sail their pirate ships right up to their victims' ships and jump on board, Rumpold covered himself in seaweed and swam to his target. This cunning ploy was always successful, for no captain ever pointed to the water and hollered, "All men to battle stations! A pile of seaweed is coming our way!"

While working in the prison kitchen, Madame noticed that the biscuit-mix bags were blue and white, just like the prison pajamas. Biscuits were a staple of the Soup-water diet. The tasteless lumps of cooked dough were fed to inmates at every meal. Breakfast biscuits were drizzled with cold gravy. Lunch biscuits had a slab of ham shoved into the middle. Dinner biscuits came with an extra dollop of cold gravy. The prison warden knew that if people suddenly stopped committing crimes and Soupwater Prison was no longer necessary, he could easily turn it into a biscuit factory.

Hundreds of biscuit-mix bags were emptied each week and tossed into the garbage bin. The garbage truck collected the bin at precisely 3:00 p.m., when the security gates opened. So Madame la Directeur, wearing her blue-and-white prison pajamas, decided to simply blend in.

Once the garbage truck had left the prison yard and was headed over a bridge, Madame jumped. The truck's engine masked the sound of her splash as she landed in goopy swamp water. She spat out a pollywog and wiped a few more from her face. "Ewww," she said with a shudder. The prison alarm hadn't yet sounded, but she knew she had no time to waste. She needed to move away from the road as quickly as possible.

Because her wristwatch had been confiscated by the prison warden, Madame had no way to tell how much time had passed before she reached the first signs of human life—a little shack and outhouse. She stepped out of the swamp and sat on a log. After rolling up her soggy pajama bottoms, she gasped. In the old days, when she'd been a member of L.O.S.T., she'd owned a pair of leech-proof socks. They would have come in handy, seeing as her calves were now covered with leeches. Flicking the fat, blood-filled pests onto the ground, she mumbled to herself, "I will never forget this. I'll show him. He'll wish he'd never been born."

A bucket of paint and a paintbrush sat on the shack's half-painted porch. Whoever had been painting it was probably taking a break. Trying to muster some dignity, Madame tiptoed past the shack and stopped at a clothesline. Stealing was no problem for her. It was a skill she'd honed over the years, and she'd been good at it—until that rotten Homer Pudding kid got in the way. She snatched a pair of jeans and a cotton T-shirt. Then she changed behind a tree. She'd never worn such garish clothing. She missed her pearls, tailored suits, and designer heels. She picked moss from her hair. How long had it been since she'd had her hair washed, trimmed, and styled at the posh Parlor de Beauty? She stared in horror at her ragged fingernails. How long had it been since she'd had them filed and shellacked at the Fingernail Emporium?

A baseball cap lay on the shack's front stoop. She grabbed it and pulled it over her wet hair.

She knew she might not make it. When the police learned of her escape, she'd be hunted like a fox. Breaking out of prison was a crime that would add years to her sentence. But she had to try. She craved revenge as a leech craves blood.

Dressed as a "normal" person, she walked down a narrow driveway until she came to a dirt road. She glanced down the road, then up the road, wondering which way to go. An engine hummed in the distance. Then a motorcycle appeared on the horizon, churning up a cloud of dirt in its wake. "Well, this is fortunate," Madame said to herself. She held out her thumb as the cycle approached.

"You want a ride?" the driver asked.

"Yes."

"Where to?"

Madame la Directeur slid onto the seat behind the driver and wrapped her arms around his waist. "Take me to The City."

PART FOUR

MAP OF THE MONTH CLUB

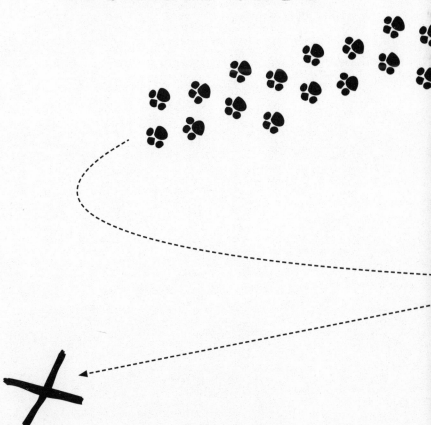

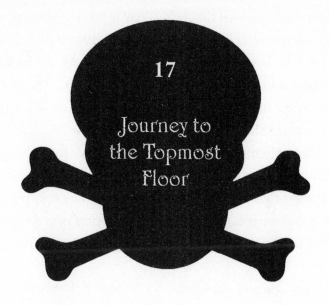

17

Journey to the Topmost Floor

The afternoon was nearly over by the time the L.O.S.T. and FOUND team sped through the lair's channel in Lorelei's red speedboat. A push of the remote control opened the gate, and the boat roared out onto City Lake. Dog sat at the helm, his ears billowing in the wind, as Lorelei thrust the boat into its highest gear. The wake tore across the lake, upsetting a canoe, a paddleboat, and a flock of geese.

They moored the boat at a public dock, then headed for their destination. Dog pranced down the sidewalk, his loose skin undulating with each step. Surely no one could have guessed that he'd recently been swallowed by a whale shark. There was a happy rhythm to his stride. Maybe he was relieved to be out of the lair. Maybe he was simply looking forward to all the fire hydrants. Maybe he was happy because, after rolling all over Rumpold's map, he'd covered himself with the scent of treasure.

The only member of the team not in attendance was Daisy, who'd stayed back at the lair to work on a nest. "It's best that way," Lorelei said. "Rats aren't very popular around here. City people leave out traps and try to kill them." Homer didn't tell her that country people did the same thing.

They turned onto the Boulevard of Destinations. "There it is," Hercules said as he tucked the spiral notebook under his arm. It would be difficult to miss the Map of the Month Club, for it had a singular unique feature. A giant world globe perched on the roof, providing a vibrant splash of color amid the other, drab buildings.

Fortunately, the map club had no revolving door, just a regular door with a regular knob that opened into a regular sort of lobby—except that entire continents were painted on the floor and a giant compass stood on a pedestal in the center of the room. A lady with cat-eye glasses sat behind an information desk.

"May I help you?" she asked as she chewed the end of a pen.

"Go on," Lorelei whispered, shoving Homer toward the desk.

Homer stuck his hands in his pockets because he thought that would hide his nervousness, even though jitters ran up and down his legs. Because he didn't want the true identity of the map to be revealed, this was going to be tricky. "Uh, hello. I have a map, and I was wondering if I could get some help reading it. It's for a...a...a school paper."

"A school paper?" The lady frowned. "Today is not school-visit day."

As Homer pondered his next move, Hercules wandered over to a bank of elevators. A brass plaque on the wall listed the names of the various offices and which floors they called home. "There's an office of celestial navigation," he called. "It's on the topmost floor."

"Could we go to the topmost floor?" Homer asked the lady. "To have our map read by someone who reads celestial maps?"

"That office is closed to the public. No one's allowed up there. Besides, we don't offer a reading service here. We publish maps and send them in the mail to our subscribers."

"I'm a subscriber," Homer explained. "I love your maps."

The lady looked over the rims of her cat-eye glasses. "Then perhaps you'd like to buy one. We have maps of the known world, maps of imaginary worlds, maps of the heavens, maps of the human body, land maps, ocean maps, river maps"—her sentences ran together as if she didn't need to breathe—"maps from the ancient times, maps from medieval times, maps from yesterday, maps from the future—"

"The future? How is that possible?" Lorelei interrupted.

"I'm not at liberty to answer that question." The lady tucked the pen behind her ear and continued. "Maps drawn by sailors, maps drawn by mountain climbers, maps of the subway, the freeway, the Milky Way, maps of circuses, maps of zoos, maps of—"

"Excuse me," Homer interrupted. "But I don't want to buy a map. I already have a map." He leaned over the desk and lowered his voice. "I'm usually really good when it comes to reading maps, but this one is...odd." Then he remembered and pulled his invitation from his pocket. "I got this," he explained, hoping she wouldn't realize it was a fake. "From Mr. Dimknob for a VIP tour."

"Mr. Dimknob is very busy." She glanced at the invitation. "Besides, the tour was at noon precisely. Tough break." A bell rang. "Closing time," she announced loudly, a grin breaking across her bored face. "Closing! Time!"

Two elevators opened simultaneously, and out marched a bunch of people with briefcases. They hurried across the lobby, pushing one another to get to the door. Because only a few could fit through at a time, a huge traffic jam ensued. Those closest to the door flattened themselves and squeezed through like paste through a tube.

The lady with the cat-eye glasses grabbed her purse and pulled out a lipstick. "You'll have to leave now. I don't want to be late for my dinner date." She spread hot pink all over her lips.

Two more elevators opened, and more people hurried out, joining the writhing group at the front door. These people either hated their jobs or they had really important places to go. The lady tossed her lipstick into her purse, then said, "Follow me so you won't get locked in." And she marched around the desk and elbowed her way into the crowd.

As the last elevator opened, Homer and Lorelei shared a look of frustration. Someone bonked Homer with a briefcase. Someone else tripped over Dog. The lady had disappeared amid a sea of gray flannel suits.

"Psssst," Hercules called. With his foot, he held an elevator door open. Without any discussion, Lorelei pushed Homer forward.

Since their death-defying experience in an elevator on their first visit to The City, neither Dog nor Homer was a fan of the contraption. Dog was about to turn his body into concrete, but Homer was fast. "Oh no, you don't." Luckily the floor had just been waxed, so one push was all it took. Dog slid on his tummy like an ice-skater, bumping gently into Hercules's sneakers. The elevator doors closed.

Lorelei stared at the panel of buttons. "What floor?"

"The directory said the topmost floor," Hercules replied.

With a shrug, she pushed the highest floor, which happened to be the thirtieth.

Ding. The second-floor button lit up, and the elevator slowed.

"Uh-oh," Homer said. "Someone's still in the building." They didn't have time to come up with a plan, because the doors swooshed open.

"Oh, it's just a cleaning lady," Lorelei said with a sigh of relief. Hercules's shoulders relaxed. Homer, however, stiffened like an overstarched shirt.

The Unpolluter pressed her hand against the elevator door, keeping it open as she stood on the threshold. Her gray hair was plastered beneath her shower cap. Her athletic socks peeked over the tops of a pair of black rubber boots. She said nothing, her gaze traveling from Homer to Hercules to Dog, then resting on Lorelei. "You kids lost?" she asked.

"No," Lorelei said.

She kept her hand on the elevator door. "The building's closed. You got business here?"

Homer followed The Unpolluter's gaze as it landed on the word FOUND, emblazoned on Lorelei's pink jumpsuit. "Yes, we have *business* here," Lorelei said.

"What kind of *business*?" The Unpolluter asked.

"The kind of *business* that's none of your *business*," Lorelei replied snippily.

The Unpolluter frowned. "I saw you on television. How's the treasure hunt going?"

Lorelei folded her arms. "Fine, thank you very much."

The Unpolluter set a bucket of sudsy water into the elevator. A mop handle poked out of the bucket. She stepped inside and pressed the fourth-floor button. The doors swooshed closed, and the elevator rose.

Dog, who couldn't ignore a bucket of water, be it sudsy or not, stuck his nose inside and managed a few gulps before Homer pulled him away. Homer didn't fret or scold. It wasn't the first bucket of soapy water Dog had helped himself to. Soapy water would simply clean out his insides—maybe make his farts smell better. What worried Homer, at that very moment, was the old woman's threat to "get rid" of Lorelei. He slid in front of Lorelei, blocking her body with his own.

"Hey," she grumbled. "You're squishing me against the wall."

Hercules cleared his throat, then peered around The Unpolluter's shoulder. "Excuse me, but I couldn't help but notice that rather large mole on your nose. Antibacterial ointment might help reduce the inflammation."

The Unpolluter ignored him and instead turned to Homer. "Do you need my help cleaning up any messes?"

He shook his head. "No, I don't need your help."

Lorelei jabbed Homer with her elbow. "You're *squishing* me. Move!" But Homer didn't move. If he'd learned one thing from Dog, it was the "I'm-not-budging-and-you-can't-make-me" technique. He wasn't going to give The Unpolluter a clear view of Lorelei.

"You're certain you don't need help cleaning up the situation?" The Unpolluter asked.

"I'm certain," Homer said through clenched teeth as Lorelei pounded on his back. "I can clean up the mess myself."

"Very well." The Unpolluter pulled a pair of yellow rubber gloves from her apron pocket and slid them onto her hands.

Ding. The elevator doors slid open. The Unpolluter clutched the bucket's handle and stepped out onto the fourth floor. But before the doors closed, she spun around and pointed at Homer. "Remember—I offered my help, but you said you didn't need it." The doors closed.

"What was *that* about?" Lorelei asked as Homer stepped aside.

"I don't know," Homer lied as the elevator rose. He exhaled, but his breath was ragged with worry. Had this meeting been a coincidence or had The Unpolluter followed them to the Map of the Month Club?

"She was creepy," Lorelei said. "She smelled like bleach. And that thing on her nose was practically glowing."

"Bleach aggravates my mucus membranes," Hercules said as he took a hit of his inhaler.

Ding. The elevator stopped on the thirtieth floor, but the doors did not open. Lorelei pushed the open button, but nothing happened. She pushed it again. "What's the problem?" She jabbed it, then punched it.

"Urrrr?" Dog pressed his nose to the crack between the doors.

"If we're trapped in this elevator, I may develop an acute case of claustrophobia, which is the fear of getting stuck in small spaces," Hercules said. "I'm warning you because if I start to get claustrophobic, I might hyper-ventilate, and then I might faint, and I don't have my helmet."

"We're not stuck," Lorelei said. She kicked both doors. "Open!"

"Don't panic," Homer said, even though his chest had begun to tighten. He stepped close to the panel and looked at the buttons. There was something different about the one to floor thirty. Right next to it was a little slot. He ran his finger over the slot. "What's this for?"

"A key?" Hercules asked.

"Maybe. But it would have to be a round key. It looks like a coin slot." He took a quarter from his pocket and shoved it into the slot. The quarter disappeared, but popped right back out. He found a nickel and a penny, but they were too small. "The quarter seems to be the right size."

"We don't have any other coins in this country that are the same size as a quarter," Hercules said.

"Maybe we do." Homer reached under his shirt. He had a hunch, and his late uncle Drake had often said, "Never ignore lunch or a hunch. One can fuel the body while the other can fuel a discovery." So, without consulting his companions, Homer pulled the chain from under his shirt and stuck the membership coin into the slot. The coin did not pop back out. A mechanical *whirr* sounded, and the elevator rose a bit higher. Then the doors whooshed open.

"How did you know to do that?" Lorelei asked, her eyes wide with surprise.

Homer shrugged. He had no idea why a L.O.S.T. membership coin would allow them entrance to the top-most floor of the Map of the Month Club, but he guessed he was about to find out. He retrieved the coin. Then, with a tug on the leash, he led Dog from the elevator.

18

The Office
of Celestial
Navigation

They stood in a narrow corridor. Other than
the elevator, there was only one door, and a sign
on it read OFFICE OF CELESTIAL NAVIGATION.
Homer knocked, but no one answered. He knocked
again and was willing to wait politely, but Lorelei
grabbed the knob and pushed it open. Dog squeezed
past Lorelei's legs and pulled Homer inside.

There could be no doubt they'd reached the topmost
floor, because the domed ceiling was made of glass
panels. A solid square platform had been constructed

at the top of the dome. That's where the enormous globe sat.

Homer took a long look around the room, which seemed to him to be a mapmaker's dream come true. The room itself was cluttered with rolled parchments. Crowded bookshelves covered the northern wall. A table, laden with all sorts of mapmaking instruments and more rolls of parchment, stretched across the room. The tabletop was painted like a blackboard. Drawings and equations had been scribbled here and there in different-colored chalks. Dust coated the floor except for a trail made by footprints that led from a cot to the table and then to a stepladder and back again. The stepladder led to a porthole where a telescope pointed up at the sky. Seven other portholes were spaced at equal intervals around the dome's perimeter.

Dog tugged the leash from Homer's grip, then began to mosey around the room. Homer didn't go after him, because he'd noticed someone standing at the top of the stepladder. The person's back was to Homer, but he could tell it was a girl because she had two long red braids and wore a black skirt and a pair of kneesocks. He assumed she was a child because she was very short. She was probably the daughter of whoever worked in this office. Because she was peering into the telescope's eyepiece, she hadn't noticed the visitors.

Homer cleared his throat. "Excuse me. Is your mom or dad here?"

The girl turned and glared down at him. A bushy beard and mustache covered most of her face. When she spoke, her voice was deep and grumbly. "Ma maw and ma paw are lang deid."

Apparently, she wasn't a *she* after all, nor was she a child. And because *she* was a *he*, the skirt was actually a kilt.

"How did ye git in here?" the small man asked.

"Uh, the door was open," Homer said.

"Open, ye say? Hmmm. Ah thought ah'd closed it. Well, whit do ye want?"

Lorelei stepped forward. "Do you read celestial maps?"

"Who wants tae know?"

"We do," Homer answered.

"And who are ye?" There was so much hair on the man's face, it was difficult to read his expressions. And his accent was thick and tricky to understand.

"Don't tell him our real names," Lorelei whispered in Homer's ear.

"I wouldn't do that," Homer told her under his breath. The last thing he wanted was to get arrested for trespassing, and if he told this man his real name, then his parents might be contacted. There'd be a big lecture and maybe some jail time. Mr. Pudding would assign Homer a whole mess of extra chores and Mrs. Pudding would telephone Ajitabh, and everyone would be disappointed and upset.

"We're students," Homer said, keeping with the original lie, which was so much easier than inventing a new one. Lies, once they begin to pile up, become very difficult to keep track of. "We have to read a celestial map for a school report and—"

"Ah dinna care nothin' aboot school reports." The man turned away and pressed his eye to the telescope's eyepiece.

"Do you care about subscribers?" Hercules asked. "Homer's a subscriber to the Map of the Month Club." Then Hercules took a quick breath and whispered, "Oops, I said your name."

"Ah dinna care nothin' aboot subscribers."

"But you work for the Map of the Month Club," Lorelei said. "Without the subscribers, you wouldn't have a job. So you should help us."

"Ah dinna work for no map club. Ah jist live up here. And ah dinna care nothin' aboot helpin' no one. A jist want to be left alone."

If the kilt-wearing man didn't work for the map club and he was simply living on the topmost floor, as he said, then he had to know something about L.O.S.T. Otherwise, why would a L.O.S.T. coin be necessary for admittance? Homer reached into his shirt to grab his membership coin, but Lorelei stopped him. She leaned close to his ear again and whispered, "Don't show him that. We don't know if we can trust him."

"But the coin got us in here," Homer said.

"That's a good point," Hercules said, huddling up to the other two as if they were about to play a game of football.

Lorelei rolled her eyes. "Yes, but if he knows about L.O.S.T., then he probably knows about Rumpold's treasure. We can't let him figure out we've got Rumpold's map."

"That's a *really* good point," Hercules said.

Yes, of course it was a really good point. Lorelei was full of good points. Homer sighed and let go of the coin's chain. Then he looked back up the ladder. "If you can't read celestial maps, then do you have a book that might help us?"

"Ah never said ah couldna read celestial maps. Ah'm an expert on celestial navigation. But ah dinna care aboot helpin ye. Now, away wi' ye."

"He's so rude," Lorelei grumbled. "Keep him distracted while Hercules and I go look on the bookshelves." She motioned for Hercules to follow, and they tiptoed over to the shelves.

A chewing sound caught Homer's attention. "Uh-oh." He whipped around. "Dog?"

For reasons Homer had yet to figure out, Dog loved paper. It didn't matter if the paper came in the form of a magazine or a library book. It didn't matter if it was a brochure on goat grooming or a school report on Tasmanian wombats. The paper could be colored, lined, or plain white. It might have wrapped a birthday present or it might have wrapped lamb chops from the butcher. Dog loved paper in all its shapes and forms, and that is why he stood on the topmost floor eating one of the rolls of parchment. Homer hurried to Dog's side and yanked the parchment from his mouth. It was a map. "How many times do I have to tell you not to eat other people's maps?" Homer scolded, though he was more embarrassed than angry. Being angry at such a great dog was nearly impossible.

"Urrrr." Dog wagged his tail apologetically, a shred of paper stuck to his chin.

"How can you be hungry already?" Homer shook his head in wonder. Dog had eaten a bunch of vending-machine snacks in Lorelei's lair. For a creature who exerted such little energy, he needed a surprising amount of refueling. "I'll get you something when we're done here."

Clunking footsteps sounded as the red-haired man stomped down the ladder. Homer hid the ruined map behind his back, certain that the man was going to start hollering about the destruction of his property. After the man stepped onto the floor, he walked over to Dog. His eyebrows were as bushy as his beard. He was shorter than Homer had first thought, standing at about three and a half feet tall, and some of that height was provided by his wild red hair. He picked the shred of paper from Dog's chin.

"I'm sorry he ate your map," Homer said. "I hope it wasn't an important map."

"Is yon a wee basset hound?"

"Yes," Homer said. No one had ever described Dog as "wee." And Homer certainly wouldn't have chosen that word, not after carrying Dog through that revolving door.

"Ah'd a wee basset hound when ah was a lad. Ah loved yon wee hound." Was that a tear sparkling at the corner of the man's eye? "Ah've a soft spot in ma heart for bassets. Can ye guess why?" He looked up at Homer.

"Because you had one when you were..." Homer almost said the word *little* but was afraid that word might insult the man. "When you were...a lad?"

"Aye, but there's another reason." The man crouched and scratched beneath Dog's chin. "We both hae the genetic markers of dwarfism. That's why we both hae these short legs."

Homer nodded. When he'd first met Zelda, she'd

explained that while Dog had a condition that kept him from growing, she had a condition that'd made her grow very fast—hence her eight-foot-two-inch status. "Genetic markers," Homer repeated.

"I've often wondered if I have some sort of genetic marker that makes me afraid of things," Hercules called from the bookcase. "I have lots of phobias."

The man stopped scratching Dog and stood. "Whit sorts of things are ye afraid of?" he asked.

"All sorts of things. Germs, bullies, feather pillows, random objects falling on my head, forgetting to take my vitamins—"

"Why do you live up here if you don't work for the Map of the Month Club?" Lorelei interrupted. She made a new path on the dusty floor as she walked along the bookcase.

"Ah dinna like people," the man grumbled. "Ah'm a hermit."

"Really?" Hercules asked. "Then you might have anthrophobia. Many hermits do. That's fear of people. I don't have anthrophobia, but I am afraid of my brothers and sister. They're sports-playing meatheads. I'm also afraid of poisonous snakes. That's called ophidiophobia. I'm afraid of the yellow bits of popcorn that get stuck in your throat, but I don't know what that's called. The one thing I'm not afraid of is skydiving."

"Hello? Can we get back to the map?" Lorelei asked irritably. She walked up to Homer and whispered, "There are a million books over there. I don't know where to begin. We need his help."

Homer smiled nicely at the man. "Could you please help us read our map? It's definitely a star chart, but I don't know how to read it."

"I can pay you," Lorelei said. "I've got lots of money."

"Ah dinna care aboot money, lassie. Ah told ye, ah dinna like people."

Dog, as if on cue, licked the man's hand. Then he turned his sad eyes up and whined. It was an expression that only the coldhearted could ignore. The man's beard and mustache rustled. "Ah'll make an exception, but only because ye have yon wee hound." From the sweetened tone in the man's voice, Homer assumed that a smile was hiding under all that hair. "Come away wi' ye. O'er here to ma table."

19

Sky Dragon

The odd little man climbed onto one of the stools, pushed aside a protractor and a ruler, then sat on the blackboard table. Lorelei, Homer, and Hercules each grabbed a stool and gathered around, while Dog stretched out on the floor beneath the table. Lorelei took the map from the inside pocket of her jumpsuit, unfolded it, then set it on the table in front of the man.

He whistled. "Whit happened to yon map? Looks like it's been eaten by Nessie herself."

"Who?" Homer asked.

"Nessie, lad. The Loch Ness Monster."

It was *eaten by a monster*, Homer wanted to say, an image of the mutant tortoise filling his mind. But a comment like that would surely lead the conversation off-track and annoy Lorelei. Best keep to the issue at hand.

"I know these are stars," Homer said, pointing to one of the black dots. "But I don't know much about the constellations. Can you figure it out?"

The man stared at the map. He turned it one way and said, "Hmmmm." Then he turned it the other way and said, "Mmmmm." Then he turned it again and again until, with a satisfied grunt, he announced, "Ye've got yersel a Draco."

"Draco?" both Homer and Lorelei asked.

"That's Latin for 'dragon,' " Hercules said.

The man grabbed a piece of blue chalk and began to draw on the map. "Hey, wait a minute," Lorelei said, reaching out to stop him, but Homer held her back.

"It's okay," Homer told her. "It's just chalk. We can wipe it off if we need to."

They watched as the man expertly connected some of the dots. When he'd finished, a dragon lay across the map, the tip of its tail at one end, its head at the other. "It's one of the oldest constellations," the man said. "The Egyptians identified it way back when the pyramids were made, but the Greeks were the ones tae name it Draco the dragon, because of yon myth."

Lorelei sat up straight. "What myth?"

"The one aboot Hercules and the dragon with one hundred heads."

"Oh, I know that myth," Lorelei said. "Hercules's eleventh labor was to steal golden apples from the dragon, but he couldn't do it alone. So he asked Atlas for help." She glanced at Homer. "By the way, Atlas was the guy who held up the world. That's why the atlas is named after him."

By the way? Of course Homer knew that fact. Anyone who knew anything about maps knew that atlases were named after Atlas. He rolled his eyes. She was such a know-it-all.

Lorelei continued. "So Hercules, being superstrong, held up the world while Atlas went to get the apples. That's how Hercules completed his eleventh labor."

"Why is that star drawn bigger than the others?" Homer asked, pointing to a star near the end of the dragon's tail.

"Yon's the North Star," the man said.

"Polaris," Homer said.

"Nae. It's a star called Thuban." The man scratched his beard. "It used tae be the North Star, but it isn't anymore."

"What are you talking about?" Lorelei asked, leaning her elbows on the table. "Stars don't change."

"But we do, lassie. The earth moves. It wobbles on its axis. And it takes twenty-six thousand years tae make one full wobble. That's why every twenty-six thousand years, the North Pole points to a different star. When Draco was discovered, the North Star wasna Polaris. It was Thuban."

"I never knew that," Homer admitted. He'd spent most of his map-reading days focused on the surface of the earth, not fixed up at the heavens. Star charting was new territory to him.

As the conversation proceeded, Hercules took notes in his notebook. He was very serious about his record-keeping duties.

"I don't understand," Lorelei said. "Where does this map take us? I mean, how does celestial navigation work?"

"Celestial navigation is the art and science of using celestial bodies tae determine the observer's position on Earth," the man said. Then he tapped a finger on Rumpold's map. "Draco is a constellation in the far northern sky. Yer mapmaker went tae the far north tae draw yon map."

"Well, I guess that's a start," Lorelei said. "But where, exactly, in the far north?" The man pointed to the date scrawled in the map's bottom corner. "I still don't understand," Lorelei said.

Homer thought he knew the answer to this. "I think the date is important because the view of the sky is always changing, but the earth's surface pretty much stays the same. So, if you stood on a mountain and looked down, the coastline would look the same whether you stood there on a Saturday or a Monday, or whether you stood there in January or in October." He glanced at the man, who nodded for Homer to continue. "But, if you stood on that same mountain and looked up, the sky would be totally different one day to the next. So that's why the date matters."

"Aye!" the man said with a smack of his knee. "Ye've got it, lad."

"So if we have the date and we have the image of the sky, then we can figure out exactly where the mapmaker was standing when he drew the map."

"Aye!" He smacked his knee again. Then he scrambled off the table and headed for his cot. "Well, ah read it for ye. Now away wi' ye. Ma brain is hurtin. Too many people. Too much bletherin." After climbing onto the cot, he lay on his back and closed his eyes.

Homer, Lorelei, and Hercules shared a confused look. "Wait," Lorelei called. "How do we figure it out?"

"Computation," the man said, his eyes still closed.

"Huh?" Lorelei asked.

"Math," Hercules told her. "He means we have to use math."

"Math?" Lorelei groaned. "I hate math."

"I'm not fond of it, either," Hercules said. "I can translate mathematical terminology for you, but when it comes to manipulating numbers, I'm pathetic."

They both looked at Homer expectantly. They were probably waiting for him to say, "Oh I love math. No problem. I'm some kind of math genius." He grimaced, remembering the bright red C- on his last math test. Sure, he could have studied more, but given the choice between studying a map on the mysterious crop circles of the American Midwest or studying fractions, well, he'd made the obvious choice. "I'm not so good at math, either," he admitted.

They still desperately needed the man's help. Experts on celestial navigation didn't grow on trees. Team L.O.S.T. and FOUND would probably have to travel to a different city just to find another one. And there was no time to do that. Homer was expected back on the farm in just five days. It was now or never. And that's why he crawled under the table to wake Dog. "Hey," he whispered in Dog's ear. "We need you. Go over there, wag your tail, and give him your sad face again."

Dog was sound asleep. His belly rose and fell steadily.

His back leg twitched as he chased something in dreamland.

"Dog?" Homer gently shook him. Dog opened one eye. "Ur?"

"Come on," Homer whispered, dragging him toward the cot. "Be charming."

Dog's ears, which were extra-long even for a basset hound, swept the dusty floor like furry mops. He opened his other eye just as he came to a stop at the foot of the man's cot. Clearly assuming that a new napping spot had been chosen for him, Dog closed his eyes and began to snore. The freight train–like sound caught the man's attention, and he sat up. "Aw, the poor wee thing. He's fair worn out." The man grabbed a pillow, jumped off the cot, and tucked the pillow under Dog's head.

"Yes, he's very tired," Homer said. "He's tired because it's been a long trip. We came all the way from the country just to find a celestial-navigation expert."

"The country, ye say? Yon's a long way for a basset tae travel." The man patted Dog's paw. Dog farted. "Aw, the poor beastie. A' that travel has upset his disposition."

"He's a mess," Homer said. "He even had to go through a revolving door."

"A revolving door?" The man's bushy eyebrows flew to the top of his head as he stared up at Homer. "Bassets hate revolving doors. Everyone knows that."

"But he went through one because he wanted an answer to the map, same as us," Homer said. Of course, this was a huge stretch of the truth, but it was the only tactic Homer could think of. The man wasn't fond of people, but his love of basset hounds might persuade him to offer more assistance. "Just think how disappointed Dog'll be if we have to go all the way back to the country without the answer to our question. We don't have any celestial navigators back home. We might have to go on another long trip to find one. We might have to go through more revolving doors."

The man threw his hands up in the air. "Nae, dinna be doing that. Let the beastie rest." He stomped back over to the table, climbed the stool, and sat on the blackboard surface. "Whit kind of person makes a basset hound walk through a revolving door?" he mumbled as he grabbed a ruler, a calculator, a protractor, a compass, and a bunch of other things. "Whit is the world coming to?"

"Good work," Lorelei said, nudging Homer's arm as he returned to the stool. He smiled and rested his arms on the table, watching as the man began to take measurements of Rumpold's map. Anticipation shot down Homer's spine. One day, a long time ago, Rumpold Smeller the Pirate had stared up at the sky. Draco the

164

dragon had greeted him. Wherever Rumpold had stood at that moment in time was where he'd buried his treasure.

Together, Homer, Lorelei, and Hercules took a long breath, their lungs filling with possibility.

The answer was just a few calculations away.

20

MacDoodle's Secret

The red-haired man's hands whipped here and there as he measured, wrote, erased, then measured and wrote some more. Chalk dust choked the air. When he'd covered one spot of the table with letters and numbers, he moved to another spot. Soon he was running back and forth between scribblings, muttering all the while. "Got tae determine the celestial sphere." Mutter, mutter. "Radius AC for the plumb line." Mutter, mutter. "Determine the zenith, then A equals the mathematical horizon of the observer."

Mutter, mutter. "PN corresponds tae the celestial north pole." And he kept up the mumblings as he scribbled, until the entire table was covered with equations. "Add in the Greenwich hour angle." Mutter, mutter.

Homer understood that last bit. "The Royal Observatory is in Greenwich, England," he told Lorelei and Hercules. "It's the official prime meridian of the world. That means that for the lines of longitude that run from one pole to the other pole, Greenwich is considered to be zero degrees." It was a basic fact that every modern mapmaker knew.

"I know that," Lorelei said, crossing her eyes. "My head feels like it's going to explode. How much longer?" she called out to the man, who now stood at the far end of the table.

"Patience, lassie."

An hour passed. Then another and another and another. Homer looked at his Quality Solar-Powered Subatomic Watch. The dials whirled and spun. It was 9:00 p.m. in Seattle and 8:00 a.m. in St. Petersburg, while midnight had come to The City. Homer's legs had gone numb thanks to sitting on that stool, but he thought it would be rude to stretch out on the floor and nap while the man was working so diligently. Lorelei didn't seem to care. She'd fallen asleep a few hours back, her head resting on her arms. Hercules was also asleep at the table.

Homer's stomach growled again and again. So did Dog's. He thought about asking the man if there was anything to eat. Maybe the building had a vending machine? He was about to say something when the man started knocking a piece of chalk against his forehead, deep in thought. Best to wait. Rumpold's treasure was far more important than the ache in Homer's stomach— and what a treasure it would be.

Because Homer had read *The Biography of Rumpold Smeller* at least a dozen times, he felt he knew as much about the pirate as anyone did. Rumpold had been born to a duke a long time ago in the old country of Estonia. Those were the days when the world was only half explored and the blank areas on maps were filled with drawings of sea serpents and monsters. Adventure awaited anyone brave enough to set sail.

And set sail was exactly what Rumpold did. With money he "borrowed" from his father, he bought a three-masted schooner and a crew and headed for ports unknown. And soon after, his reputation for thievery and villainy was the topic of gossip all over the world. The tales of his unpleasant temper were recorded in a few songs, one of which Homer began to hum.

♪ *Rumpold Smeller's a dastardly feller.*
His teeth be yeller, his breath be foul.

If you steal his booty, he'll kick your patootie, ♫
Slit your throat with his sword and make you howl.

Homer stopped humming. The little man was staring at him. How stupid he was to hum that song. What if the man began to suspect the connection between the song and the map? "It's just a song," Homer said. "I…I don't even know what it's about."

"Ah dinnae care nothin' aboot songs," the man said grumpily. He stepped over Lorelei's sleeping head and cleared a new spot on the table for his calculations.

Time passed. Homer's eyelids drooped. He closed them for a moment. Sleep crept closer and closer. His eyelids pressed heavier and heavier. He imagined his goose-down pillow from back home and the quilt his grandmother had made. Sleep wrapped its arms around him and…

"Got it!" the man announced.

"Huh?" Homer sat up, his eyes popping open. "What?"

"What's going on?" Lorelei asked, jolting awake. Her hair was matted to her forehead.

Hercules rubbed his eyes. "Did something happen?"

"Ah've got it," the man said from the center of the table. "Ah've got the coordinates. Ah've got the spot where yer mapmaker was standing." He drew a circle around two sets of letters and numbers.

Homer took a long, deep breath to make certain he was actually awake. "He's got it," he whispered with amazement. Trying to get a better view, Homer climbed up onto the table and leaned over the circled coordinates, but as he did so, his membership coin and its chain slipped out from his shirt.

The man pointed at the dangling coin and bellowed, "Ye'r a member of L.O.S.T.! Ye came here tae spy on me!" He gripped the ends of his braids. "Ah shoulda known. Ye said ah left the door open, but ah never leave the door open. Ye got in here with yer coin."

Homer quickly tucked the coin back into his shirt. "We aren't spying on you," he said. "I promise we aren't." Lorelei and Hercules added their assurances that no one was spying.

"Mockingbird," the man hissed. "He sent ye here. Well ye can tell Mockingbird that ah'm nae interested in goin to one of his meetins. Ah dinna like meetins. Too many people at meetins. And ye can tell Mockingbird that ah have no more Celtic coins. No more, ye hear me?" The man jumped off the table and stomped over to his cot.

Suddenly it dawned on Homer—he knew who this man was. He grabbed Hercules by the arm, pulling him to the corner so they could talk without Lorelei over-hearing. "Do you think he's Angus MacDoodle?"

Hercules, still groggy, yawned and rubbed his eyes again. "Angus who?"

"Angus MacDoodle. You know. The L.O.S.T. member who never goes to the meetings."

One of Hercules's duties as records keeper was to take attendance at the meetings. "Oh, that guy," he said with a nod. "His Lordship was always trying to get him to come and vote on agenda items. I tried to send him a notice about Lord Mockingbird's funeral, but no one knew where to send it. He's been in hiding for a long time. But I didn't know he was a celestial navigator."

"I didn't know that, either," Homer said. "He's famous for finding those Celtic coins in his backyard."

"What are you two whispering about?" Lorelei asked, sliding between them.

While Homer didn't want Lorelei to find out any more secret facts about L.O.S.T., it would be impossible to keep this one from her because Angus was giving it away all by himself.

"Ah had me a perfectly lovely life in the Highlands," the man grumbled, "minding ma own business. No one tae talk to but the birds and no sounds but the breeze in the heather." Angus grabbed a plaid suitcase from under his bed and began stuffing clothes into it. "Ah had ma wee cottage on the bluff. No city lights or pollution tae block the stars. But then ah found those blasted coins, and everything changed."

"What coins?" Lorelei asked.

"Ah dinna care nothin' aboot coins," Angus said. He stuffed some shoes into the suitcase. "Ah study the sky. Ah watch the stars. That's what ah care aboot. But one day ah was digging a hole tae bury ma dead cat and ah found the coins. Ma whole life changed. Ah became famous. Ma yard was filled wi' folk. Kin ah'd never met came askin' for money. A strange man flew a cloud to ma cottage and invited me tae join Mockingbird's club."

"That's Ajitabh," Homer said.

"Aye. He told me that L.O.S.T. would take the coins and donate them tae a museum. Ah told him he could have the coins but he had to gie me a secret place to live, where no one would bother me. A secret place where ma greedy kin couldna find me."

"So *that's* why you live here," Lorelei said. "You're hiding."

"Ah was hidin'. Now ah have tae find a new place." He zipped his suitcase. "Ye can tell L.O.S.T. tae leave me alone. I did whit they asked. I gave them the coins." He reached down and patted Dog's head. "Good-bye wee beastie."

Dog, who'd been napping, raised his head off the pillow and grunted.

Angus hurried up the stepladder and collected his telescope. With the telescope tucked under his arm and suitcase in hand, he hurried to the door.

"Wait," Homer called. "I won't tell anyone you're here." But Homer couldn't make promises on Lorelei's behalf. Knowing her, she'd probably hold a press conference and tell the world.

Without another word, the man darted into the hallway, slamming the door shut behind him. The instruments on the blackboard table trembled.

"That guy's weird," Lorelei said.

"He's not weird. He suffers from a very serious phobia," Hercules said. "He doesn't like people. Maybe we should apologize for disturbing him." He walked to the door and tried to open it. Turning the knob, he pulled, then pulled again. "I think it's locked."

Panic spread across Lorelei's face, and she ran to the door. She pushed Hercules aside and yanked on the knob. "He locked us in!" she cried. With a grunt, she threw her body against the door, but it didn't budge. "Let us out!"

"It's just jammed," Homer said as he tried the knob. "Why would he lock us in?"

"Because he thinks we're spying on him, remember?" Lorelei pointed at Hercules. "Use your superstrength. Bust it open."

"It's not superstrength. I'm not a superhero. I'm just

stronger than I look." Hercules put his shoulders into the attempt, pushing with all his might. But the door, which was made of some kind of metal, did nothing but give him bruises. "I'm going to need an ice pack," he said, rubbing his shoulder.

"Look for another way out," Lorelei said. She ran around the room. "There's got to be a way out."

Homer searched around the knob. Maybe there was a slot for his membership coin. But he found nothing.

"There's no other way out!" Lorelei cried.

"Don't panic," Hercules said, still rubbing his shoulder. "If you start to panic, then I'll start to panic. I'm very susceptible to suggestion."

"Yeah, we shouldn't panic," Homer said, though his stomach was tightening as he spoke. "The building opens in the morning. One of the workers will let us out."

"Only a L.O.S.T. membership coin will let someone open the elevator door," Lorelei reminded him. "And none of the L.O.S.T. members know we're here. Except for Angus MacDoodle, and he's run off to hide." She grabbed Homer's arm and yanked. "This is bad. Really bad."

"It's going to be okay," he tried to assure her, though he had no idea how it was going to be okay.

"Don't you get it, Homer?" Lorelei threw her hands in the air. "If we don't find a way out, we could be trapped here... *forever.*"

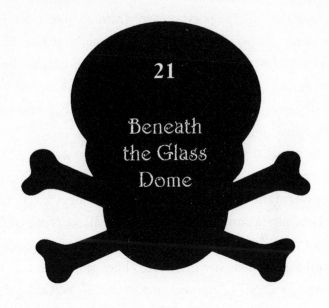

21

Beneath
the Glass
Dome

It was way, way, way past bedtime, but The City still twinkled all around. Far below, a river of light flowed as taxis and buses made their nightly rounds down shop-lined boulevards. Victorian lampposts highlighted the edge of City Lake, where Lorelei's speedboat waited. All this could be seen through the glass dome on the topmost floor of the Map of the Month Club building.

It was a terrible feeling being locked beneath that dome. Lorelei's warning of *forever* echoed in Homer's mind. He stood on the stepladder, sticking his nose through one of the portholes for fresh air like a dog in an open car window. On the other side, people had choices about where to go. If he was locked in this place *forever*, he'd never be able to say, *I'm going to walk down my driveway*, or, *I'm going to sit under that tree just because I feel like sitting under that tree.*

Is this what it felt like to be a hamster in a cage? Mrs. Peepgrass, the Milkydale schoolteacher, kept Poof the hamster at the back of the classroom. The cage was made of clear plastic, and even though it had all sorts of plastic tubes that wound in and out so the hamster could take a stroll and stretch his little legs, Poof spent most days sleeping in a pile of chewed-up toilet paper. What did the poor thing have to live for? But at least he had a bowl of food and a water dispenser. Homer's stomach growled. A packet of freeze-dried brine shrimp from Lorelei's vending machine was starting to sound delicious.

Homer tried to fight the feelings of doom. The Unpolluter could probably find them. But he'd told her that he didn't need her help. He'd told her he would "clean up the mess" himself.

"We're trapped," he said, his low blood sugar souring his mood.

"We're not trapped," Lorelei snarled. "No one traps me. No one!"

She lay on Angus MacDoodle's cot, staring up at the top of the dome, where the giant globe perched. She'd exhausted herself trying to find a way out, searching every nook and cranny, crawling on hands and knees, prodding and poking for possible secret escape hatches. But the only door they'd found had a sign that read CLEANING CREW ONLY. The door opened to a narrow balcony, where a window washer's scaffold hung, suspended from the top of the dome. As evidenced by the streaks of bird poop on the dome and the dust all over the office floor, no cleaning crew had visited in a very long time.

"Why aren't you two helping me figure this out?" Lorelei complained. "Why must I do everything?"

"Urrrr."

Homer nearly toppled off the ladder as he spun around and pointed a frustrated finger at Lorelei, about to tell her that they wouldn't be in this mess if she hadn't stolen his map. But his arm fell to his side as he glowered at Dog, who lay beside Lorelei on the cot, his long body stretched against hers. "Dog?" Homer was in no mood for disloyalty. "Why are you cuddling with her? She kidnapped you twice, remember?"

"I think *dognapped* is a better description," Hercules said.

"Dognapped. Kidnapped. Whatever," Homer said crossly. "The point is, she took him—twice!"

Dog raised his head, then let it fall back onto the pillow. His tail *thwapp*ed Lorelei's leg. Even though it was simply a matter of laziness, and even though Homer knew this, it still hurt Homer's feelings. "Traitor," he grumbled. Then he stuck his nose out the window again. "We have to get out of here."

"Don't even think about jumping," Hercules said. He'd wiped all the dust from a spot on the floor and was lying on his back, reading one of Angus's books. "We'd get flattened like pancakes. I'm too young to get flattened like a pancake."

"You jumped from an airplane," Homer pointed out.

"Yes, well, that was a moment of insanity. Besides, I had a parachute."

Homer took a quick breath. "Oh, I've got it. We could write *HELP* all over the windows. Someone will see it and send a rescue team."

"We can't do that," Lorelei said. "Think about it. If the wrong sort of person rescued us, we could get arrested for trespassing. And you two would be sent home early and I'd be sent to an orphanage, and we'd have to stop our quest."

Homer narrowed his eyes. Sending Lorelei to an orphanage might be the best thing to happen to the treasure-hunting community since the invention of the handheld metal detector. But she was right. Rescue would undoubtedly lead to an end to their quest. Mr. Pudding would have a fit if he learned that Homer had been treasure hunting when he was supposed to be on a VIP tour of the map club. Mr. Pudding was extra-aware of the dangers of treasure hunting, since his only brother had been killed in the pursuit of treasure—Rumpold Smeller's treasure, to be exact. So Mr. Pudding made certain that he told Homer at least once a day about the stupidity of treasure hunting and about the benefits of goat farming—a safe and family-friendly career.

They fell into silent frustration. Homer had no more ideas. Not a brilliant plan. Not even a dim-witted plan came to mind.

"Poor Daisy," Lorelei said. "She'll be so sad if I don't come back to the lair. I hope she's not worried about me."

Homer doubted that a rat would worry about such things.

Lorelei rolled onto her side and glared at Hercules. "Why are you reading? Why aren't you thinking about escape?"

"For your information, *Lorelei*, I am thinking about escape. In fact, I'm thinking about nothing else." Hercules held up a book titled *History of the Map of the Month Club*. "There's a section in here all about this very building. I'm reading about its construction in case there's a hidden escape hatch or something."

"Oh," she said. "That's actually a good idea." Her stomach growled, and she screwed up her face. "If we don't get out of here, I'll starve to death. And then I might have to turn to cannibalism."

More than a few treasure-hunting quests had ended in cannibalism. Homer knew this fact from his book *The Worst Ways to End a Treasure Hunt.*

"No one's eating me," Hercules said. "And I'm not eating Dog, no matter how hungry I get."

"Urrrr?"

"No one's eating Dog," Homer grumbled. Though he was a meaty sort of dog...

A hazy patch of clouds floated across the night sky. Homer's thoughts turned to Ajitabh and Zelda and how they were probably trying to find him. Anger bubbled to the surface. "This is all your fault!" he hollered.

"Are you yelling at me?" Lorelei asked.

Homer glared over his shoulder. "You stole my map. You threatened to tell the world about L.O.S.T. I hope we do get rescued because then they'll send you to an orphanage and you won't have your lair anymore. And then someone will adopt you, and you'll have to go to school and you'll have to be a regular kid, just like everyone else."

Lorelei's face went red. "That's the meanest thing you've ever said to me."

Maybe it was, but at that moment, Homer didn't care. Maybe he should have let The Unpolluter clean things up. Maybe he should have let The Unpolluter "get rid" of her.

Then he turned away, ashamed by that thought. No one was getting rid of anyone, no matter how annoying that anyone was. Not on his watch.

Frustration and blame were getting them nowhere. With a sigh, Homer climbed down the stepladder and walked over to the bookcase. He ran his fingers along the dusty spines, searching until he found a world atlas. Then he set it on the blackboard table, right next to the coordinates that Angus MacDoodle had calculated.

Lorelei sat up. "What are you doing?"

"I'm going to see where these lead," he said.

The first coordinate, the latitude line, was N 60. Homer already knew the treasure was in the northern hemisphere because the dragon constellation revolved around the North Pole. He opened the atlas to a map of the Arctic Ocean. Then he ran a finger down from the North Pole, past eighty degrees, past seventy degrees, until he came to sixty degrees latitude.

Lorelei peered over Homer's shoulder as he read the next coordinate, the longitude line: W 044. West. They were already in the west, so that meant they wouldn't have to travel all the way around the world. Homer ran his finger to the left, along the sixty-degree latitude line, passing twenty degrees longitude, passing forty degrees longitude, and stopping at forty-four.

"Greenland," Lorelei said.

"The southernmost tip of Greenland," Homer corrected. Here was the answer so many had yearned for—the location of the greatest pirate treasure ever. A shiver danced up Homer's neck. This moment would go down in history. This moment would change everything. It would be the greatest quest the world had ever known!

But then Hercules had to go and ruin the thrill by pointing out a *wee* problem. "How are we going to get there?" he asked.

Homer's and Lorelei's smiles collapsed. A long moment of silence followed as the three adventurers fell into deep thought. Dog, who was still stretched out on the cot, also appeared to be in deep thought, his eyelids trembling, his back leg twitching. But his thoughts were most likely about rabbit-chasing or paper-eating—not about how he'd get himself to Greenland.

"I can steal a cloudcopter," Lorelei said. "I did it before, I can do it again."

"No way," Homer said. "You're not stealing anything from Ajitabh."

"Well, I'm not going to ask for a cloudcopter, that's for sure." Lorelei scrunched up her face. "If Ajitabh and

Zelda find out about this, they'll want to come along. I'm not sharing the glory with them."

Homer strummed his fingers on the table. How could they get to Greenland if not by cloudcopter? Air travel would be fastest. Lorelei had lots of money, so they could buy plane tickets, but no airlines landed on Greenland's southernmost tip. They could buy tickets on a ship, but there was no major port, either. Perhaps a private boat could be hired, something that traveled at high speeds.

"I've got it!" Homer cried. Dog raised his head. Hercules and Lorelei leaned forward. "We can use the submarine. The one in the lair."

"Brilliant," Lorelei said, smacking her hand on the table. "Absolutely brilliant."

"The submarine?" Hercules swallowed hard. "You want to travel *under*water?"

"Why not? Ajitabh designed the submarine for treasure-hunting quests."

"And we won't be stealing it, because it belongs to me," Lorelei said. "Finders keepers."

Whether or not the submarine actually belonged to Lorelei was up for debate. But Homer did not want to argue about it. They had a quest to get to. And the fact was, *finders keepers* was a claim honored by most treasure hunters.

"Underwater?" Hercules asked again. Sweat broke out on his nose. "Under? Water?"

"Obviously underwater," Lorelei said. "Submarines don't fly." She raised an eyebrow and glanced at Homer. "This one doesn't fly, does it?"

"I don't think so," Homer said. His uncle had never mentioned anything about a flying submarine.

"Well, we can't do anything unless we get out of here," Lorelei said with a stomp of her foot. "There's got to be a way."

"Actually, I think I might have found a way," Hercules said. "Look at this page." He folded his legs and set the open book in his lap. "There are a couple of paragraphs about the giant globe."

"Who cares about the globe?" Lorelei said with a roll of her eyes. "It's sitting on the top of the building. We want to get to the bottom of the building."

"That's what I'm trying to tell you," Hercules said. "It says here that the globe belonged to a woman named Lulu Bell and that she donated it to the map club. It says that she flew it to the top of the building, where it's been ever since."

Homer knew the name Lulu Bell. It was written on one of his ceiling maps back home—the one of Cutthroat Canyon. "She was a mapmaker who specialized in the topography of canyons," he said. "She used a hot air balloon to move up and down canyon walls. She could explore the deepest crevasses much quicker than having to hike in and…" He stopped talking, his gaze colliding with Lorelei's. Their irises expanded at the exact same time as the exact same thought popped into their heads.

"Hot air balloon!" they cried.

22

The World on a String

Lorelei and Homer dashed to the door that read CLEANING CREW ONLY. Even though she'd stopped to grab the map and shove it into her jumpsuit pocket, Lorelei was faster. Cool night air rushed in as she yanked the door open.

"Be careful," Hercules said, setting the book aside. "It's dangerous out there!"

It was a tight squeeze on the balcony. Lorelei reached up and pulled on a rope, lowering the window washer's scaffolding. The scaffolding rocked from side to side as she climbed on. "You stay here," she told Homer.

"Wait," Homer said, grabbing the rope. She knew the coordinates. She knew the riddle. What was to keep her from floating away on the hot air balloon, leaving her number one competitor to starve to death on the topmost floor?

"What?" Lorelei asked innocently.

Dog waddled onto the balcony and squeezed his big head between Homer's shins.

"Nothing," Homer said, letting go. She wouldn't dare leave without Dog.

The rigging squeaked as Lorelei pulled on the rope, raising the scaffold foot by foot. Her pink jumpsuit shone bright against the night sky. Hercules joined Homer and Dog on the balcony. They craned their necks, watching as the scaffold rose higher and higher until it came to a stop at the edge of the globe's platform. In a blur of pink, Lorelei pulled herself onto the platform, then disappeared from view.

After a nerve-racking couple of minutes, the squeaking resumed and Lorelei lowered herself back down the side of the glass dome. When she reached the balcony, Homer knew, from the smile on her face, that she'd found what she was looking for. She handed Homer a small brass plaque. He held it up so that the twinkling city lights shone on its surface.

> ### Commemorating the last flight of Lulu Bell

"There's a fan under the balloon—that's why it's fully inflated. And the balloon is still attached to its basket," Lorelei reported. "Let's go. We can't lose any more time."

"Have either of you ever flown a hot air balloon?" Hercules asked.

"I've flown a cloudcopter," Lorelei said.

"I've flown *in* a cloudcopter," Homer said.

"Yes, but a cloudcopter has an engine," Hercules pointed out. "And a steering wheel."

"Why do you worry about *everything*?" Lorelei asked. "Don't tell me you have some kind of phobia about hot air balloons."

"Not exactly. I mean, I don't have globophobia, which is fear of balloons, and I don't have megaglobophobia, which is fear of really big balloons. I don't have aerophobia, which is fear of flying, but I am afraid that we might drift into something and get crushed, or we might drift into something sharp and get impaled. Or the balloon might overinflate and explode and—"

"Oh, for Pete's sake, let's go!" The scaffold rocked as Lorelei stomped her foot.

As difficult as it was going to be to persuade Hercules to get into that hot air balloon, it was going to be more difficult to persuade Dog. At least Hercules wouldn't lie on the ground like an overstuffed bag of grain, refusing to cooperate. Or maybe he would.

"You and I could fly the balloon and then come back and get Dog and Hercules," Homer suggested.

"That will take way too long," Lorelei said. "Besides, we'd have to wait for the building to open, and then how would we get past that woman with the cat-eye glasses?" Her points seemed valid. There was no way out but up. "Why are you just standing there? Rumpold's treasure is waiting!"

In order to get Dog onto the scaffold, he had to be blindfolded. Homer tore a strip of fabric from Angus MacDoodle's pillowcase and wrapped it over Dog's eyes. Dog struggled, shaking his head and body. "It's okay," Homer told his furry friend. "We've done crazy things before, and we've always survived." Although that was the truth, it didn't seem to comfort Dog. He stuck his nose into Homer's sleeve and whined.

Once Homer was balanced on the scaffold, Hercules lifted Dog and slid him onto the wooden planks. While

Homer whispered comforting words in Dog's ear, Hercules climbed on board. Then he and Lorelei pulled on the ropes. As the scaffold began its slow ascent, the rigging squeaked ominously.

"Don't look down," Hercules warned. "You could get vertigo, which is a terrible sense of dizziness. I got vertigo once just from thinking about being up high."

"I won't look down," Homer said, his eyes focused on Dog's brown head. He'd been in some very high places, like the top of Ajitabh's tower, where the cloudcopters landed. And he'd stood in the open doorway of Hercules's plane, staring down at Mushroom Island. But dangling from the side of a thirty-story building wasn't a stunt for the fainthearted.

"Heights don't scare me," Lorelei said. "Before I lived in the soup warehouse, I climbed dozens of fire escape ladders."

"Why'd you do that?" Hercules asked.

"So I could have a place to sleep." There was no embarrassment in her statement. Some people might not want to admit that they'd been homeless or that they'd slept on other people's balconies, but Lorelei was not one of those people. She wasn't ashamed of the humble places she'd lived.

Homer's cheeks flushed red as he remembered the time he'd been ashamed of his family's small farmhouse.

There'd been a new student in school. She'd been real nice to him on that first day, and he'd desperately wanted to impress her. So he told her he lived in the biggest house in Milkydale. She found out the truth, of course. Sure, the Puddings' little farmhouse wasn't anything like Hercules's palace, which was so big you could actually get lost in it, but it was a home. Lorelei had never had a *home*.

As much as he distrusted Lorelei, Homer felt a twinge of respect. She was a kid and she'd survived on her own. It was an amazing feat.

"Don't look down, don't look down," Hercules chanted as he pulled the ropes.

Homer tightened his grip around Dog. What if someone looked out the window and noticed them on the scaffold? Would that person call the police? But there was probably no chance of that happening, since morning was still a few hours away. So Homer tried not to worry, focusing on the task at hand.

With a unified sigh of relief, they reached the top of the dome. Hercules transferred Dog safely onto the platform. "There's no railing up here," he said. "That's terribly dangerous."

The balloon's passenger basket was held in place by bungee cords. An electrical cord, plugged into an external outlet, trailed over the basket's rim and into the basket itself, where a fan pushed air into the hovering balloon. Four ropes attached the balloon to its basket.

"Lulu Bell's balloon," Homer said quietly. He'd read a lot of treasure-hunting history books, paying particular attention to the chapters dedicated to mapmakers. If he'd been in a museum, he would have walked around the balloon, admiring the beautiful painting of the continents across its silk surface. He would have imagined Lulu Bell flying into unexplored canyons, her hair blowing in the wind, her drawing pad perched on her knees, as she created some of the most beautiful, detailed maps in the world. But this was not a museum, and all he could think about was the edge of the platform. He kept a tight hold on Dog's collar.

"So, how do these things work?" Lorelei asked as she climbed into the basket.

"Hot air," Hercules said, clutching the basket's rim.

"Duh. I knew that much," Lorelei said. As she leaned over the fan, her hair flew straight up. "But this air is cold." Then she bumped her head on a little tank that was suspended from the center of the balloon. "Hey, this says propane. I wonder..." She reached for the red button on the bottom of the tank.

Homer took a quick breath. "Uh, Lorelei, I don't think you should—"

Ignoring Homer's warning, she pushed the button.

Whoosh! A flame shot out of the tank and up into the balloon, lighting it like a Chinese lantern.

"That's how they do it," she said with a satisfied grin. She pushed the button again and the flame stopped. Then she turned off the fan and handed it to Hercules. "Come on. Get in."

"Shouldn't we talk about this?" Hercules asked as he set the fan on the platform.

"What's to talk about? We're here. Let's go."

"I mean, shouldn't we have some sort of plan?"

"The plan is to get off this building and back onto the ground," Lorelei said.

"Yes, but—"

"It's our only way down," Homer reminded him as he climbed in.

Hercules lifted Dog over the rim, then joined them. Without the fan, the balloon had begun to slowly deflate, and part of it draped over Hercules's head. He dropped his notebook onto the floor, then raised his arms to hold up the balloon.

Lorelei smiled at him. "Hercules is holding up the world," she said. "Just like in the myth."

On the basket's floor, Dog shook his head and pawed at the blindfold until it came free. Because the basket was deep enough to block Dog's view, Homer left the blindfold off. He turned his attention to the propane tank.

"We need to inflate the balloon," he said. "Stand aside." Lorelei and Hercules pressed against the side of the basket as Homer pushed the red button. The flame shot upward, and the balloon expanded. The basket wobbled, straining against the bungee cords, as the balloon lifted to its full height. "Flame on, we float. Flame off, we sink. This shouldn't be too complicated," Homer said.

Hercules gripped one of the ropes. "Let's hope those don't become your famous last words."

Famous last words is a phrase well known to those in the treasure-hunting community. Chapter 15 in *The Worst Ways to End a Treasure Hunt* is dedicated to famous last words. Here are some examples:

"I'm most certain there's no quicksand around here.
In fact, I'd bet my life on it."
—Elvis Flutt, mapmaker

"Rhinoceroses are harmless beasts. Let's go pet one."
—Sir Bellamy Whistle, debonair adventurer

"These berries are too delicious to be
poisonous....Ackkkkkkk."
—Princess Agatha of Russia, amateur anthropologist

Homer hoped that a new edition would not be printed to include:

> "Flame on, we float. Flame off, we sink.
> This shouldn't be too complicated."
> —Homer W. Pudding, big dummy

"We'll keep the flame going until we're past the skyscrapers," he said. "Then we'll turn it off and drift to the ground." He was trying to keep his voice steady, not only for himself but for Hercules, whose eyes were as wide as teacups. With a nod, Homer and Lorelei unhooked the bungee cords.

As the basket rose, Dog pushed between Homer's shins. A rush of fear took Homer's breath for a moment, but it was quickly replaced by amazement. This wasn't anything like flying in the cloudcopter, which vibrated and tilted upon liftoff. This ride was as smooth as a sigh escaping from someone's body.

Far above the skyscraper roofs, Homer turned off the flame. On the horizon, the faintest tint of pink heralded the arrival of Tuesday morning. The kids peered over the basket's edge. The bird's-eye view revealed The City's maze-like construction. It reminded Homer of something his little brother might build with blocks on the kitchen floor.

"Watch out!" Hercules cried. Homer whipped around. A building rushed toward them. Correction—they rushed toward a building. How had they lost height that quickly? Behind one of the apartment windows, a man stood in his bathrobe at his kitchen counter, pouring himself a cup of coffee, too sleepy to notice what was going on outside. Lorelei lunged for the red button and pushed it. *Whoosh!* They rose but not quite fast enough. The basket bumped into a balcony, upsetting a pot of geraniums.

"That was close," Homer said as they rose above the building.

"Too close," Hercules said.

"Hey, there's the speedboat." Lorelei pointed as the balloon drifted toward the edge of City Park. The park was much bigger than Homer had realized. The lake was the central focus, with the Museum of Natural History at one end and a channel at the other. The channel led to a river, which led to the sea, which led to Rumpold's treasure.

"Couldn't we land here?" Hercules asked.

"I don't know." Lorelei circled around the basket, getting a full view. "There are trees everywhere. We'd get tangled for sure."

"Does this thing float?" Hercules asked. "If it does, we could land in the lake."

"That would ruin Lulu Bell's balloon," Homer said.

The balloon was a precious piece of mapmaking history. He didn't want to be responsible for its destruction.

"And I can't swim," Lorelei said.

"You can't swim?" Hercules yanked his notebook from Dog's mouth. "Really?"

"Yeah. Really." She pouted at him. "You got a problem with that?"

"No, I don't have a problem with that. I'm just surprised. I mean, it seems like you can do all sorts of things. Swimming isn't hard. Are you afraid of the water? That's called aquaphobia."

"No, I'm not afraid of the water," Lorelei snapped. "I just never learned."

Homer ducked as a tree branch nearly gouged his face. "Hey, Lorelei, we need hot air again."

She pushed the button, but no flame came out. "Uh, guys, I think we have a little problem." She pushed the button again and again. "Okay, so it's a big problem."

The bottom of the basket skimmed the top of a tree, then lifted off and skimmed another and another, like a rock skipping across a pond. Lorelei kept punching the button, but the flame didn't awaken.

"We must be out of fuel," she said. Dog pressed against Homer as the basket skimmed across two more trees and then, with a jarring motion, stopped. They were stuck.

Hercules stepped toward Homer, but as he did, the basket tipped.

"Stop moving," Lorelei ordered, holding out her arms like a tightrope walker. "Don't anyone move."

And so they stood there, balancing on top of a tree like a little hat on Gertrude's head. South America and Australia began to shrink as the balloon slowly deflated.

"We can't stand like this forever," Hercules said from the corner of his mouth. He raised his hands to hold up the world. The basket wobbled.

"Don't move," Lorelei ordered again. But while Homer and Hercules understood the reason for not moving, Dog had no idea what was going on. Since he was only one foot tall, he couldn't see over the top of the basket. And because he couldn't see over the top of the basket, he was not privy to the unfolding events. This was a common theme in his life. While the world at ground level was one he could keep track of, the world above the counter and tabletops was often a total mystery.

So he ambled toward Homer.

The basket tilted. Lorelei squealed.

"Stay," Homer said. "Stay, Dog, stay." Dog turned around and ambled toward Lorelei. The basket tilted in her direction.

"Stay!" she ordered. Dog stopped for a moment and cocked his head. Homer knew Dog understood the command *stay*, so it wasn't a matter of comprehension. It was a matter of mood. Was he in the mood to stay or was he in the mood to get his rump scratched?

"Ur." He twisted his long body and scratched at a flea. The basket shook. Then he straightened and walked a few more steps toward Lorelei.

"Oh no," she said as the basket tilted farther. A branch cracked. Dog lost his footing and slid toward Lorelei. Lorelei lunged at Homer, who stood on the opposite side. But her attempt to balance the basket didn't work, because that was when, with a crumpling sound, the silk balloon folded in on itself and collapsed onto a neighboring tree, draping across it like a scarf. And pulling the basket onto its side.

Spilling the basket's contents into the treetops.

23

More Bloomin' Bad News

og!" Homer cried.

He grabbed Dog by the collar just before they were cast out of the basket. Somewhere to his right, Lorelei screamed. As did Hercules. But where were they? All Homer could see was a blanket of leaves so thick it looked as if he and Dog could walk right across it. He held his breath, not daring to move. If only this moment could be suspended in time. But gravity, the enemy of those perched at the top of a tree, took control of the situation. A branch broke.

"Ahhhh!" Homer cried.

He never let go of Dog's collar. Even as he bumped from branch to branch, even as his sleeve tore and his eyes were nearly gouged out, he held on tight. Down, down, down they tumbled. Dog yelped. A branch hit Homer's leg; another scraped his cheek. And then he landed on one of the lower branches, Dog in his lap. They'd stopped falling. Homer breathed a sigh of relief as he caught his balance. All was still. All was safe.

But then Dog lifted his leg to scratch a flea, throwing them off balance again, and they fell the last few feet to the ground.

Lorelei and Hercules had already landed. "Everyone okay?" Hercules asked.

Homer, who lay face-first in the grass, moaned. "I think I broke my entire body."

Lorelei sat up and picked a caterpillar off her nose. Then she reached into her jumpsuit to check on the map. "Got it," she said. Then she searched her pockets. "Hey, where's my remote control?" As if it had heard her, the remote fell from the tree, landing with a thunk near Homer's head. Lorelei grabbed it.

From the way his legs ached, Homer knew some big bruises would soon be making their appearances. He shook leaves from his hair, then got onto his knees and checked on Dog. This was the second time this summer that his best friend had fallen from the sky. "Please be okay," Homer pleaded under his breath. Dog lay on his side. His belly rose and fell with steady breaths, so that was a very good sign, but otherwise he wasn't moving. Homer ran his hands over Dog's back and down each of his legs. Nothing seemed broken. "Dog?"

"Maybe he just got the wind knocked out of him," Lorelei said as she knelt next to Homer.

"But he's not waking up." Dog's ear was flopped back onto the grass so that its soft inside was exposed. Homer gently stroked the ear. "Wake up, Dog."

Hercules crawled over. "If he's knocked out, it's probably a concussion, which is a traumatic brain injury. *Concussion* comes from the Latin *concutere*, which means 'to shake violently.'"

"Why do you always talk like you're in the middle of a spelling bee?" Lorelei asked. "What's the matter with you? It's weird."

"I like words," Hercules said with a shrug. "What's wrong with that?"

"Traumatic brain injury?" Homer repeated, his stomach tightening. Dog's brain wasn't very big, and because of his lack of smell, he already had trouble when it came to finding his way back home, knowing which foods to eat, and knowing who was friend or foe. A conk on the head could add more troubles. A rush of emotion over-took Homer, and he grabbed Dog's shoulder and shook him, pleading, "Dog! Wake up!" Dog's jowls jiggled as Homer shook again. "Wake! Up!" *Please, please, please, please...*

"Ur." Dog opened one eye. Then he sneezed and a caterpillar shot out his nostril.

"Disgusting," Lorelei said as the caterpillar whizzed past.

"Dog?" Homer gushed. "Are you okay?" Dog raised his head and *thwapp*ed his tail against Hercules's knee. Then with a grunt, he rolled onto his paws and stood. Homer threw his arms around Dog's thick middle and hugged. "I'll never let you fall out of a hot air balloon again. I promise."

Lorelei scrambled to her feet. "Since we're all okay, we'd better get going."

Homer and Hercules wiped the last bits of leaves and caterpillars from their clothes. While Hercules gathered his notebook and pen, Homer picked a twig from his hair. "We've destroyed Lulu Bell's balloon," he said sadly.

"It's fine, just deflated. I'll send a harmonic crystal to the Map of the Month Club. That will cover the cost of any repairs." Lorelei started across the park. "Come on. It's a long walk back to the speedboat."

Homer grabbed Dog's leash and followed Lorelei. "I can't believe I didn't break anything," he told Hercules.

"We're very lucky," Hercules said. "Hey, Homer, is it true what Lorelei said earlier? Do I always sound like I'm in the middle of a spelling bee?"

"Only sometimes," Homer replied.

"Does that make me weird?"

Homer wasn't sure how to respond. Pointing out the Latin root of words definitely made Hercules a bit weird. Digging holes all over Milkydale definitely made Homer weird. Pink hair made Lorelei weird. Smelling treasure made Dog...well, it certainly didn't make him weird. It made him kinda cool. But eating paper made Dog weird. "Everyone's weird," Homer said. "Some people are just better at hiding it than others." Hercules smiled.

Lorelei led the way across the park. Grass stains glowed on the rump of her pink jumpsuit. A hole gaped at the back of Hercules's rugby shirt. Homer's left sleeve was slit down the seam. The scratches that each of them bore on their hands and faces were badges of honor, for they'd just survived one of the most productive twenty-four hours in treasure-hunting history. Not only had they reconstructed one of the world's most famous maps, they'd translated its riddle and found an expert to calculate the coordinates, and now they had a destination.

But having a destination was like having a cake without frosting, which, in Homer's opinion, was the best part. They still had a treasure to claim.

It was early morning, so only a few exercise fanatics were jogging in the park. A newspaper truck pulled into a parking lot. A man jumped from the truck, opened a newspaper kiosk with a key, shoved the day's fresh, crisp newspapers inside, then drove off. Homer couldn't help but notice the giant headline:

NOTORIOUS THIEF ESCAPES FROM SOUPWATER PRISON

Homer might have ignored the headline. After all, he had more pressing things on his mind than a thief's escape. But the photo below the headline caught his attention. It was a mug shot of a perfectly groomed woman with slicked-back black hair and a strand of pearls. Homer shuddered as if he'd just swallowed spoiled goat milk. "Lorelei!" he hollered, his voice cracking. "Lorelei!"

"What?" she called, whipping around. "Why are you two always so slow?"

Hercules stood next to Homer and peered over his shoulder. "What's going on?"

Homer fumbled through his pockets. "Do you have a quarter?" he asked. Hercules shook his head. It cost two quarters to buy the paper and Homer had just the one. "Lorelei, come here!" he shouted.

She stomped back toward him. "What?"

"Do you have a quarter?" he asked, his eyes wild.

"Why—?"

"Just give me a quarter!" Spit flew from his mouth.

"Jeez. Why are you so grumpy?" She reached into her pocket and set a quarter into his hand. He stuffed the coins into the slot and opened the kiosk door, grabbing the top newspaper. Then he read the article aloud.

Madame la Directeur, once the esteemed director of The City's Museum of Natural History, is the first person to have escaped from Soupwater Prison. Thanks to an anonymous tip that she'd been stealing gems from the museum's Cave of Brilliance and replacing them with fakes, she was arrested earlier this year and sentenced to twenty years in the maximum-security facility.

It is not clear how she escaped, but an investigation is under way. A motorcycle rider claims he gave a ride to someone fitting her description and dropped her off just outside The City.

"I don't know how she survived our swamp," the prison warden said. "It's full of alligators and piranhas."

The whereabouts of Madame la Directeur is unknown at this time. Law-abiding citizens are instructed to telephone the police if they know anything that might lead to her arrest.

Had the air suddenly been sucked from the park? Homer couldn't quite catch his breath. "Where do you think she is?" Hercules asked.

All the color washed from Lorelei's and Homer's faces. "The lair," they replied.

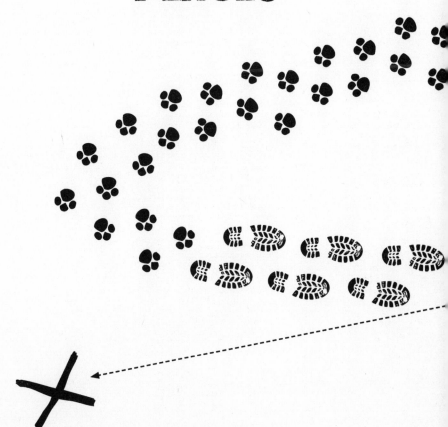

PART FIVE

WATERY PLACES

24

Go Jump In the Lake

The word *enemy* is filled with ugliness. Hercules would tell you that it comes from the Latin *inimicus*, which means "foe." *Enemy* isn't a word to be used lightly. For example, if your teacher assigns you a fifty-page report on the composition of moon dirt and you do not care one bit about the composition of moon dirt, then you might consider your teacher to be a bit of an annoyance, but he is not your enemy. Another example—if the girl sitting behind you in the movie theater keeps flicking popcorn seeds into your hair, you will probably dislike that girl, but she is not your enemy. A true enemy is someone who seeks to confound, overthrow, or injure an opponent.

Madame la Directeur had done all three of those things. *Confound*: She lied to Homer about the membership coin, about his uncle, and about L.O.S.T. *Overthrow*: She stole the membership coin from Homer as well as all of his uncle's possessions, including the map. *Injure*: She murdered Homer's uncle, and then she tried to feed Homer, Lorelei, and Dog to her mutant carnivorous tortoise.

Madame la Directeur wasn't simply Homer's enemy. She was his überenemy.

After reading the newspaper article, Homer and Lorelei sank onto a bus bench, their bodies slumping like Lulu Bell's deflated balloon.

"Now we'll never get the submarine," Lorelei said. "That old witch will never let me back into the lair."

"She'll never let me in, either," Homer said. *Or if she does*, he thought, *it would be just like the Hansel and Gretel story, where the old lady lures the little children into her candy house, only to enslave the girl and cook the fat boy over a fire.*

"It was a crazy idea anyway," Hercules said, squeezing onto the bench between them. "We don't know the first thing about driving a submarine. There are all sorts of health issues with underwater travel. Too much pressure can blow an eardrum. And then there's the bends. Have you ever heard of the bends? It's when nitrogen bubbles get trapped in your veins and—"

"It wasn't a crazy idea," Lorelei said, jabbing Hercules with her elbow. "It wasn't crazy at all."

Homer remembered a day, not so long ago, when Uncle Drake had come to Milkydale to visit. He'd arrived in his usual manner, with an armful of strange presents for his two nephews and niece—a stuffed iguana for Gwendolyn, a miniature zeppelin for Squeak, and a new world atlas for Homer. After drinking lemonade and eating cherry pie with the rest of the family, Homer and Uncle Drake stretched out beneath the willow tree. They watched the ants trailing past, collecting twigs to carry back to their nest. Uncle Drake pointed to one ant carrying a stiff brown leaf. "See that little critter? It's got one thing on its mind, to get that leaf back to the nest. It's determined. Now watch this." Drake took off his shoe and stuck it right across the trail, blocking the ant's path. The ant wandered in a circle for a bit, but then took a sharp left turn and marched right around the shoe until it was reunited with the original path, the leaf still in its possession. Drake had smiled. "Homer, my boy, if we had one-tenth of an ant's determination, we could do anything. With determination, anything is possible."

Homer straightened his shoulders and took a long, deep breath. "It's not a crazy idea. That submarine belonged to my uncle, and I'm going to get it." Dog, who'd been eating the front page of the newspaper, must have noticed the serious tone in Homer's voice because he stopped chewing and looked up.

Lorelei frowned, her pink bangs dangling over her defeated eyes. "I don't see how. She'll kill us if she sees us."

"Look, we can do this. We just flew a hot air balloon, and we survived." Hercules and Lorelei shared a bewildered look as Homer darted to his feet. "Lorelei, you're really good at being sneaky and you're really good at stealing things. And Hercules, you won the World's Spelling Bee. I mean, come on, that's amazing. We've outsmarted Madame before. We can do it again."

"Okay, so how do we get into the lair?" Lorelei asked. "She'll be watching. She'll know if we come down the tortoise slide, and an alarm will ring if the gate opens. We can't race in with the speedboat."

Hercules shrugged. "Don't look at me. I have no idea how to get into that place."

"I'll swim in and get the submarine," Homer said. The idea came to him as suddenly as a burp.

"You think you could swim in there and not have Madame notice?" Lorelei asked.

"Yes," Homer said. "With determination, anything is possible."

"Are you a good swimmer?" Hercules asked. "It's a long way down that tunnel."

"I can swim," Homer said. But he didn't say he was a *good* swimmer.

When Homer turned five, his mother signed him up for lessons at the Milkydale Community Pool. And each summer following, until he turned ten, she continued to sign him up for lessons. He began in Jellyfish class—that's when you can float by yourself—and made it up to Bullfrog class—that's when you can put your face in the water and swim like a frog. But he never made it to Porpoise, which included all the other strokes.

"I can swim," he repeated.

"Well, what are we sitting around for?" Lorelei asked. She smacked Hercules on the back. "Let's go get ourselves a submarine."

Morning was in full swing, and there was no time to waste. They gave up the idea of hiking all the way around the lake to the public dock, where the speedboat was moored. Instead, Lorelei rented a paddleboat from a nearby stand, and they paddled as close to the gate as possible.

"You'll have to swim under it," Lorelei said.

Homer peered over the edge of the paddleboat and cringed.

Some bodies of water are meant for swimming. Mountain lakes, though cold, invite the swimmer with soft ripples and crystal clear water. Lazy rivers tempt the swimmer with deep pools of blue and green. Country clubs, community centers, and private residences skim bugs from the water and add drops of chlorine. City Lake, however, was not meant for swimming, hence the signs posted throughout the park:

> **WARNING:**
> **This lake is not meant for swimming.**
> **Itchy rashes, unusual fungal infections,**
> **respiratory distress, swollen toes, and hair loss**
> **may occur after swimming in this lake,**
> **so DO NOT swim in this lake.**

Homer, however, had not seen any of these signs, because most had rotted away and were lying on the lake's bottom. The others were covered in pigeon poop.

He removed his shoes, socks, T-shirt, and jeans so that he was standing in his boxers. The only thing that embarrassed him about standing in his boxers was that he was wearing a pair with hearts all over them, picked out by his mother. Otherwise, a pair of boxers was pretty much like a bathing suit, so it was no big deal. He patted Dog's head. "I'll be right back."

"I'm a good swimmer," Hercules said. "Even though I don't have my swim goggles or my nose plug, I should go with you." He started to pull off his rugby shirt.

"No," Homer said. He turned his back to Lorelei and whispered to Hercules, "You stay here and watch Dog. Make sure she doesn't take him."

Lorelei leaned over Homer's shoulder. "You don't trust me?" she asked innocently.

"Not in a million years," he said. Then he lowered himself over the side of the boat, breaking through a patch of yellow scum the way a spoon breaks through piecrust. The water was oddly warm. Dog balanced on his hind legs and leaned over the edge of the paddleboat, whining.

"Don't let him follow me," Homer said, remembering how Dog had jumped out of an airplane in a desperate attempt to chase after Homer.

Hercules wrapped an arm around Dog. "Good luck," he said as Homer began to dog-paddle toward the tunnel.

"Don't forget Daisy," Lorelei called. "Bring her back."

"What?" Homer nearly swallowed a mouthful of water. "How am I supposed to do that?"

"What about Speckles?" Hercules asked.

"Oh, I almost forgot about Speckles," Lorelei said. "He can't live in there with Madame. She'll feed him nuclear waste like she did to the tortoise. She'll turn him into a monster. Homer, you have to save Speckles."

"What?" Homer stopped paddling and began to tread water. "How am I supposed to get the submarine *and* rescue a rat and a whale shark at the same time?"

"With determination, anything is possible," she said.

"You did say that," Hercules confirmed.

Homer regretted those words. But he knew how badly he'd feel if Dog were left behind to live with Madame.

After peeling a plastic grocery bag from his arm, Homer frog-kicked toward the tunnel. He passed through a bunch of fast-food containers and plastic soda-can rings that had tangled together like a field of man-made water lilies. The gate loomed before him—as ominous as the entrance to a medieval fortress. He grabbed hold and peered between two iron bars. Then, before he could panic, he took a deep breath and sank into the murky water. Keeping his eyes squeezed shut, he lowered himself to the bottom of the gate, swam beneath, then emerged on the other side.

"Blech," he said, wiping lake water from his lips. It tasted soapy, with a hint of cod-liver oil.

Something floated toward him from the depths of the tunnel. It was a red ball. As the ball picked up speed, it became clear that it wasn't floating—it was being pushed.

A wide expanse of polka dots skimmed the surface of the water. With the red ball balanced on his head, Speckles the whale shark swam up to Homer. As he tilted his head, the ball rolled into the water. He nudged it toward Homer. *Wait a minute*, Homer thought. *Rescuing Speckles might be the easiest part of this mission.* Homer grabbed the ball. Then he tossed it between the gate bars, into the lake. With a smack of his tail, Speckles dove under Homer's feet and disappeared.

"Lorelei!" Homer called. "Here comes your shark."

"Thanks!" she called back.

Hoping that the rat and the submarine would be equally cooperative, Homer pushed away from the gate and went into frog-kick mode. His arms began to ache at the halfway point, and by the time he reached the end of the tunnel, they felt as heavy as lead pipes.

Homer's gaze fell upon the submarine. As silent as a water bug, he swam along the far edge of the lair's pool, his eyes adjusting to the bright lights. The place looked vacant. Maybe Madame had been caught by the police already. He could only hope. Then he remembered Lorelei's request.

"Daisy?" he called quietly, scanning the lair for a pair of beady eyes and a long gray tail. Where was she? "Daisy?" He was about to swim across and search the lair when a voice shot out of the back room, piercing Homer like a precisely aimed porcupine quill.

"That'll teach her to bring rats into my lair!"

For as long as he lived, Homer W. Pudding would

never forget that voice. Clinging to the submarine's edge, he watched as Madame la Directeur stomped into the lair. Then he grimaced as a gruesome scene unfolded.

A lifeless gray rat swung by its tail from Madame's fingers. In her other hand she held a shovel. She must have whacked the creature over the head. "Infested," Madame hissed. "My lair is infested!" She opened a garbage can and tossed in the body. It hit the bottom of the can with a horrid *thunk*. *Poor Daisy*, Homer thought. *Lorelei will be crushed.*

Even though Madame had the same slick black hair and was still shaped like a pear, with her upper half much smaller than her lower half, Homer almost didn't recognize her. She used to wear a ton of makeup and fancy clothes with high heels. Now she looked like she'd been camping in a baseball dugout. She dropped the shovel and wiped her hands on her jeans. Then she yanked the baseball cap off her head. "Look at all this junk," she said, turning in a slow circle. "My lair is full of toys! Children's toys!" She kicked a beach ball and overturned a beanbag chair. She kicked Hercules's first-aid kit into the pool. Then she stomped to the vending machines. "Packages of brine shrimp? How dare she fill my vending machine with brine shrimp!" She pushed one of the vending machines over.

Homer cringed as the *clang* echoed off the stone walls.

He tightened his grip. Madame was out of control. She'd whacked Daisy on the head, and she'd probably whack him on the head, too. Her face clenched in a frenzied rage. "When I get my hands on that girl, I'll…what's this?"

She picked up Homer's backpack. His mother had insisted on embroidering his initials on the flap, just in case it got lost. "H.W.P.?" Madame opened it and pulled out a black jacket, then a piece of paper. "'Traditional mourning attire…for Mr. Homer W. Pudding'…Homer Pudding? Homer Pudding?" Then she looked around and softened her voice. "Oh, Homer? Are you still here? Come out, come out, wherever you are."

Homer slid behind the submarine. Submerged to his nostrils, he peered around the bow.

A buzzer sounded and the flat-screen lit up. Horizontal lines blinked, and then Torch's face appeared. She held a glue stick and a piece of cut paper. The table in front of her was covered with little map pieces. "Hey, Lorelei! Where the heck are you?"

Madame's arms fell to her sides, and she dropped the coat and paper.

"I need your help with this stupid map," Torch said. "Hey! Lorelei!"

Madame tucked her T-shirt into her jeans, pushed a few stray hairs from her face, then strode across the room and sat on the red throne, facing the screen. "Hello, Torch."

Torch's mouth fell open. The glue stick tumbled from her hand.

"Why do you look so surprised?" Madame asked snidely. "I told you that I would escape. I told you that I would lead you and Gertrude on this quest."

Torch narrowed her eyes. "Where's Lorelei?"

"I don't know where that street urchin is," Madame said. "But she stole my red speedboat, and when I find her and that Pudding kid—"

"Homer?" Torch asked. "Homer's with Lorelei?"

"Obviously the boy wants the treasure as much as we do."

"But if he's with Lorelei, then that means he's abandoned L.O.S.T."

"Yes, clearly."

"I don't believe it."

Madame leaned back in the red throne. "Homer doesn't matter right now. What matters is the map. Where's Gertrude?"

"She had a little accident," Torch said in a humdrum way. "We were standing on the deck, and she suddenly toppled overboard. I tried to save her—really I did." The corners of her mouth turned up slightly. "But all that jewelry pulled her right down to the bottom."

Homer shivered as silence filled the lair. Gertrude was dead? Possibly murdered? Even though she was a traitor, this was a major loss to the organization. The L.O.S.T. membership was dwindling by the day.

"I see you are in the process of reassembling the map," Madame said. "I will be there shortly to assist you."

"No," Torch blurted out.

"No?"

"That's right. No." Torch's brow knitted, and she glared into the camera. "I don't need your help. So what if you've escaped? I have the map. I have Gertrude's yacht. I don't need you anymore. The plan has changed."

"The plan has changed?" Madame repeated. She darted to her feet with so much gusto that the throne fell backward. *The plan has changed?*

Torch winced, as if Madame's fury had reached through the screen and slapped her.

"Do not forget, you tattoo-covered nitwit, that I'm the one who created *the plan*," Madame said, pointing a finger at the screen. "The girl is working for me. I persuaded her to go to the Pudding farm. I told her about the map. Then I called you and Gertrude and told you to offer your services to her. I told her she could trust you two. She was idiotic enough to give you the map—that's her fault. But I'm the one behind this, so never *ever* forget who's in charge. You wouldn't have the map if not for me."

Homer's fingers turned white as he gripped a porthole. Lorelei was working with Madame la Directeur? Maybe he shouldn't have been shocked. After all, she'd worked for Madame before.

But Madame thought Lorelei had given Rumpold's map to Gertrude and Torch. So that meant that Lorelei was double-crossing Madame. Homer clenched his jaw. She would try to double-cross him, too. No doubt about it. She was playing a game with everyone—a game comprised of her own rules for her own benefit. No matter how many promises or pacts she made, Lorelei wanted the treasure for herself and no one else.

Well, Homer could play games of lies and deception, too. At least he thought he could. He'd never really tried, but right then and there, he knew it was necessary. He'd have to stoop to Lorelei's level. Homer W. Pudding, nephew of Drake H. Pudding, wasn't about to let Rumpold Smeller's treasure, a treasure the entire world was waiting for, fall into Lorelei's greedy hands. No way. *No way!*

"You don't scare me," Torch said from the flat-screen. Her hawk appeared and pecked at the camera lens. "You're an escaped convict. I'm going to call the police and tell them where you are."

"You don't know where I am," Madame said, folding her arms and smirking with satisfaction.

"Whatever," Torch said, pushing the hawk aside. "It doesn't matter that you've escaped. I don't need you. That's the point. I have the map."

"Oh, but you do need me." Madame picked up the red throne, brushed off its cushion, then sat. Resting her hands on the armrests, she spoke in a steadier, calmer voice. "You haven't put the map together. You're having trouble."

"I ain't having trouble," Torch insisted. "It's just that there are a lot of pieces."

Madame made a *tsk-tsk* sound as she shook her head. "My dear Torch, you're not a map reader. You don't come from a treasure-hunting family. Your head is filled with fantasies about Atlantis. That's why you've never found a single thing in your life. You need my expertise. I can put the map together."

The hawk leaped onto Torch's shoulder and nuzzled her cheek. Torch, deep in thought, stroked the hawk's head. Then she stared at all the map pieces lying in front of her. "Okay, fine. You can help me."

"Then we'll have to get rid of the girl," Madame said. "She knows too much. And the boy, too."

Homer's heartbeat pounded at his temples.

"Those kids ain't my problem. All I care about is the treasure." Torch uncapped a glue stick. "So, if we're going to put this map together, I want to make a new plan. This time it's just you and me. Deal?"

"Deal," Madame said. Torch gave her directions to Gertrude's yacht. Then Madame reached out and turned off the screen. "'You and me,'" she said with a snicker. "Until, of course, it's just me."

25

Underwater
Driving

No one really knows how many people have perished in the attempt to find Rumpold Smeller's treasure. Treasure hunting, in general, is a dangerous activity. As Homer well knew, treasure hunters often live exciting though abbreviated lives. The book *The Worst Ways to End a Treasure Hunt* is all about exciting though abbreviated lives. In a future edition, Drake Pudding's untimely death by carnivorous tortoise would be added. Gertrude Magnum's death by falling overboard would be added as well. If Madame la Directeur had her way, Homer and Lorelei would follow.

A sick feeling rose in Homer's gut, and a sour taste filled his mouth. Maybe it was because he'd swallowed a bit of lake water while swimming. Or maybe it was because he'd just overheard his überenemy say she was planning to "get rid" of him.

Homer waited in the murky water, his jaw shivering, his legs itchy. Madame would be leaving soon to join Torch. Then he'd climb into the submarine. Then he'd tell Lorelei that he knew she'd been working for Madame. Then he'd grab Dog and Hercules and forget all about Lorelei, forget all about their L.O.S.T. and FOUND pact. He didn't need her. He was the one who'd pasted the map back together. Hercules had translated the riddle. Angus MacDoodle had calculated the coordinates. Lorelei hadn't done anything. Yes, that's what he'd do. Somehow he'd leave Lorelei behind.

Except for one thing—Lorelei knew the riddle and the coordinates. And she could go straight to Madame and Torch with the information. And if she went straight to Madame and Torch, they'd "get rid" of her. He sighed. As much as he distrusted her, she'd once been his friend. And no matter how many bad things she did, those friendship feelings were as stubborn as a herd of goats in a lettuce patch—there was no way to budge them.

Homer's thoughts scattered as Madame la Directeur hurried from the back room. She'd changed into professional treasure-hunting clothing, which looked exactly like the clothing Homer owned, so it had probably been made by Mr. Tuffletop. There was a pair of khaki shorts, a forest-green shirt, a khaki vest, knee-length leech-proof socks, brown leather boots, and a leather belt with the initials *M.L.D.* on the buckle. She stood in front of a mirror and pulled a Panama hat over her black hair. No one would recognize her as the woman plastered on the front page of the newspaper.

"Time to show those amateurs that they've met their match," she said. Then she stomped up the staircase. Her steps echoed long after she'd disappeared through the tortoise exit.

Homer's hands trembled as he untied the submarine's mooring line. With a grunt, he climbed onto the deck. The sub was shaped like a biscuit with a thick candle sticking out of the top. The biscuit part was the sub's body, and it floated just below the water's surface. The thick candle was actually a wide metal pipe called a conning tower, with a hatch on top. Homer climbed a ladder and opened the hatch. Then he climbed down another ladder into the sub's body.

As he stepped off the ladder, the first thing he noticed was a gold wall plaque.

> ## LA MADAME
> Designed by Ajitabh for Drake Horatio Pudding
> to navigate the deep sea in search of treasure

The submarine had been named after Madame la Directeur? Homer scowled, reading the plaque again. Uncle Drake had once been in love with Madame, so it made sense that back in those days, Ajitabh would have named the submarine after Drake's *girlfriend*. Homer shuddered. No way would he ever call it *La Madame*. As soon as the quest was finished, he'd get a new plaque and rename it *The Drake*.

The next thing he noticed was a metal tank built into the back wall. A label affixed to the tank read SEAWEED PROCESSING BIOFUEL UNIT. A switch on the tank read UP FOR ENGINE. DOWN FOR UNDERWATER BATTERY. Homer thought about this for a moment. Ajitabh had created a unit that sucked seaweed from the ocean and turned it into fuel. The fuel powered the engine while the submarine cruised at the surface. Then the battery took over when submerged. How very clever.

A little room off the side was labeled THE HEAD. Homer knew this was a seafarer's way of saying "bathroom." Another door read SUPPLY LOCKER and another SEAFLOOR EXIT. Three seats were mounted at the bow, each facing a curved observation window. The middle seat had a steering wheel that looked like it had come off a tugboat.

Homer sat in the pilot's seat, his gaze scanning the panel of buttons before him. Ajitabh had affixed a tidy label beneath each button, but even so, the idea of driving a submarine was daunting. It would have been much easier to have Ajitabh at the controls, but that was not going to happen. Homer was on his own. So he carefully read each of the labels until he found what he believed was the first step in the process. ENGINE ON. When he pushed the button, it glowed green. The submarine rattled so loudly it sounded like the inside of a kettledrum. But then the noise subsided to a steady hum.

As he pondered the next step, his gaze rested on a throttle that jutted from the console right next to the steering wheel. There was a similar throttle in his dad's old red truck that made the truck go forward and backward. With a tug, he pulled the throttle down. The engine roared and the submarine shot backward, slamming into the end of the lair's pool. Homer pushed the throttle up. The engine roared and the submarine shot forward, crashing into the opposite side of the pool. Homer cringed. At this rate, he'd break the thing into pieces before leaving the lair.

It took a bit of practice, but he finally figured out how

to ease the throttle into position. Gripping the wheel, he drove down the tunnel, leaving the lair behind. When the gate came into view, Homer pulled the throttle to neutral. Then he climbed up the ladder and stuck his head out of the hatch.

"Hey, Lorelei! Open the gate!" She did, and Homer drove the submarine into City Lake.

When he climbed out of the hatch, warm August air blew across his face. "Hi, Homer," Hercules called from the paddleboat. Dog barked and wagged his tail.

"You did it!" Lorelei called. She pumped her legs, paddling quickly toward the sub. "You got it. Did you see Madame? Is she in there?"

Homer glared at the pink-haired girl in the pink jumpsuit. He wanted to yell at her, wanted to tell her he knew she'd been working with Madame. But if she knew that he knew, then she'd be ready for the time when he'd double-cross her. He stepped onto the sub's deck. "Yeah, I saw her. But she's gone now."

"Where'd she go?" Lorelei asked.

"I don't know," he said with an innocent shrug. "I didn't talk to her. I was hiding."

"Did she seem upset?" Lorelei asked as the paddleboat pulled up alongside the submarine. "I changed a bunch of things in her lair. Did she notice?"

"Oh, she noticed," Homer said.

With a grunt, Dog heaved himself over the side of the paddleboat and landed on the deck next to Homer. Hercules followed and handed Homer his clothing. Then Lorelei stepped onto the deck. She gave the empty paddleboat a shove, sending it toward the far side of the lake, where the rental stand awaited.

Dog peered into the water and growled as the whale shark circled the sub. "Thanks for getting Speckles," Lorelei said.

"What are you going to do with him?" Homer asked.

"Well, it should be easy. He'll follow us down the river, and when we reach the ocean, he'll be free." She climbed up the ladder and disappeared through the hatch.

"Can you help me get Dog up that ladder?" Homer asked Hercules.

"Yeah, no problem." Hercules scooped Dog up and started up the ladder. "Do you have life jackets on board?" he asked. "I sure hope so."

Before climbing back inside the submarine, Homer stood at the top of the ladder and scanned the view. More joggers had appeared on the lake's distant shore. An ice cream truck drove past crowded benches. The skyscrapers loomed beneath a blue cloudless sky. Homer W. Pudding was about to leave The City behind and head for open ocean. *Am I crazy to do this?* he wondered.

His uncle's voice rolled through his mind: "It is a sad

truth of human history that those who dare to be different are often judged to be not quite right in the head."

Homer smiled, suddenly remembering that he was about to embark on a quest while wearing only his boxers. *Maybe I am just a tiny bit crazy.*

"Hey, where's Daisy?" Lorelei's voice boomed from the bottom of the ladder.

Homer glanced down the conning tower. Lorelei was holding out her arms as if the gray rat would jump into them at any moment.

All the anger Homer felt toward Lorelei, that churning pin-prickly sensation that had made his heart race and had made him feel as if he were standing in the eye of a storm, all of that receded like a dream.

"Lorelei," he said gently after he'd climbed down the ladder and looked into her big eyes, "I have some bad news."

26

Full Speed
Ahead

As it turned out, the pin-prickly sensation that covered Homer's skin wasn't caused by his anger toward Lorelei. It was an unpleasant side effect from swimming in the City Lake water.

"It's not the worst rash I've ever seen," Hercules pointed out. "But if those little bumps turn into pustules, then you're going to be miserable. I sure wish I had my first-aid kit."

"Me, too," Homer said with a moan.

The mood inside the submarine was somber at best.

Definitely not the sort of mood that should befall a trio of intrepid adventurers who were setting out to find the world's most coveted pirate treasure. Where was the joy? The excitement? Where were the delirious fantasies as they imagined how their lives would change? But the reality was this: While Homer sat on the submarine's floor in a state of itchy despair, Lorelei was curled up in the corner, her arms wrapped around her legs, deep in grief.

Homer had delivered the news of Daisy's death, but he'd avoided the gory details—especially the shovel-whacking bit. "I can't believe she's gone," Lorelei said, her lower lip trembling.

Homer didn't know if he should hug Lorelei or stand next to her and say things like, "It's going to be okay. There, there. Don't cry." How do you help someone feel better when she's lost her pet rat? When she's lost the only other member of her family?

Anyone who has spent time with an animal knows that an animal can be loved as much as a person. Sometimes even more. Homer knew this. Besides the obvious reasons to love an animal—their cuteness, their cuddliness, their all-around appeal—animals are loyal beyond measure. They don't tell lies. They don't work out elaborate ways to double-cross. And they most certainly don't sneak into bedrooms and steal things from secret compartments under beds.

But here's their most impressive quality—animals accept you for who you are. They don't care if you have a blueberry-sized mole on your face. They don't care if you have to shop in the Husky Boys' section at Walker's Department Store or if you're homeless.

So when Homer's ugly rash made its appearance, Dog lay down next to him and rested his chin on Homer's lap.

"Look what I found," Hercules cried from the supply locker, where he'd been rooting around. He brought out a red metal box. "It's a first-aid kit!" Kneeling next to Homer, he opened the kit. "Hmmmm. This isn't anything like mine."

While Hercules's first-aid kit was designed for those who live on land, this kit was designed for those who live underwater. Pill bottles had labels like OXYGEN RELEASERS, SUNLIGHT VITAMINS, and SHARK REPELLANT. Droppers were labeled SALTWATER EYEBALL SEALER, PLANKTON WASH-AWAY, and BARNACLE BE GONE. Tubes contained PRUNE PREVENTION CREAM FOR FINGERTIPS AND TOES, JELLYFISH PHEROMONES, and OCTOPUS ANTISUCTION OINTMENT.

"Hey, this might work," Hercules said as he opened a tube. "It says it's a gel for jellyfish stings." He squeezed a glob into Homer's open palm. The goo was green and smelled like something one of the farm dogs might have rolled in, but Homer didn't care. If the itching lasted one more minute, he'd rip his skin right off. So he spread the gel all over his legs, arms, belly, and neck. Hercules applied it to Homer's back. The relief was instantaneous.

"Thank you," Homer said after a long, happy sigh.

Skin soothed and boxers dried, Homer dressed in his jeans and plaid shirt. He stayed barefoot because it didn't make much sense to wear shoes on a submarine. Lorelei and Hercules had taken off their shoes, too.

Hercules found a box of rations in the storage locker. He, Homer, and Dog each ate three energy bars. "I'm not hungry," Lorelei mumbled. She turned away and rested her face against a small porthole.

Homer knelt beside Dog and whispered in his ear. "Go sit with Lorelei. Go cheer her up." He gave Dog's rump a push. Dog waddled across the sub and, with a grunt, lay across Lorelei's feet. Homer always appreciated that same gesture on cold mornings. Dog made the best slippers in the world.

But Lorelei turned away from Dog. "Leave me alone," she mumbled. "I'm too sad to pet you."

"What do we do now?" Hercules asked as he closed the first-aid kit.

Homer wasn't sure how to cheer up Lorelei. So he turned his thoughts back to the quest. "I guess we'd better start driving this thing."

The autopilot mechanism wasn't too difficult to figure out. Homer typed in the destination's coordinates. The control-panel screen lit up. Point A represented their current location, and Point B represented their destination. A black dot, which represented the submarine itself, began to pulse.

Homer took the pilot's seat. Hercules took the seat at Homer's right, his seat belt tightly buckled. Speckles swam in and out of view as they made their way to the river that fed City Lake. It wasn't a wild, churning river with jutting rocks and grizzly bears pawing at spawning salmon. City River had been dammed-up so that it formed a wide, calm waterway, perfect for the delivery of goods from all over the world.

"Watch out!" Hercules cried as a tugboat honked its horn. Homer was about to yank the steering wheel, but the autopilot did it for him, avoiding a collision.

"It's crowded," Homer said with surprise. They passed barges carrying lumber. A ship stacked with huge metal containers sat at a dock, where an orange crane unloaded the cargo into waiting trucks. As a cruise ship glided past, its passengers leaned over the railing and stared at the strange submarine. Sailboats, speedboats, and fishing boats joined the parade. Speckles appeared now and then, circling the sub like a border collie.

"Hey, I think he's guiding us," Homer said.

When they reached the junction of the river and the ocean, the waves grew choppy. After a few minutes of turbulence, the water calmed and brilliant blue spread before them all the way to the horizon.

"Wow," Hercules said.

"Look, Lorelei, it's the ocean."

But Lorelei didn't look.

The Seaweed Processing Biofuel Unit began to hum, and as it did, the fuel meter changed from half full to nearly full. "It must be sucking in seaweed," Homer said. "And turning it to fuel."

"Cool," Hercules said.

What was really cool was seeing above and below the water at the same time. Schools of fish swam past, darting and weaving in a synchronized dance. Seagulls rested on the surface, their orange feet gently treading water. Speckles swam into view, his red ball balanced on his nose. Then he stopped and stared into the distance. A shudder ran through his body. Was he hearing the call of the vast ocean? He'd lived in a zoo all his life. Was he feeling the thrill of freedom?

His ball forgotten, Speckles darted off, his tail waving as if saying good-bye.

"I think Speckles is leaving," Homer said.

"What?" Lorelei pushed Dog aside and darted to her feet. "Speckles?" She rapped her knuckles on the glass, louder and louder. "Speckles! Don't leave without saying good-bye. Speckles!"

The whale shark turned around and swam back. He circled the sub, then pressed an eye against the glass, right where Lorelei stood.

"Go," she whispered with a trembling voice. "Go be free." She waved sadly. Speckles circled one last time. Then his massive polka-dot body gradually faded into the distance, as if he'd turned into water. Lorelei sighed.

"I bet he's happy," Hercules said.

"Yeah, I bet he is," Homer agreed.

"Have a good life," Lorelei said quietly. Then she sat in the other seat, her bare feet resting on the console. "If you drive this slowly, we'll never get there."

"I've got the throttle pushed all the way forward," Homer explained.

"Well, it's not fast enough," Lorelei complained, folding her arms. "We have to go faster."

Even though Homer was glad Lorelei was no longer grieving in the corner, he didn't entirely welcome the reunion with her bossy side. "How am I supposed to go faster?" he asked.

"What about this?" Hercules asked as he opened a

small compartment on the console. Inside, a button was labeled HYPER-SPEED. "*Hyper* is a Greek word," Hercules explained. "It means 'excessive.'"

"Hyper works for me." Lorelei reached out with her finger, but Homer grabbed her wrist.

"Uh, shouldn't we talk about this?" he asked. "That sounds really fast." While it was reassuring to have the autopilot at the helm, what would happen if the autopilot failed? Lorelei was a city girl. Hercules lived in a gated private community. Homer was a farm boy. Not a drop of sea blood could be found in any of their veins. "Maybe we should rethink this."

Lorelei raised her eyebrows and stared at Homer. Hercules nervously fiddled with the hem of his shirt. Dog snored. "Rethink? Are you serious?"

He *was* serious. They were about to do something very dangerous, and *danger* was not Homer's middle name.

But then again, everything he'd done since his uncle's death had led up to this moment.

Lorelei and Hercules watched Homer carefully, waiting for his response.

He closed his eyes, filling his mind with an image of Uncle Drake. *You can do this*, his uncle's voice whispered. *You're my nephew. You're a Pudding through and through.* Homer's eyes flew open, and he smacked his hand on his thigh. "Let's do it!" He reached out and jabbed the button.

It was just like one of those science-fiction movies where the captain says, "Warp speed ahead." The view through the observation window went blurry as the submarine jolted forward. Homer and Lorelei, who'd forgotten to fasten their seat belts, tumbled out of their seats, ending up on the floor in a tangle of arms and legs. Dog, who didn't have the luxury of a seat belt, flew across the sub and landed on Homer's chest. *Wham!* It was pretty much like having a meteor fall from the sky. Homer wheezed as his breath shot from his lungs.

After checking to make sure Dog wasn't hurt, Homer looked out the observation window. "Wow. We're really moving." The submarine cut and jumped across the sea's surface like a dolphin gone berserk.

"I think I'm getting seasick," Hercules announced. "Really, really seasick. Somebody better get me a bag or something."

Dog lay on his side and moaned. His tongue hung out like a discarded dishrag. Homer's stomach went into a knot, and a cloud of dizziness swaddled his head. "I'm getting seasick, too."

"I bet the ride would be smoother if we went below," Lorelei said.

"Below?" The word squeaked out of Hercules's mouth.

"You got it." Lorelei said as she strapped herself into a seat. "This is a submarine, remember?" She punched the button labeled SUBMERSION. Engine off, battery on, and down, down, down they went. The ride immediately settled to a smooth *swoosh*. The black dot on the autopilot screen blipped steadily, following its preordained path. The seasickness abated.

Time passed. Fatigue settled over the crew. Except for Dog, no one had slept since the little naps in the Office of Celestial Navigation. Hercules slid his notebook under his head and stretched out on the floor. "We'll take shifts," Lorelei said. "You sleep first."

Although Homer didn't trust her, his eyelids were heavy and his brain felt foggy. He curled up on the floor and tucked a life vest under his head. The humming of the battery, the gentle snores from Dog, and the congested wheezing from Hercules created a soothing, floating melody.

Homer drifted away until it felt as if his body were as liquid as the sea itself.

27

The Treasure Queen

Madame la Directeur stood in the Museum of Natural History's Grand Hall, her upper lip curled with contempt. She'd taken the basement elevator to the main floor. There was no reason for her to crawl through that spider-filled tunnel like some kind of rat. She deserved better than that. *I used to rule this place*, she thought. *It would be nothing without me.*

Morning visitors strolled around the lobby, museum maps in hand. They gazed in wonder at the *Tyrannosaurus rex* skeleton that reached halfway to the vaulted ceiling.

They gawked at the mammoth that stood near the grand stairway and the glass-encased giant squid that spanned the length of a wall. Ticket-takers, cashiers, and museum guides busily went about their duties. Not a single employee paid any attention to the woman in the professional treasure-hunting gear who stood beneath the pterodactyl, her face hidden in the shadows of her Panama hat. *I was your boss*, she thought. *I was your queen!*

A man walked past. His name tag read MR. WOOD, MUSEUM DIRECTOR. Madame's foot darted out. Brochures tumbled from Mr. Wood's hands as he landed on the marble floor. His glasses flew across the room and shattered against a tyrannosaurus thighbone. *How dare he try to take my place.* Then, without an apology, she stepped over Mr. Wood and walked out the museum's front doors.

As she strode down the sidewalk, she tried to make sense of her current situation. The girl had followed directions and had stolen the map from Homer Pudding's house. The girl had continued to follow directions by agreeing to work with Gertrude and Torch. Everything up to that point had gone as Madame had planned. But why would the girl hand the map over to Gertrude and Torch? That made no sense. She was supposed to keep it safe until Madame arrived.

It was possible that the girl was a simple creature

without much intelligence. Yet she'd survived on the streets for many years, so she wasn't stupid. She was up to something. But what?

There was no doubt what the Pudding kid was up to. He wanted the map back. What if he'd told the other L.O.S.T. members about the lair's existence? They'd swarm the place like locusts. Madame couldn't go back there. It would be too risky. She'd have to find a new place to live. As soon as she got her hands on Rumpold's treasure, she'd move far from The City. Maybe to a tropical island where she could work on her tan. Why not buy an entire island? Then she could do whatever she wanted.

Madame crossed Main Street and turned onto Success Street as a police car drove past. She didn't miss a beat of her determined steps. She'd already outsmarted them. A stack of newspapers sat on the sidewalk, the paperboy shouting, "Escaped prisoner on the loose. Read all about it." Madame kicked the stack over as she hurried by.

It was not much farther until she reached the marina where Gertrude's yacht was moored and where Torch was trying to piece the map together. Madame's fingers wiggled with anticipation. Finally, after all this time, the map would be hers. And as soon as she found the treasure, L.O.S.T. would beg her to come back. They'd beg her to be their leader. And she'd laugh in their faces—*I don't need you*. Then she'd give herself a new name—the Treasure Queen.

As the Treasure Queen, Madame would rule the treasure-hunting world. From her throne on her private island, she would plan future quests. She would employ an army of minions—ruthless men and women who cared not for international laws or treaties, who would stop at nothing to collect the desired treasures and bring them back to their queen. A film company would make a movie about her and then a television series, and everyone would be jealous of her riches, power, and fame. She'd license the rights to Treasure Queen action figures and bobblehead dolls—maybe start a Treasure Queen clothing line.

The train station loomed on the other side of the street. Madame wouldn't have given the building a second glance had it not been for the man sitting on a bench just outside the station's main entrance. The man's feet reached only halfway to the sidewalk. He had a telescope tucked under his arm and a plaid suitcase beneath his feet.

Madame stopped so abruptly that she nearly caused a pedestrian collision. Angus MacDoodle hadn't been seen in public in more than a decade. He was supposed to be in hiding. Why would he be in The City? "Angus?" she hollered.

Angus MacDoodle, who'd been reading the train schedule, looked across the traffic and spotted Madame. He mumbled something, slid off the bench, and hurried into the station.

Madame la Directeur gave chase, running against the traffic light and darting between taxis. "Out of my way!" she ordered, pushing people aside as she entered the building. A cacophony bounced off the brick walls. Trains whistled, espresso machines steamed, a loudspeaker announced arrivals and departures. Where was he? She cut through a line at the ticket booth, stepping on a little boy's foot and elbowing an old lady in the process. Then she spotted him. He was about to board a train. Picking up speed, she reached out just in time to grab the telescope from beneath his arm.

Angus whipped around, his red braids soaring. "Give it back."

"Not until you tell me what you're doing here."

"Tha's none of yer business," he said. He stepped toward her, his eyes blazing. Then he pointed to a newspaper kiosk. "The police are lookin' for ye. Give it back or ah'll make a fuss."

She stepped away, her grip tightening on the telescope. Then she stepped close to a track and held the telescope over it. "I'll drop it," Madame threatened.

"Tell me what you're doing here or I'll drop it and it will break into pieces."

Angus took a sharp, worried breath. "Ye've always been a troublemaker. Ah was glad whin they kicked ye out of L.O.S.T. Ah never liked ye. Never."

"Well, you've always been a strange little man, and I've never liked you, either." She narrowed her eyes. "But you're a hermit, and hermits don't like cities. What are you doing here? Tell me."

"Ah'm going away. Those kids found me. Ah dinna care nothin' about those kids and their map."

"Kids?" Madame raised an eyebrow. "Map?"

"Ah dinna care about it. Ah'm going far away whir no one will bother me. Where ah can watch the stars in peace." He skirted around her and tried to grab the telescope, but she simply held her arm higher.

"Did one of the kids have pink hair?" He nodded. "And did the other kid look like he'd eaten too much birthday cake?" He nodded again. "And was there a dog?"

"Aye. A wee basset hound."

Madame couldn't believe her luck. Fortune, who'd been ignoring her lately, was smiling upon her once again. Had she not run into Angus, she would have wasted time with Torch, putting together a map that was obviously a fake. That Lorelei girl had proven to be a master of deceit. She'd distracted Torch and Gertrude by creating a forgery, all the while keeping the real map for herself. Perhaps the girl deserved a second chance. Such deception was admirable. She might make a good minion for the Treasure Queen.

But not the boy. Homer Pudding still had to go.

"Tell me about the map," Madame la Directeur insisted.

Angus MacDoodle grunted, then folded his arms and glared at her from beneath his bushy eyebrows. "It was a celestial map," he said. "Ah read it for them."

A celestial map? Yes, of course. Rumpold Smeller was a pirate, a man of the seven seas. It made perfect sense that he'd chart his buried treasure by the stars. "You calculated the coordinates?"

"Aye."

With an amused smile, Madame la Directeur relaxed her arm and held the telescope in front of Angus's reddened face. "I'll make you an offer. The telescope for the map's coordinates. Do we have a deal?"

"All aboard!" a conductor yelled. "Last call for the train to Gnome. All aboard!"

"I bet the stars are beautiful in Gnome," Madame said. "But how will you watch them without your beloved telescope?"

Angus glanced nervously over his shoulder. Then he wrapped his hands around the lens and gave Madame the coordinates.

"Are you certain they are correct?" she asked, leaning over so their noses were nearly touching. "Because I will find you if they are wrong."

"Dinna insult me, woman." Angry spit flew from Angus's lips. "Ah know the stars better than anyone else in the world. Of course ah gave ye the correct coordinates." She released her grip, and he reclaimed his telescope. Then he scurried past the conductor and climbed onto the train.

A blanket of steam surrounded Madame as she stood on the platform.

The treasure was almost hers.

28

Jellyfish
Traffic Jam

Despite their progress across the ocean, Lorelei's mood remained gloomy. Her pale, frowning face reminded Homer of Zelda, who was always draped in sadness. It's a well-known fact that if you spend too much time with someone who is sad, you start to feel sad, too. The sadness floats around and gets in your hair and on your face. Then it seeps into your thoughts. So Homer tried to keep his brain busy by studying the console's buttons and gadgets. At least his toxic rash was all better.

It was Lorelei's turn to sleep, so Homer took watch in the pilot's seat. The problem with traveling at hyperspeed was that sightseeing was difficult, even with the headlight beams on high. The submarine zipped through the water so fast, Homer couldn't get a good look at ocean life. And just like a car traveling down the highway, collecting bugs on its windshield, the sub's observation window collected jellyfish. Poor jellies. Unlike fish, they couldn't swim out of the way. *Splat!*

"Ooooh, there's another one," Homer said as the tentacled creature slid down the glass. "Too bad this thing isn't powered by jellyfish guts."

Hercules sat next to Homer in a copilot's seat, with Rumpold's map draped across his lap. "This riddle still doesn't make much sense. 'Twins of flame above and below. An endless mirror between. In heavenly eyes the stars do shine. Behind saliva hides what you seek.'"

"Some of it makes sense," Homer said. "We know it's the Draco constellation, so the dragon has heavenly eyes, right? 'In heavenly eyes the stars do shine.' We've figured out that line."

"Yeah, that makes sense."

Homer cringed as another jellyfish hit the windshield, leaving a gooey smudge the size of a pillow. "Wow! That was the biggest one yet. I never knew they could get that big."

"What about the other lines?" Hercules asked, his gaze focused on the map. "What about the first line, 'twins of flame'?"

"Well…" Homer paused. He'd never had much luck with games involving wordplay. On stormy nights back on the goat farm, when the power went out, the Scrabble board usually made an appearance. His sister, Gwendolyn, always won because she used mysterious scientific words. If anyone challenged and said, "Gwendolyn, *nurftle* isn't a word," Gwendolyn would say, "Of course it's a word. It's a word all taxidermists know." And then she'd end up on a triple-word square and her score would soar.

Just once, Homer had tried to cheat. "*Ybkzurp* is a word all mapmakers know." But Gwendolyn had a hissy fit, and Homer had to change his word to *burp*. Gwendolyn won.

Homer read the riddle again. "Well, dragons breathe fire, so that might be the flame part. 'Twins of flame above and below.' So we know that there is a dragon in the sky, and if the dragon has a twin, then it must be a… dragon on land."

"Well, it can't be a real dragon," Hercules said. "Dragons are mythological creatures. So it must be something like a dragon statue. Or maybe something shaped like a dragon."

"We won't know until we get there," Lorelei mumbled sleepily. How long had she been awake?

"Ur." Dog rolled over and stuck his legs in the air, presenting his belly for scratching. Lorelei, who was lying next to Dog, ignored him. Dog got to his feet and nudged Lorelei with his nose, but still she ignored him. "Ur?"

The boys shared a long helpless look. Was Lorelei going to be in this sad mood for the entire quest?

Hercules folded the map and set it on the console. "I have an idea," he said. "Maybe we could have a funeral for Daisy." It was the first time anyone had mentioned the rat by name since Homer had delivered the bad news.

"Really?" Lorelei pushed her bangs from her swollen eyes and looked up at the boys.

"Sure," Hercules said with a shrug. "Why not? It might make you feel better if we do something like that."

Would a funeral make Lorelei feel better? Homer wasn't sure. Lord Mockingbird's had been pretty weird, but it was also the only funeral Homer had ever attended. At this point, he'd do nearly anything to get Lorelei to stop moping. They needed her help with the riddle.

"But she's not here," Lorelei said. "We can't bury her."

"That doesn't matter," Hercules said. "We can use the funeral to *remember* Daisy."

Homer checked the autopilot setting. According to the blinking black dot, they'd crossed the halfway point and were still on course. *Splat!* A yellow jellyfish hit the windshield. Homer wanted to holler, "Look at that one!" because it was the size of two pillows. But given that they were about to hold a funeral, he thought it best to restrain his amazement.

Everyone, including Dog, sat in a circle on the submarine's cold floor.

"What do we do now?" Homer asked.

"Well, maybe Lorelei could tell us how she met Daisy," Hercules said.

"Okay." A little sparkle lit up in Lorelei's eyes as the memory drifted to the surface. "I was living behind the utility closet at the soup warehouse. Lots of people used to dump their garbage out in the alley, and sometimes it was pretty good stuff. I had my eye on a sofa cushion, but when I went to get it, I found a family of rats living in it. A mom and her five new babies. They were so cute."

Homer shuddered. He'd seen newborn rats back on the farm—pink, hairless, and squirmy like overfed maggots. *Cute* wasn't the word he'd choose.

"I left the couch cushion in the alley so the mother rat could take care of her babies. But a week later, someone came and took the cushion away. I felt so sad wondering what had happened to the rat family. Then I saw something moving in the shadows. One of the baby rats lay on the bricks, shivering. She must have fallen out of the cushion. I carried her inside and fed her some soup. She became my rat."

"Why'd you name her Daisy?" Hercules asked.

"Because most people think rats are ugly. But I thought she was beautiful. Like a flower."

"That's a misnomer," Hercules said. "A misnomer is when you call something the opposite of what it is. Like when you name a pig Perfume. Or when you name a turtle Speedy."

"Daisy wasn't a misnomer," Lorelei said with a pout. "She *was* beautiful."

"Your turn," Hercules told Homer.

Homer frowned. What was he supposed to say? "Uh, well, I remember when I first met Daisy at the soup warehouse." What else could he say? The rat had stared at Homer with her beady eyes, black nose, and twitchy whiskers. Honestly, she'd given him the creeps. "She was...uh...she was a nice rat."

Hercules elbowed Homer. "Keep talking," he whispered. Lorelei flared her nostrils and looked at Homer, waiting for some sort of story.

Homer cleared his throat. "I remember how she stole my Galileo Compass when I was trying to sneak into the lair. And how she stole that silver spoon from Ajitabh's cook when we were at his tower." He wasn't sure if this was the kind of story Lorelei wanted to hear, but she suddenly smiled. So he kept going. "And how she got into the cave on Mushroom Island and stole those harmonic crystals."

"She was a brilliant thief," Lorelei said like a proud mother. "I didn't need to teach her anything. She was a natural."

Feeling like he'd done his job, Homer elbowed Hercules. *"Your* turn."

"Well, I didn't spend much time with Daisy," Hercules said. "But I do know that the word *rat* comes from *raet*, which is Old English. And the word *rodent* comes from *rodere*, which in Latin means 'to gnaw.'"

"She was good at gnawing," Lorelei said.

"Funerals usually end with someone saying something, like 'rest in peace,'" Hercules said. So they all said it together. "Rest in peace." And that's all it took, just a bit of talking, to cheer Lorelei up.

"I still miss her, but I do feel a little better." She gave Dog a hug.

And so they sat for a while, the hum of the battery the only sound. Dog stayed close to Lorelei, as if he sensed that she needed something warm and furry to hold on to. But then the mood was broken by a loud *splat*.

Gigantic yellow globs bombarded the window.

"Yuck," Lorelei said. "It looks like it's raining boogers."

The next jellyfish to hit was a whopper, and the impact sent a vibration throughout the sub. The gold name plaque trembled, then slid down the wall and landed on the floor at Homer's feet. He grabbed it.

"I hate that this is called *La Madame*," Homer said. "Madame used this submarine to double-cross my uncle. And then she stole it from him. She doesn't deserve to have it named after her."

"I remember reading the report," Hercules said. "When I became the official records keeper for L.O.S.T., I had to put all the files in order. The last records keeper never alphabetized anything. He simply shoved the documents in wherever there was room. It was a total disaster. I created a system based not only on the alphabet, but also on Latin prefixes. For instance—"

"Never mind all that," Lorelei interrupted. "Tell us about the report."

"Oh. Right." Hercules screwed up his face for a moment, deep in thought. "Let's see if I can remember. The report was called 'The Unforgivable Treacheries of Madame la Directeur.' I didn't file it under '*t*' for '*the*,' because I think it best not to do that. So many things begin with '*the*' and the '*t*' file was bulging. So I filed it under '*un*,' since that is the prefix for '*unforgivable*,' and—"

"You're going to drive me crazy," Lorelei blurted out, her sadness dissolving by the moment. "We don't care about the filing system. Just tell us about the report."

So Hercules did. He remembered it as best as he could. And here's what it said:

The Unforgivable Treacheries
of Madame la Directeur

Submitted by Lord Mockingbird XVIII following an interview with Drake Horatio Pudding, witness to the horrid event.

Let it be known that Madame la Directeur did break the solemn vow she made to the Society of Legends, Objects, Secrets, and Treasures by stealing treasure for personal gain. The dastardly deed occurred as follows:

Madame la Directeur accepted a position as questing partner alongside Drake Horatio Pudding in a L.O.S.T.-sponsored quest to find the sunken remains of the HMS Bombastic. *Drake offered the use of his brand-spanking-new submarine,* La Madame. *Upon finding the* Bombastic's *remains, Madame manned the submarine while Drake explored the wreckage. At great risk to his life, Drake searched the ship's quarters, including the captain's, where he discovered the captain's chest. Take heed, for what follows is undeniably dastardly.*

As Drake carried the chest back to the submarine, Madame attacked him with the submarine's robotic arms. Drake fought valiantly but was no match for the metal demons. The captain's chest was ripped from his grip. His oxygen tank nearly empty, he watched in agony as the robotic arms and the captain's chest disappeared into the submarine. Madame la Directeur piloted the submarine to an unknown location, leaving Drake to drown. She later sold the chest's contents on the black market.

"That's how I remember it," Hercules said. "You've got to have a good memory to be a World's Spelling Bee champion."

"Robotic arms?" Lorelei asked. "This submarine has robotic arms?"

While Homer was also interested in learning more about the robotic arms, he couldn't shake the image of his brave uncle floating in the middle of the ocean while Madame drove away.

"I wonder what was in the captain's chest," Hercules said.

"Some people thought the captain's chest contained

Rumpold Smeller's treasure," Homer answered. He knew all these details from reading *The Biography of Rumpold Smeller*. "The owner of the chest was Captain Ignatius Conrad. He was the last person to see Rumpold alive. He made Rumpold walk the plank—"

"—and then Rumpold drowned," Lorelei interrupted. "Or got eaten by sharks. Or maybe both. No one actually knows."

"Well, I'm going to rename the sub," Homer said. "I'm going to call it *The Drake*."

"You can't do that," Lorelei said. "It's mine now. Everything from the lair belongs to me. Finders keepers."

"But—"

The submarine shuddered, and the battery began to whine like an angry housefly. The whining rose an octave, and Dog started to howl.

"What's going on?" Lorelei asked.

Homer and Hercules scrambled to their feet and rushed to the console. The battery light blinked red. "We've stopped," Homer said, pointing to the autopilot screen, where the black dot had stopped moving.

"How come we've stopped?" Hercules asked.

"Howoooo!" Dog cried, throwing his head back as the battery's whine continued to climb the musical scale. Lorelei covered Dog's ears.

"I think it's the jellyfish!" Homer shouted above the

noise. "There are too many of them. They're pushing against us." Gelatinous yellow and white blobs now covered the entire window. "It's like we're trying to drive through a bowl of Jell-O. The propeller isn't strong enough."

Then the battery went silent. The submarine shuddered to a stop. The headlights dimmed and everything went dark.

"Ur?"

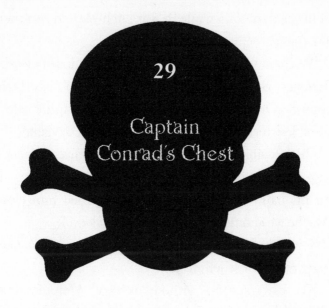

29

Captain
Conrad's Chest

It took a few minutes to find the emergency backup battery. As soon as Homer pulled the switch, the overhead lights flickered, then glowed. The yellow and white jellyfish pressed against the windshield, their gelatinous bodies undulating, their tentacles creeping along the glass. It reminded Homer of the moths that were drawn to his bedroom window at night. "Do you think they're attracted to the light?" he asked.

"Maybe. Let's turn the light off and see if they go away," Lorelei suggested.

So Homer turned off the emergency battery, and they sat in the dark for a while. It was pitch-black down there and kinda creepy.

"Without power, the oxygen generator doesn't work," Hercules whispered, as if he didn't want to disturb the jellyfish. Or as if whispering a terrible truth made it sound less terrible. "What if we run out of oxygen?"

This possibility hadn't occurred to Homer. *Run out of oxygen?* He reached for Dog and found a warm ear. He ran his hand down Dog's back and pulled him close. "Maybe we should turn the battery back on."

"Give it a few more minutes," Lorelei said. "We need to get rid of those jellyfish."

"We can't survive without oxygen," Hercules said, followed by a soft puff of his inhaler. "My throat feels like it's closing up. Does anyone else feel that way?" Another puff. "Do you think we're running out already?"

Homer's throat began to feel weird, too. But it was probably because he had his face buried in Dog's neck and he'd inhaled a few stray dog hairs. That always happened. "Let's turn it back on," he said.

"Thanks a lot, Hercules! All your worrying is making me worry," Lorelei said. "Fine. Turn the battery back on."

Homer gladly switched on the emergency battery, and the interior lit up. "Crud," he said as he looked at the undulating blanket of yellow and white that was still pressed against the window.

"Why won't they go away?" Lorelei asked.

"They seem to like us," Hercules said.

An unsettled sensation tickled Homer's stomach. "Hey, we're rising," he said. As the upper half of the submarine surfaced, the jellyfish slid down the windshield until they covered only the submerged half of the window. Night had fallen. A full moon hung in the sky like a lightbulb. The submarine began to rock back and forth with the ocean current.

The black dot started moving again—but in the wrong direction. "They're pushing us backward," Homer said.

"What?" Lorelei rushed to the console. "We can't go backward. There isn't enough time to go backward. We've got to get rid of them."

"Hey, wasn't there something in the first-aid kit about jellyfish?" Hercules rummaged through the red metal box. "Here it is." He held up a tube. "It's jellyfish phero-mones. Maybe we could use this."

Homer didn't want to admit that he had no idea what pheromones were. Thankfully, Lorelei did it for him. "I have no idea what phero-thingies are," she said.

"Pheromones are chemicals that are released by ani-mals," Hercules explained. "*Phero* is Greek, and it means 'to carry.' The chemicals carry a scent that can be smelled by others in the same species. And the scent makes them behave differently. I think it's used for mating, mostly. It's pretty cool when you think about it."

"Oh, so the scent will attract the jellyfish." Lorelei leaned close to Homer and whispered, "Kinda like the scent of treasure attracting you-know-who."

Homer thought about this for a moment. "So if we squirt that tube into the water, then the jellyfish will stop liking us and will like the scent instead, and we can get rid of them."

He grabbed the tube from Hercules, climbed the conning tower, and opened the hatch. Fresh salty air rushed in, filling the interior like a cool drink of water. Homer stuck his head out the hatch. The ocean churned, rocking the sub from side to side. Waves rolled over the deck. A sour taste filled his mouth. He'd have to do this quickly or he'd get seasick for sure. After uncapping the tube, he stepped onto the top rung and tossed the pheromones. The sea quickly swallowed the little tube. Homer closed the hatch and rejoined the others at the observation window.

The effect was immediate. Tentacles trembled. Then a quiver ran across the jellyfish, reminding Homer of his visits to the ballpark when everyone stood up and did the wave. The giant blobs released their grip on the submarine and swam away.

"We did it!" Lorelei cried.

Soon after, they were submerged again and racing along at hyper-speed.

Homer and Lorelei sat at the helm studying Rumpold's map. "I'm hungry," Hercules announced, and he wandered into the supply locker.

"Bring me a couple of energy bars," Lorelei said. "And some water."

Now that they weren't bobbing on the surface, Homer's stomach had settled back to normal. "Is there anything other than energy bars?" he asked, trying not to imagine what his mother might be making for dinner. As shuffling sounded from inside the locker, Homer tried not to think about creamy macaroni and cheese or roast beef with tender red potatoes and gravy. *A dry energy bar will be delicious,* he told himself. It was certainly better than having to eat sand-flea soup, which had been the main dinner course during many a treasure-hunting expedition.

Lorelei mumbled as she read the riddle. "'Behind saliva hides what you seek.'" She scratched her upturned nose. "Saliva? How do you hide a treasure behind saliva? That's just weird."

"Uh, guys," Hercules called from inside the supply locker. "I think I found something." A screeching sound filled the sub as Hercules dragged a large wooden chest from the closet.

Dog shot to his paws and galloped toward the chest, his nose quivering. He circled the chest, sniffing every square inch. Hercules fiddled with the padlock. "Dog, move your nose. I'm trying to open this thing." Hercules gave Dog a gentle push, but Dog pushed back, squeezing between Hercules and the chest. His tail wagged furiously as he stuck his nose right up against the lock and sniffed. "The chest was inside a metal locker. It's got the initials *C.I.C.* on it. Do you think that stands for 'Captain Ignatius Conrad'?" Hercules pushed Dog again. "Hey, why is Dog sniffing this thing if he can't smell?"

"Smell?" Homer and Lorelei blurted out.

The map flew into the air as Homer and Lorelei leaped from their seats like Olympic athletes in a long-jump competition. Arms reaching and fingers twitching, each tried to get to the chest before the other. Lorelei, being the swifter of the two, threw herself over the chest. But Homer, having a bit of a weight advantage, knocked her off with a shoulder butt.

"What's the matter with you two?" Hercules gasped. He scooted away as they started wrestling like a couple of first graders fighting over the last cupcake. "Someone's going to get hurt."

Lorelei clutched the padlock, but Homer grabbed her around the waist and pulled her away from the chest.

"It's not yours!" he said with a groan. "It belonged to my uncle Drake."

"Let go of me! I want to see what's inside!" She kicked his kneecap. Pain shot up his leg, and he fell backward, smacking his shoulders against the Seaweed Processing Biofuel Unit. "Finders keepers," she said as she grabbed the padlock.

Homer was sick and tired of "finders keepers." He took a huge breath and lunged at Lorelei. They rolled onto the ground, where he pinned her, as Hercules watched in silent confusion.

"Madame stole it from my uncle," Homer said, his chest heaving with short breaths. "I'm not going to let you steal it from me. I know you're working for her."

Lorelei stopped struggling. She narrowed her eyes. "What are you talking about?"

"I heard Madame when she was in the lair," Homer said, tightening his grip on Lorelei's wrists. "She was talking to Torch on the flat-screen. She said she'd sent you to get the map from me. She said she told you to work with Torch and Gertrude."

Lorelei's expression softened. "Okay, so what? So she sent me to get the map. But I didn't give it to her. I kept it."

"You're working for Madame?" Hercules asked.

"No. I just pretended to work for her." Lorelei cringed. "Homer, you're hurting me."

"Tell us the truth," Homer insisted, not releasing his grip.

"I am telling you the truth." She cringed again. "Why would I work with Madame? She double-crossed me before, remember? She tried to feed me to her tortoise. I'm working with you. It's L.O.S.T. and FOUND together. Now let go of me. *Please.*"

Homer let go, then scooted between Lorelei and the captain's chest. Lorelei sat up. Her pink hair was all messed up from their fight. Her face was still covered in scratches from the hot air balloon disaster. But Homer was equally a mess, with a collection of scratches and a thin layer of green goo spread over his toxic rash.

Lorelei rubbed her wrists and stared at him with a sad pout. He felt a bit bad for hurting her. His sister, Gwendolyn, had spent a fair amount of time pinning him to the ground, torturing him with tickles or by dangling squirrel guts in his face. Being pinned down was a terrible, helpless feeling. "Sorry I hurt you," he said quietly.

"Homer?" Hercules asked. "What should we do? Should we open it?"

"I don't think so," Homer said. "Not with her here."

Lorelei folded her arms. "Oh, I see what's happening. You're thinking of double-crossing me. You're trying to figure out how to push me out of the pact."

"The pact was to find Rumpold's treasure, not Captain Conrad's chest," Homer said. "The chest belongs to L.O.S.T. It was found on a L.O.S.T.-sponsored quest."

"The chest was re-found on this quest, and our pact covers all treasure we find on this quest," she said.

"*Re-found* is not a word," Hercules pointed out.

"Whatever," Lorelei grumbled. "The point is, we have a pact. And you're supposed to be a man of your word, Homer." They stared at each other. "Are you going to break a pact? A sacred agreement in which you've given your word?"

"Maybe," Homer said, though his voice came out small and without conviction.

Lorelei smiled. "You won't break our pact. I know you won't. Honesty is your Achilles' heel."

Thunk.

"Hey, guys," Hercules said. "What is Dog doing?"

Dog, who'd been sniffing the chest this entire time, had pushed the chest over. That slight impact was all it took to shatter the rusty lock. Lorelei lunged forward and pulled the lid open.

A unified sigh of disappointment filled the submarine as the kids stared into the empty chest. "Nothing," Lorelei grumbled. "Madame took it all."

All that fighting for nothing, Homer thought, his cheeks turning red with embarrassment. But even though it was empty, the chest itself was a valuable artifact. A maritime museum would probably like to have it. After all, Captain Conrad was one of the most famous British naval officers in history. Homer was about to tell Lorelei that he still intended to claim it in the name of L.O.S.T., but that's when Dog lay on his stomach and pawed at the chest's underside. "Urrrr." Dog sniffed and pawed, his tail wagging.

"He's still sniffing," Lorelei said with a burst of excitement. "Do you see that, Homer? He's still sniffing!"

"Will someone tell me why Dog is sniffing?" Hercules said. "It doesn't make sense."

Homer leaned close and inspected the place where Dog was scratching. "It looks like there's a secret compartment under here." He patted Dog's head. "Good boy." Then he wiggled a piece of wood until it slid free. A package lay beneath. Homer carefully lifted it from its snug hiding spot.

The package was wrapped in some sort of animal skin that had been pounded as thin as paper. The skin felt rubbery. Homer peeled it open. Beneath was a second layer of the rubbery skin. Then a third layer of silver fur. Holding his breath, he peeled back the fur.

A small leather-bound book lay inside. Lorelei didn't try to grab it. Instead, she stared, wide-eyed and speechless.

"It's in perfect condition," Homer whispered as he turned the book over. "The skins kept a watertight seal."

"What is it?" Hercules also whispered. It was definitely a whispering kind of moment, for a secret was about to be revealed. The submarine's battery hummed. Dog's tail *thwapp*ed against the floor. Breaths were held.

Carefully, with fingers barely touching the precious leather, Homer opened to the first page. He could have sworn that an orchestra swelled at that very moment. Harps sang out, and cymbals clanged—for in loopy handwriting across the page were the following words:

The Diary of Rumpold Smeller the Pirate

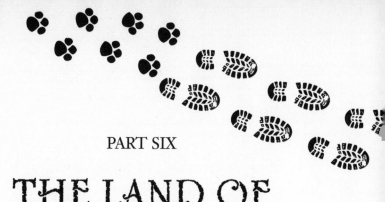

PART SIX

THE LAND OF DRAGONS

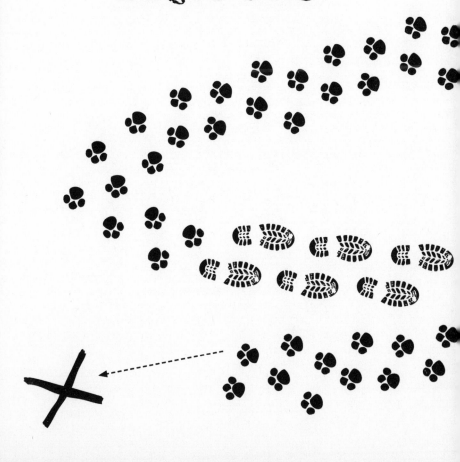

30

Rumpold's
Secret

Imagine if you found someone's diary—someone you'd read about your entire life. Let's say, for example, Santa Claus. What a find that would be. *Dear Diary, Today I told Mrs. Claus that I was sick and tired of being a glorified delivery boy and that I wanted to go back to college and become a taxidermist. It's always been my dream to be a taxidermist.* Or how about the Tooth Fairy? *Dear Diary, I'm so totally in love with the boy next door, but every time I see him, I'm always carrying a big, stinky tooth, and I think he thinks I'm weird. What should I do?*

To Homer and Lorelei, Rumpold Smeller the Pirate was as much a character from a storybook as he was a real person. He'd lived on this planet—no doubt about that. But his adventures were woven from the threads of historical fact, hearsay, and exaggeration, forming a tapestry of legendary proportions. What was true, what was fiction, no one really knew.

Until now.

Homer sat on the submarine's floor, crisscrossed his legs, and held the diary in his lap. Hercules and Lorelei sat on either side, pressing their shoulders against Homer's. Dog pushed beneath the diary and draped himself over Homer's lap. He'd found the treasure, after all, so he had every right to the best seat in the house. Homer cleared his throat and turned to the next page. Then he read out loud.

Dear Diary,

Today, on the eve of my thirtieth year, I begin this diary. It may seem odd that I waited so long to write about my life, but until this moment, I've been much too busy to put quill to parchment. You will discover how busy I've been as you read about my adventures traveling the world and collecting treasure—from the forbidden palace in China, where the emperor himself gave me a yellow ball of dragon's saliva to—

"Hey, that's part of the riddle," Hercules said. "Shhhh," Lorelei shushed. "Keep reading."

—to the piranha-infested Amazon, where a chieftain gave me the key to a lost city.

But how is it, you must wonder, that I now find the time to write? As I look out my porthole, a British naval ship, the HMS *Bombastic*, sails on the horizon in fast pursuit. Captain Ignatius Conrad appears determined to capture me. I fear my life will be coming to an end sooner than I'd like.

So in the time I have left, I will tell you my true story as I lived it. But be warned, I will not reveal the location of my treasure in this diary. What I will do, however, is to clear up some of the rumors about me. As you shall read, I'm not the cold-blooded killer the world thinks me to be. As you shall also read, I'm not the person most people think me to be.

I am known as Rumpold Smeller the Pirate, but I was not born with that name. I was born Rumpoldena Smeller, the only daughter of Duke Smeller of Estonia.

Homer stopped reading. "Wait a minute. That can't be right." He read it again.

I was born Rumpoldena Smeller, the only daughter of Duke Smeller of Estonia.

Lorelei grabbed the diary from Homer's hands. "He's a girl? I mean, she's a girl? Wow, listen to this." Lorelei read the next sentence.

In order to live the life I wanted, I cut my hair short, wore the costume of a boy, and took my brother's name.

"She's a girl. A girl!" Lorelei beamed.

"That's amazing," Hercules said. "She looks like a boy in all the drawings."

Homer's thoughts traveled through the pages of his books back home. Every drawing of Rumpold showed him as a man with pants and a sword and a Jolly Roger flag. Sometimes a severed head dangled from his hand, and sometimes the bodies of his victims lay at his feet.

"Wait a minute," Homer said. "All those drawings were based on his legend. Rumpold himself only posed for three portraits, and he doesn't have a beard in any of them. I bet if we looked at those portraits, now that we know the truth, we'd be able to see that he was actually a girl."

"This is huge," Lorelei said. "This is going to change history."

Never ever would Homer have guessed this secret. Because he'd kept a number of secrets, he knew how often they tried to free themselves. How tempting it was to tell someone, just so the secret would stop tickling for a bit. What a feat Rumpold had accomplished. She'd pretended to be a boy for most of her life. It was a secret worthy of some sort of award.

Mr. Bernard Dullard would be in shock when he learned the news. As the author of *The Biography of Rumpold Smeller*, he would have to rewrite the entire book and change all the *he*s to *she*s, and that would certainly take a very long time.

"Now that I think about it, it makes total sense that the most successful treasure hunter in the world was a girl," Lorelei said.

"What is that supposed to mean?" Homer asked.

"Girls are better at finding things," was her explanation.

"You mean girls are better at *taking* things," Homer said with a frown. "And they're better at lying."

"That's not true." Lorelei was about to whack Homer with the diary when Hercules, who'd been oddly quiet, cleared his throat.

"I think you've both been lying," he said. Homer and Lorelei shared a fleeting glance, then fell silent. "I'm part of this quest, and you've been keeping a secret from me."

"What do you mean?" Lorelei asked innocently.

Hercules pushed up the sleeves of his rugby shirt and leaned his elbows on his knees. "There had to be a reason why Lorelei kept kidnapping Dog. There had to be a reason why she wanted Dog to be a part of this quest. He can't smell, but he was sniffing Captain Conrad's chest. And he was sniffing the treasure map back at the lair. I'm not stupid. I know there's something going on." A hurt expression washed over Hercules's face. "Don't you trust me enough to tell me the truth?"

Homer felt about as small as an ant. And his heart grew heavy as he looked into Hercules's sad brown eyes. Hercules had been true and loyal. Without his help, the quest to Mushroom Island would have been a failure. Without his bravery, Dog would have fallen from that airplane and been squashed. It was the biggest secret Homer held, but it felt wrong to keep it from Hercules. "Dog can smell treasure," Homer said.

Lorelei smacked Homer's arm. "What are you doing?"

"I should have told him," Homer said. "He's my friend, and he's risking his life on this quest."

"But—"

"But what?" Homer said sharply. "I trust Hercules a million times more than I trust you, Lorelei. Dog's my dog—don't forget that. I get to choose who I tell." Lorelei grumbled something under her breath, but Homer didn't care about her opinion at that moment. He cared only that he'd hurt his friend's feelings. "I'm sorry I didn't tell you," he said to Hercules. "My uncle Drake knew that Dog could smell treasure. That's why he kept Dog, and that's why he made sure I inherited Dog. And Lord Mockingbird knew because he once owned Dog. But now only the three of us know."

Hercules reached out and patted Dog's rump. "If word got out, Dog would be in danger."

"That's right," Homer said. Then he leaned close to

Hercules and whispered, "I'm glad I told you. If anything happens to me, someone other than Lorelei should know. Someone who will protect Dog." Hercules nodded.

"I don't care if you're whispering about me," Lorelei said huffily. "I'm going to read Rumpold's diary because it's *a million times* more interesting than anything you two have to say."

A buzzer sounded. Homer scrambled to his feet and rushed to the console. The speedometer moved from HYPER to SLOW. A button labeled ICEBERG AVOIDANCE SYSTEM lit up.

"Look," Lorelei said, pointing. The headlight beams grazed across a large glistening shape.

"Iceberg!" Homer cried. He grabbed the steering wheel, but the submarine didn't respond. "We're on autopilot," he realized. "I can't do anything while we're on autopilot."

"Uh-oh." Hercules threw himself into a seat and latched the belt.

Unfortunately, a seat belt would offer little protection. *The Worst Ways to End a Treasure Hunt* had an entire chapter dedicated to iceberg disasters. Upon contact, merchant schooners were reduced to fireplace kindle, pirate ships were gutted like dead fish, and ocean liners plunged to the bottom of the sea. Icebergs were a seafarer's foremost enemy. The little submarine stood no chance if it crashed into such an imposing foe. Homer pushed the ICEBERG AVOIDANCE SYSTEM button.

"Hang on!" Homer cried as he jumped from the seat and threw himself over Dog. Dog, who'd been chewing on an energy-bar wrapper, moaned. Homer squeezed his eyes shut, waiting for the impact, but nothing happened. The submarine took a gentle turn to the right, avoiding the ice chunk.

"That was close," Lorelei said, wiping sweat from her forehead.

"Uh-oh," Hercules said, pointing as another chunk of ice appeared. The Iceberg Avoidance System continued to operate, and the sub turned just in time.

And that is how the next hour passed. Ice chunk after ice chunk loomed, and the submarine maneuvered around and between the chunks like a confident sea lion. The kids sat in the seats, their gazes glued to the awesome sight. It was as if they'd entered another world. Each chunk contained its own magic. Each chunk contained its own story. Dog sat on Homer's lap, mesmerized by the sparkling landscape of blue and white.

"I've never seen anything so beautiful," Lorelei whispered.

Schools of silver fish passed by, darting between icy

crevasses. Dog barked as a larger fish appeared at a corner of the windshield.

"Oh, look," Hercules said. "It's a narwhal." The whale was sleek and dark against the ice, like a torpedo. It turned its head for a moment, staring at the submarine's occupants, then swam out of view, its tusk leading the way.

"Wow," Homer said.

"Double wow," Lorelei said.

Hercules, who could have told them that the word *narwhal* comes from the Old Norse language, simply took a deep breath and said, "Triple wow."

The speedometer's dial moved from SLOW to DRIFT. The coordinates flashed on the autopilot screen, followed by DESTINATION REACHED.

"We're here," Homer said. He could barely believe it. "We've reached Greenland."

Lorelei pressed her palms on the window. "The treasure's out there." As she said that, a shiver ran up Homer's spine.

They resealed the diary in its waterproof skins and set it into the chest for safekeeping. If all went well, there'd be plenty of time to read about Rumpold's adventures. If all didn't go well...

Homer didn't want to think about that.

The submarine surfaced, and the battery shut off.

Homer climbed the conning tower and opened the hatch. Cold air rushed in, and it felt as if ice water had been poured over their faces.

"Brrr!" Lorelei complained. She wrapped her arms around herself. Homer's jaw tensed against the frigid temperature as he stepped to the top rung and stuck his head out of the hatch.

They were adrift in a small inlet. According to Homer's Quality Solar-Powered Subatomic Watch, it was 10:00 p.m. Wednesday. Gulls cried overhead, circling the strange contraption that had invaded their quiet world. Jagged, snow-covered mountains loomed, sheer walls of gray standing in silent greeting. Chunks of ice clung together at the water's surface as if a giant had dropped his snow cone. "It's freezing out there," Homer reported as he closed the hatch and climbed down. He couldn't feel his nose or cheeks.

"Your lips are purple," Hercules pointed out. "We need warmer clothes." While he shuffled around in the supply locker, Homer turned the engine back on.

"We'll need to find a place to moor the submarine. I saw a rocky ledge I think we can tie up to."

Hercules found some parkas that were lined with white fur. And he found fur-lined boots and gloves. They were a bit big, but they'd have to do.

"What about Dog?" Homer asked.

"He's already fur-lined," Lorelei pointed out as she pulled on a pair of boots.

"Yeah, but his paws aren't fur-lined."

"Oh, good point."

Dog would certainly be more comfortable waiting inside the submarine, but since he was the only treasure-sniffer in the group, he was needed on the surface. So, using Homer's Swiss army knife, Lorelei cut some fur-lining from her parka and secured it around Dog's paws with the laces from her sneakers.

"That's quite clever," Hercules said.

"You have to be clever to survive in The City on your own," she told him.

Homer drove the sub close to the ledge. After shutting off the engine, he and Lorelei climbed out and onto the water-drenched deck. Even with the layer of fur, the cold soaked through to their skin. Homer stepped onto the rocky ledge and Lorelei tossed the mooring line. He pulled the sub close and tied the line around a boulder.

"Okay!" he hollered. "You can bring Dog." Then the members of L.O.S.T. and FOUND walked along the ledge until they reached the beach.

The beach on this southernmost tip of Greenland was nothing like the beaches back home, which were made of fine gray sand, clamshells, and the occasional hopping sand flea. Saucer-sized rocks covered this beach, making it difficult to traverse. The rocks rolled underfoot, creating ankle-twisting wedges.

"The air is so dry," Hercules said. "My sinuses are closing up. And my throat is getting sore. I wish I had a lozenge."

"My watch says it's forty-five degrees Fahrenheit," Homer said. "I thought it would be colder than this."

"It feels colder," Lorelei said. "That wind is going to freeze my brain." She pulled her hood tighter.

The wind did carry a sharp bite. It jabbed its way up Homer's nose, so he pulled the parka's collar as high as it would go. He worried about Dog, but Dog showed no signs of shivering. He wagged his tail, seemingly happy to be on land.

Just beyond the beach, the ground was interwoven with patches of thick-bladed grass, grayish moss, and piles of rocks. White-petaled flowers peeked from between the rocks, their yellow faces turned toward the horizon. Lorelei stopped walking and stared at the sky. "The stars aren't very bright."

"It's not going to get any darker," Homer said. "It's summer, and we're close to the Arctic Circle. Up here, the sun rises almost as soon as it sets."

Lorelei pulled Rumpold's map from under her parka

and unfolded it. "The Draco constellation winds around the Little Dipper," she said, and they all peered up at the sky. Homer had seen the Little Dipper many times in his own backyard, so it was easy for him to find.

"I see Draco," he said. "There's the tail over there. The nose is over there." His legs began to tremble, but it wasn't on account of the icy wind. "Rumpold Smeller stood here," Homer said. "He looked at these same stars."

"*She* looked at these same stars," Lorelei corrected.

"Do you think we should start calling her by her real name?" Hercules asked. "Rumpoldena?"

"No way," Homer said. "I say we keep calling her Rumpold. She claimed that name, and that's how everyone knows her."

"I agree," Lorelei said. "Lots of girls have names that used to belong to boys. It's no big deal. A person can change her name if she wants. I might change my name one day."

"What would you change it to?" Hercules asked.

"Something heroic," she said. "Something brave and strong—like your name."

Hercules paused thoughtfully, then said, "A butterfly would still fly without the butter."

"What's that supposed to mean?" Lorelei asked.

"It means your name doesn't define you," he replied. "It's what you *do* that defines you."

Yeah, like dognapping and double-crossing and stealing, Homer thought. But he didn't say those things to Lorelei. The moment was too exciting to be ruined by another argument.

The fur on Homer's hood rippled as he returned his focus to the map. "So," he said, putting his best reasoning skills into action. "Rumpold stood here, looking up at this sky, and wrote the riddle. 'Twins of flame above and below.' We see our dragon above, but where is our dragon below?"

"We should walk around and see if anything looks like a dragon," Hercules said.

"And see if Dog smells anything," Lorelei added.

So they walked as far as they could, to the cliffs, then back to the beach. The inlet was small and horseshoe-shaped. Other than scaling the mountains, there was nowhere else to go. Dog ate some tufts of grass and clumps of moss, but he didn't sniff at anything.

"What about that rock?" Hercules asked. "Do you think that looks like a dragon?"

"It looks like a rock," Lorelei said grumpily.

"Yeah, I guess you're right."

Homer held the map up to the sky and recited the

riddle. "'Twins of flame above and below.' Above and below." He looked at the sky. He looked at his feet. "'An endless mirror between.'" He slowly lowered the map and looked at the water. The water in the inlet was calm, the stars reflecting like...

"The mirror is the sea," he called.

"Oh, that's brilliant!" Lorelei rushed to his side. "'An endless mirror between.' If the mirror is the sea, then the other dragon must be below the water. You know what that means?"

Hercules groaned. "It means we're about to go swimming?"

Homer smiled. "It means we're about to find sunken treasure."

But before this realization had settled over them, a rumbling sounded in the distance. Dog dropped a moss clump and turned his face toward the sound. It was an engine of some sort, approaching from the south.

Seabirds fled their cliff-face nests as a seaplane buzzed over the inlet, sending ripples across the water. Homer, Lorelei, and Hercules ducked as it skimmed over their heads.

Homer reached down and grabbed Dog's collar. Something was terribly wrong. The seaplane took a sharp turn and headed back toward the beach. Homer couldn't run, couldn't breathe, couldn't think clearly, as fear filled his entire body from head to feet.

For as the plane approached, the pilot's face, which was a mere speck behind the windshield, became clearer and clearer, closer and closer, until the wicked smile of Madame la Directeur was in perfect focus.

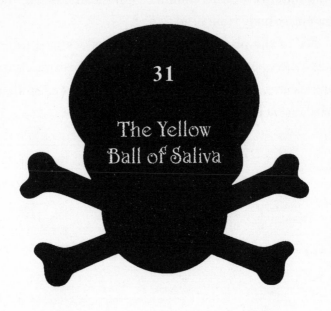

31

**The Yellow
Ball of Saliva**

*R*un!*"* Lorelei screamed as the seaplane barreled
down on them. Her hood bounced at the back of
her neck as she sprinted toward the rocky ledge,
her pink hair a dollop of alien color in the muted
landscape.

Although still riddled with fear, Homer forced his
thoughts to clear. Madame la Directeur had come for
the treasure, and she'd do whatever was necessary to get
it. There was no time to freak out. Escape was manda-
tory. He wrapped his arms around Dog and started lift-

ing, but Hercules knocked him aside and scooped Dog into his arms.

"Who's flying that plane?" Hercules cried.

"Madame la Directeur!"

Dog's ears and jowls shook with each of Hercules's frantic steps. Rocks rolled beneath Homer's boots as he ran—it was like running across a field of bowling balls. The engine's roar nearly shattered his eardrums as the seaplane swept over his head. A gust of air blew across his back. As the plane banked, preparing for another attack, Homer and Hercules reached the rocky ledge. Lorelei was already on the submarine's deck. She climbed the ladder and opened the hatch.

"Hurry!" she yelled. "We've got to dive!" Then she tumbled down the conning tower.

While Hercules carried Dog through the hatch, Homer pulled the mooring line free. The deck trembled as the engine started. Bubbles formed around the sub. The seaplane's roar began its crescendo as Madame set it in a direct path for the submarine. A warning light flashed on the hatch and Homer's ankles suddenly felt cold. The sub had begun its dive. The inlet's frigid water rose up Homer's legs. Panic beating at his temples, he struggled up the ladder. His fingers trembled inside the gloves as he clutched the metal rungs. The rising water followed, nipping at his heels. The submarine was almost fully submerged by the time he reached the hatch. An alarm bell rang.

"Close it! Close it!" Lorelei hollered. Seawater flowed over Homer's face as he gripped the hatch and pulled it down, latching it into place. The seaplane roared overhead, its pontoons skimming the water's surface. Homer half slid, half fell down the conning tower, landing at Hercules's feet. Dog waddled over and licked his face.

"She can't get us now," Lorelei said from the pilot's seat.

"She tried to kill us!" Hercules said, taking a puff of his inhaler. "She's insane."

"She's totally insane," Homer said. The seawater had numbed his legs. As he scrambled to his feet, he lost his balance and bumped into the control panel. Clutching the panel's edge, his hand brushed over a speaker. The closest button read EMERGENCY FREQUENCY 16. "Hey, I think this might be a radio," Homer realized.

The airplane engine roared overhead. "Call someone," Hercules said. "Tell them she's trying to kill us!"

"We don't want anyone to know we're here," Lorelei said.

"But we need help," Hercules argued. "She's *trying to kill* us!"

She was. And she wouldn't stop. Homer knew this. He'd heard her in the lair. "Mayday, Mayday!" he cried as he pushed the button. He'd never used a ship-to-shore radio, but how difficult could it be? "We're under attack. Mayday, Mayday!" He released the button.

The wait seemed endless, but just as he was about to press the button again, static filled the speaker. Then a voice replied, "Greenland Coast Guard to unnamed vessel. What sort of attack?"

"Unnamed vessel to Greenland Coast Guard. Madame la Directeur is an escaped prisoner. She's in a seaplane, and she's trying to kill us."

"Greenland Coast Guard to unnamed vessel. What are your coordinates?"

Lorelei grabbed Homer's shoulder and spun him around. "You can't tell them where we are. We're not sharing the treasure with anyone else."

"I'm going to tell them where to find Madame," Homer said. He held down the button. "Unnamed vessel to Greenland Coast Guard. Madame la Directeur is flying over the southernmost tip of Greenland." The speaker went silent.

"Do you think they heard you?" Hercules asked.

"I sure hope so," Homer said.

Lorelei switched on the headlights. "There's no time to waste. We've got to find that dragon."

As Lorelei drove, Homer sat on the floor and pulled off his soaked boots. Hercules knelt beside him and whispered, "How'd Madame know we were here?"

"Someone must have told her," Homer said, casting a suspicious glance at Lorelei.

"But that doesn't make sense. If Lorelei is double-crossing Madame, why would she tell her where to find us?"

"I don't know." Homer rubbed his frozen toes. "But what I do know is that we have to protect the treasure." Sweat trickled down his back. While the air inside the submarine was pleasant, having someone try to run you over with a seaplane would make even the bravest person break out in a cold sweat. And knowing Madame was up there, trying to squash them—well, that made him sweat even more.

"Stop whispering about me and help me look for the treasure," Lorelei snapped.

Homer and Hercules slipped out of their parkas. Dog shook and kicked his paws, freeing himself of the booties. Then the boys sat beside Lorelei while she maneuvered the submarine along the bottom, the headlights guiding the way.

"It's here somewhere," Lorelei said. "Looking for a dragon, looking for a dragon."

Hercules opened his notebook. "Looking for a dragon," he repeated as he scribbled.

Homer's gaze scanned the seafloor. A handful of silver fish darted through the crystal water. If the dragon was buried in sand, how would they find it? Surely the scent of treasure couldn't travel through water *and* a submarine window. Could it?

"What's that?" Homer asked, darting to his feet. He pressed his palms to the glass. "Something's sticking out of the sand. Right over there."

Lorelei pulled back on the throttle, and the propellers slowed to a stop. As the submarine drifted, the head-lights rested on a strange object. The kids leaned over the console, desperate to get a better view.

If you lived in a world inhabited by dragons, then you wouldn't be surprised to see them flying across the night sky. You wouldn't be surprised to see them trampling through burning villages or guarding jewel-filled caves. Those are dragon activities. But a dragon's head sticking out of the ocean floor? Well, that's just weird.

Even though Homer knew he was searching for some sort of dragon, when the submarine's headlights fell across a yellow eyeball and snout, he couldn't remember how to breathe. And when dizziness swept over him, caused by excitement and the fact that he'd stopped breathing, he forced his lungs to expand. "Do you see that?" he asked with a gasp. "Do you guys see that?"

"Yes," Hercules whispered as the notebook slid off his

lap. Lorelei clung to the steering wheel, staring in silent wonder. Dog pressed his wet nose to the glass and whined, his doggy breath leaving a perfect circle of fog.

"Take us in closer," Homer said. Lorelei pushed the throttle a smidge, just enough to move them forward a few yards until the dragon head stood directly before them. Homer yanked the anchor lever. Four feet sprang out from the bottom of the submarine, anchoring it into place.

The cold blue water provided a perfect view. The dragon's head had been carved from an enormous timber. One eye held what looked like a ball of yellow glass; the other eye was closed, as if the dragon were winking. Its long snout was upturned, and its mane stood erect as if caught in a windstorm. Intricate scales ran down the long neck, which disappeared into the sand.

"It's a figurehead," Homer realized.

"Oh, that's a cool word," Hercules said. "It's a nautical term for a carved full-length figure or bust that's built into the bow of a sailing ship."

"But where's the rest of the ship?" Homer asked.

"There is no rest of the ship," Lorelei said. "The riddle is about a dragon, not a ship. Rumpold buried the figurehead on purpose."

Dog whimpered and scratched on the glass. But his nostrils didn't quiver. His nose didn't twitch. There was no treasure scent for him to detect. Even so, Homer was certain that Rumpold's treasure was within reach. He could feel it calling him like a Siren to a sailor. *Homer. I'm waiting for you.*

"Remember in the diary where Rumpold said the emperor of China gave her a yellow ball of dragon's saliva?" Lorelei said.

Homer took a quick breath as the riddle came together. "The dragon's eyeball! Look at it. It's yellow and round."

"Do you think the eyeball is the treasure?" Lorelei asked. "It can't be actual dragon saliva. That's ridiculous. What kind of gemstone is yellow?"

"It looks like amber to me," Hercules said. "My mother has amber jewelry. It comes from tree resin that's been petrified. Sometimes little creatures get preserved in it."

"Maybe people once thought that amber was made from dragon saliva," Homer wondered.

"Is amber a rare thing?" Lorelei asked.

Hercules shook his head. "I don't think so. Mom has lots of it."

"Then that eyeball can't be the treasure," Homer said.

"The treasure must be behind the eyeball, inside the dragon's head," Lorelei said.

Dog whined and pawed at the window. Then a low growl rumbled in his wrinkly neck. "It's okay," Homer told him with a pat. "It's not a real dragon."

"How do we get into the dragon's head?" Lorelei asked. "Do you think we can use the robotic arms?"

Homer had forgotten all about the robotic arms. "It's worth a try," he said.

The EMPLOY ROBOTIC ARMS button was located on the console between two joysticks. When Lorelei pressed the button, an exterior compartment opened on the left side of the submarine and another on the right side of the submarine. A series of articulating rods unfolded, stretching in front of the observation window like arms. At the end of each arm, a mechanical hand awaited, its fingers lifeless.

Lorelei worked the left joystick while Homer took the right one. "I'm pretty good at this," she said. "I'm at level eighty-five in *Galaxy Games*." Homer, who'd never worked a joystick, had never heard of *Galaxy Games*. As Lorelei moved hers, the left hand came to life, its fingers clicking hungrily. Homer wiggled his, and the hand balled up into a fist, shot out and punched the dragon's neck.

"Oops," Homer said as some rotting dragon scales came loose and drifted to the seafloor. Homer wiggled the stick again, and the hand unclenched.

Lorelei managed to reach the dragon's eyeball with her mechanical hand, but she couldn't get the index finger and thumb to cooperate. They snapped at the eyeball like a crab's pincher. That's when Homer's hand balled up into another fist and punched Lorelei's hand.

"Watch it," she grumbled. She tried to grab the eyeball again, but the fingers simply slid off. "It can't get a grip. The ball is too smooth." She let go of the joystick and spun the seat around. "Someone will have to swim out there," she said, poking her finger into Homer's chest. "And since I can't swim and since Hercules has to take notes, you'll have to do it. It's the only way. How long can you hold your breath?"

"I don't know," Homer said. He often held his breath in his sister Gwendolyn's laboratory. The smell of roadkill was beyond disgusting. "I've never timed it."

"Well, you look like you've got big lungs," she said, poking his chest again. "I bet you can hold it for at least a minute."

"He doesn't have to hold his breath," Hercules said. "There's an underwater suit in the supply locker. It's one of those old-fashioned ones for walking along the seabed. I've seen them in movies."

"Walking?" Lorelei jumped out of the seat. "Then I'm going out there."

"Oh no you're not," Homer said. He ran to the locker and blocked it. Lorelei tried to push him aside. Then she threw her hands in the air.

"Are you serious? What do you think I'm going to do?

Get the treasure and swim away? I don't know how to swim, remember?"

"Maybe you *do* know how to swim. Maybe you've been lying about that," Homer said, folding his arms. "Maybe you'll get the treasure and swim to the surface, where Madame is supposed to be waiting for you. Maybe that's why you didn't want me to tell the Coast Guard where we are?"

"For the millionth time, Homer, I'm *not* working with her." She stomped her foot. "It feels really bad when your questing partners don't trust you. What do I have to do to get you to believe me?"

"If you didn't give Madame our coordinates, then who did? Huh?"

"I...I...I don't know."

Homer's gaze fell upon the embroidered FOUND on Lorelei's pink jumpsuit. *Beware the lost and found.* No one had to remind him. He would never *ever* give her another chance to trick him. "Stay here with Hercules. I'm going to get the treasure."

32

Inside a Dragon's Head

Ajitabh had invented many amazing things—a cloudcopter, a seaweed-powered submarine with robotic arms, a solar-powered subatomic watch. But the diving suit looked outdated, like something from an old science-fiction movie. Surely there were better ways to walk along the seafloor than in such a weird contraption. What about an underwater jet pack powered by plankton? Homer would mention this idea to Ajitabh the next time they got together.

The diving suit's green jumper was made of a rubbery

material. Pulling it over his belly, Homer felt as if he were squeezing into a balloon. The suit covered every inch of his body, leaving only his face and head exposed. Hercules slipped a pair of weighted boots onto Homer's feet. Then he handed Homer a round, clear plastic helmet. A narrow tube ran from the helmet to a tank. "It's your oxygen line," Hercules explained. "It says on the tank that you have one hour of air."

One hour? Homer swallowed hard.

"You look scared," Lorelei said. "Let me go. I'm not scared."

"I'm not scared, either," Homer lied.

"We'll need a way to communicate with you once you're out there," Hercules said. "Just in case you run out of oxygen, or something worse."

Something worse? What could be worse than running out of oxygen? Getting skewered by a narwhal tusk? That sounded pretty bad, too.

As Homer examined the helmet, he imagined what his mother and father would say. They thought he was in Ajitabh's care, exploring the nooks and crannies of the Map of the Month Club. Never in a million years would they have given Homer permission to walk along the seafloor off the southernmost tip of Greenland to search for treasure. If they found out, he'd certainly be grounded for life. And his chore list would be so long you could stretch it from the Puddings' front door all the way down Grinning Goat Road.

"How about thumbs-up, thumbs-down?" Hercules suggested, demonstrating. "That's an easy way to communicate. Thumbs-down lets us know you're in trouble, and we can pull on the line to bring you back in."

"Okay," Homer agreed. Lorelei was back in the pilot's seat, sulking. Homer whispered to Hercules. "Don't take your eyes off her. She's going to try to get the treasure." Hercules nodded.

Dog pawed at Homer's feet. He looked up at him and whined.

"I can't take you with me," Homer explained gently. "I'll be right back."

Homer slid the helmet over his head and face. It sealed the diving suit with a collar and watertight zipper. Once the helmet was in place, Homer couldn't hear anything but his own breathing and his heart beating in his ears.

"One hour," Hercules mouthed. Then he slid Homer's subatomic watch over the wet suit and onto Homer's wrist. "You okay?" Homer gave a thumbs-up.

Hercules opened the hatch labeled SEAFLOOR EXIT. Homer ducked and stepped into the closet-sized space. The door sealed behind him. *This is really happening*, he told himself. *I'm going out into the ocean to collect Rumpold Smeller's treasure.*

After turning a wheel, the exterior door opened. Water rushed inside, filling the little room. Homer had expected the water to feel icy cold, but as it engulfed him, the temperature inside the suit remained unchanged. Fresh puffs of air filled the helmet. The oxygen line was working.

Homer had never thought of himself as a risk taker. While Uncle Drake had been famous for his crazy stunts, Homer was famous for digging holes in the backyard. If risk could be turned into a food product, Uncle Drake would have poured milk over it and eaten it for breakfast. Homer would have left it on the pantry shelf and eaten something else. Until this particular year, Homer had spent most of his life living the fantasy of adventure inside the safe pages of books. But there he stood, the ice-filled sea sparkling before him, a treasure waiting to be snatched. And so, the oxygen line trailing behind, Homer W. Pudding took a steadying breath and stepped out of the submarine.

The water was fairly shallow in this part of the inlet. The surface sparkled above. Is this how the astronauts felt when they walked on the moon? Each step was awkward as the weighted boots pressed deep into the sand. Each movement was robotic because of the tight wet suit. His labored breathing was the only sound he heard. He walked around the submarine and through one of the headlight beams until he stood before the observation window. Three faces peered out at him. Lorelei wore a pout. Hercules smiled and waved. Dog cocked his head, his ears flattening in confusion as if to say, *How come I'm in here and you're out there?*

Hercules pointed at his wrist, a reminder that Homer had only one hour. Homer gave him a thumbs-up, then turned his back to the submarine and faced the figurehead.

The dragon's eyes were level with Homer's. He walked around it, making sure the oxygen line didn't tangle. There were no holes, no latches, nothing that would indicate a secret compartment to hold treasure.

Behind saliva hides what you seek.

The eyeball was the size of a baseball. Homer gripped it with the rubbery fingers of the diving suit and pulled. The suction was tight, but after a few tugs, it popped free. It was solid like glass, with swirls of yellow and orange. Homer dropped the ball to the seafloor. The empty socket stared back at him.

He squeezed his hand into the hole. His fingers wiggled and searched until they rested on something. It was a lever. With a click, the dragon's head shifted. Homer yanked his hand from the eye socket, then lifted the dragon head from its neck. The neck was hollow. Homer tried to steady his breathing. This was the most exciting thing that had ever happened to him! He dropped the dragon head to the seafloor and reached his arm into the neck.

His fingers ran into something. "I've got it!' he cried. His words bumped up against the inside of the helmet. Gripping the something, he pulled it free and held it in both hands, staring at it as if new life had just come into the world.

What Homer held was a bundle, wrapped in the same watertight skins that had kept Rumpold's diary safe. The bundle was larger and thicker than the diary, but there was no time to imagine what was inside, because at that very moment, the water trembled and a shadow fell over Homer.

Two shapes loomed on the water's surface. *Pontoons!* Homer stepped away from the dragon, craning his neck to get a better view. As the ripples cleared, the side of a seaplane came into focus. Someone stepped onto one of the pontoons. After removing goggles and a leather pilot's helmet, the person leaned over and looked down. The burning gaze traveled through the water like a flaming torpedo. Homer could have sworn he'd been hit by something. Madame la Directeur smiled wickedly. She pointed and mouthed, "I see you." Then she waved.

So what if you see me? Homer thought. *I've got the treasure and you don't.* He waved back, forcing a victorious grin through his clenched jaw. The package gripped in his hand, he turned to face the submarine, ready to make his escape. Lorelei and Hercules stood at the observation window, waving their arms, pointing upward. "Yes," he mouthed, "I see her." He lumbered forward. Lorelei and Hercules pressed against the glass, screaming something. Then it looked like they were doing some sort of crazy dance as they pointed upward.

Another shadow fell over Homer. A strange shape drifted down through the water. What was it? A net? Was that *a net*?!

It's really difficult to run underwater, especially in a diving suit with weighted boots. Imagine trying to run against the wind with bricks in your shoes. Homer pumped his arms, desperate to gain momentum. A boy who reads most of the time and digs the occasional hole is not a boy with Olympian endurance. A boy who reads most of the time and digs the occasional hole is a boy who runs out of breath when he climbs four flights of stairs. So all in all, the escape attempt was doomed from the start.

The net fell over Homer's head. Small dangling weights pulled it to the seafloor, trapping Homer in place. One of the weights pressed against the oxygen line, strangling the fresh puffs of air. Homer dropped to his knees and slid the treasure bundle under the net just before it completely encircled him. She would never get her hands on it. Never.

Homer's mind raced. If Madame la Directeur hauled him to the surface... He shuddered at the thought. Grabbing the net, he tried to pull it off but it tightened around him. Thrashing only made things worse as netting tangled around his feet and arms. He felt like a tuna. Panic beat in his chest.

It was a sad ending to a brilliant quest. Homer stopped struggling and stared through the green mesh, hoping to catch a final glimpse of his comrades. Hercules puffed on his inhaler, his eyes wide with fear. Dog barked madly and scratched at the window. Lorelei was doing something at the console. Oh, she was working the joysticks. She was trying to get the treasure. Would she give it to Madame? Would she keep it for herself?

Homer blinked. What was that? It looked like a black hole and it was moving toward him. Was he seeing things? The oxygen line was tangled, the fresh puffs of air less frequent. Could his brain be suffering from oxygen depletion? The black hole loomed. Then the hole closed and a gray-and-white speckled shape glided around the net. Could it possibly be...?

Speckles!

Speckles the whale shark stopped swimming and pressed an eyeball to the net. Had he followed them all the way to Greenland? Homer thrashed. Speckles swam around and around. He stopped to look through the net again. But he wasn't looking at Homer. He was looking at the dragon's eyeball that was also caught in the net. Speckles wiggled his back end, just like a dog waiting to play fetch.

Clearly Speckles had no idea that someone's life was at stake. Clearly he had no idea that the most important pirate treasure in treasure-hunting history was at risk. Or maybe he knew these things but simply didn't care. Who truly understands the mind of a whale shark?

The net began to move upward. Madame la Directeur was hauling in her catch. Homer gritted his teeth. How could he escape?

Speckles eyed the amber ball again. Turning in a circle, he darted to the surface, smacked his tail, then returned to the net. In his playful frenzy, his tail had barely missed one of the pontoons. The seaplane rocked. An idea sprung to life in Homer's submerged head. He grabbed the eyeball and held it, pretending he might throw it. Speckles went nuts. He turned in a circle, zipped to the surface and smacked his enormous tail. "Yes!" Homer cried as the tail smacked into one of the pontoons, crushing it like a boot crushing a soda can. The seaplane tilted and the net, with Homer in it, fell to the seafloor.

Pain shot through Homer's legs as he landed on some

rocks. The net loosened, and he managed to crawl out. As the dragon eyeball rolled onto the sand, Speckles scooped it up with his nose and carried it around the submarine. Homer struggled to his feet. He searched for the treasure bundle. Where was it? He turned toward the observation window, hoping Hercules or Lorelei would point him in the treasure's direction. But Hercules was not at the window. Lorelei sat in the pilot's seat, working the joystick as a robotic hand retreated, the treasure in its mechanical fingers. With desperate steps, Homer lumbered forward.

Speckles raced around again, but this time he caught the oxygen line with his tail, ripping it from the submarine. The puffs of air stopped. The robotic arms folded back into their compartments, and the compartment doors closed. Lorelei had the treasure. Hercules and Dog were nowhere to be seen. And Homer had only a helmet's amount of air.

This was Lorelei's moment of victory—her double-cross complete. And it was déjà vu for Homer. For just as Madame had used the robotic arms to steal the captain's chest from Uncle Drake, so, too, had Lorelei used them to steal Rumpold's treasure from Homer.

"Lorelei!" he cried. He gasped for air but found none. The quest was over.

The observation window faded, and the sea darkened.

33

A Bundle
of Booty

"Homer? Wake up."

Light trickled through the crack in Homer's eyelids. Something brushed against his face. He opened his eyes and took a deep, surprised breath.

He was lying on the submarine's floor, the diving helmet at his side. Lorelei crouched, hovering so close that her pink hair tickled his face. "Homer? Can you hear me?"

"Uh-huh." He smacked his lips, his mouth as dry as the inside of a walnut shell.

"Drink this." Hercules handed him a water bottle and helped him sit up. Homer drank as if he'd just been rescued from a deserted island.

"I...couldn't...breathe," Homer said between gulps. "I...thought..." Water dribbled down his chin. As he wiped it away, he stared at Lorelei. "I thought..."

She sat back on her heels. "You thought what?"

"Lorelei saved your life," Hercules explained. "She grabbed you with the robotic arms and pulled you on board. I was trying to keep Dog calm. He went nuts when you got caught in the net. I thought, he was going to break through the glass."

Lorelei folded her arms. "You thought I was going to leave you out there? Is that what you thought, Homer?"

"It occurred to me," he said, his cheeks heating up.

"How could you think such a terrible thing?" She punched his shoulder. "I told you. I'm not working with Madame. You may not believe me now, but one day you'll realize I'm telling the truth because the truth always comes out. *Always.*"

Had he jumped to the wrong conclusion? Had he been too quick to judge her? If not Lorelei, then who gave the coordinates to Madame? As Homer pondered these thoughts, he peeled off the diving suit and boots. He felt oddly light, as if he'd shed an entire other body. Lorelei watched from beneath her bangs, and he recognized the hurt in her eyes. "I'm sorry I thought you might leave me," he said. "Thank you for saving my life."

"You're welcome." She flared her nostrils and turned away.

A snuffling sound caught Homer's attention. Dog, who hadn't welcomed Homer with his usual face licks or tail thumps, was busy circling the treasure bundle. He sniffed the watertight skins, his rump wiggling. Ears and jowls swaying, he pranced around the bundle. Then he flopped over onto his back and rolled, covering himself with the bundle's scent the way farm dogs do when they come across a particularly nasty-smelling dead squirrel or a putrid pile of raccoon poop. No doubt about it, this wasn't just treasure—it was the greatest treasure ever!

Lorelei reached for the bundle, but Homer stayed her hand. "Wait," he said. He was as eager as everyone else to see what glorious booty lay inside, but there was an unfinished matter to tend to. "What about Madame?" He expected to see her swimming outside the observation window. But only Speckles swam past, the dragon eyeball still balanced on his nose. "She could still come after us."

"She's not going anywhere," Hercules said. "Take a look." He raised the periscope, then motioned Homer over. Homer pressed an eye to the lens. The seaplane was still floating in the inlet, but tilted almost to the point of falling over. Madame la Directeur stood on the remaining pontoon, the empty net at her feet. For a long moment, she stood as lifeless as the dragon figurehead, her gaze fixed on the horizon. She was stranded. Without the second pontoon, the seaplane couldn't take off. And without a wet suit, there was no way she could survive the frigid water. Homer wanted to surface, then climb out the hatch and shout, "I've got the submarine you stole from my uncle! And I've got Rumpold's treasure!" He wanted to cheer and do a victory dance. Then he noticed something moving on the horizon.

"Dog's lying on the treasure," Lorelei complained as she tried to slide the bundle out from under Dog's belly.

"Urrrr," Dog complained.

"Homer, will you please get your dog to move?" Lorelei asked.

Although Homer was dying to reveal the treasure, he couldn't tear his gaze away from the scene taking place at the water's surface. A Coast Guard ship sped toward the seaplane. An old woman stood on the bow, her apron blowing as the boat cut across the water. She held a mop as if it were a sword, ready for battle. Two officers stood beside her. The Unpolluter had come to clean up the mess.

Homer snickered and switched the periscope to its telephoto lens so he could get a better view of Madame's defeat. This was a moment he wanted to savor. Years from now, when Homer was an old man and kids came to visit him at the Home for Aging Treasure Hunters, he wanted to describe in great detail exactly what it looked like when an überenemy realized she'd lost.

Madame slowly turned her head, her cold eyes searching until they found the periscope. Homer had expected anger. He'd expected her to wave her fists and curse the day he'd been born. But her expression was oddly calm. She raised her eyebrows and nodded at him. It was a gesture of recognition. She knew he'd won. The Coast Guard vessel pulled up alongside the seaplane. One of the men jumped onto the pontoon and slapped a pair of handcuffs on Madame's wrists.

"You can put in your notebook that on this day, Madame la Directeur was defeated once and for all," Homer said.

"Defeated," Hercules said as he scribbled.

Homer lowered the periscope, then set the autopilot coordinates to City Lake. Lorelei pulled the anchors in. The battery hummed as Homer drove out of the inlet. When they reached the open ocean, he switched to hyper-speed, and they were on their way.

Finally, the team of L.O.S.T. and FOUND sat on the floor, the booty bundle before them. Dog, exhausted from his frolicking, collapsed next to the bundle, his tongue hanging from his panting mouth. Hercules waited, notebook perched on his lap. Homer and Lorelei breathed deeply, filling their lungs with anticipation. This was a million times better than Christmas morning, when Homer would reach for his stocking to find out what goodies were stuffed inside, but they were always predictable—chocolate coins, a new deck of playing cards, licorice ropes, a comic book, stuff like that. He had no idea what waited beneath the waterproof skin. He and Lorelei reached for the bundle at the same time. Their hands touched.

"You do it," Lorelei said, pulling away. "You're the one who found it."

After all the trouble she'd gone through to get the map, her offer surprised him. But he wasn't going to argue. He picked up the bundle.

"Homer picked up the bundle," Hercules mumbled as he took notes. "You could cut the tension with a knife." Then he looked up. "Should I write that? Is that cliché?"

Lorelei put a finger to her lips. "Shhhh."

The wrapping was smooth and rubbery, just like the wrapping that had covered the diary. There were three skins, each held in place by a golden chain and clasp. As Homer removed the chains, Lorelei slipped them over her head. He wanted to tell her that the necklaces looked pretty on her. But he didn't. With trembling fingers, he peeled open the last skin.

"What's that?" Hercules asked.

Homer held up a little dried creature that had been

stuck to the wrapping. Hercules and Lorelei leaned close. It was about six inches long, jet-black, with eight spiky tentacles.

"Those spikes look dangerous," Hercules said. "They might be poisonous. Be careful."

"I bet Rumpold was trying to protect his treasure. Or maybe the creature crawled in and died by accident," Lorelei said. "Either way, it's totally creepy. Get rid of it and keep unwrapping."

"Don't eat this," Homer told Dog as he set the creature aside. The final layer of wrapping was a Jolly Roger flag, folded so that the hollow eyes of the skull stared up at him. "It's a warning," he whispered. "It's supposed to scare us."

"It's scaring me," Hercules said.

"Oh for goodness' sake, *open it*!" Lorelei practically exploded.

As Homer peeled back the flag's corners, Lorelei and Hercules hovered so close he could smell their energy bar–scented breaths. "Paper?" Lorelei said. "It's a pile of paper?"

It was a pile of paper. Folded paper, to be exact. One of the papers had threads woven through it; another looked as if it had been made from grass. Homer carefully unfolded one that was as delicate as a butterfly wing. He burst into a grin. "It's a map!"

The map was composed of needle-thin lines, drawn in black and green ink. It appeared to be a map of a building. Chinese characters ran along the edge. At the bottom, in the same loopy handwriting as found in the diary, were some notes.

This map was taken from Emperor Ming's treasure ship. I found it stuffed in a drawer of recipes, long forgotten. It is the only map of the buried Golden Crane Palace.

"Golden Crane Palace?" Hercules said. "I've never heard of that."

"Neither have I," Lorelei said.

The next map was drawn on paper made from some sort of reed. Egyptian hieroglyphs ran across the map, which showed a river and a desert.

This map was taken from Prince Badru's pleasure craft. Some fool had wadded it up and was using it to stop a leak. It is the only map to the Lost Pyramid of Isis.

"Isis was an Egyptian goddess," Lorelei said. "Can you imagine the kind of treasure you'd find in that pyramid?"

Homer was speechless. What words could he possibly utter that would express his amazement and delight? He unfolded the next paper, which was glossy and thick. "It's in Latin," Hercules said, pointing to the Roman numerals and letters. It appeared to be some sort of maze. "It says *Ninth Labor of Hercules*." He smiled. "Cool. What was the ninth labor?"

"Well," Lorelei said. "That was when Hercules had to go get a belt from Hippolyte. She was a warrior queen."

This map was taken from an Italian merchant vessel. An illiterate servant had used it to line a stocking drawer. It leads to the famous belt of Hippolyte.

There were a dozen maps in all. After the twelfth had been unfolded and gazed upon, Homer leaned against the Seaweed Processing Biofuel Unit. His giddiness made him a bit dizzy. His mind raced. Rumpold Smeller's treasure was not a chest of jewels and gold, as many had suspected. It was a collection of treasure maps that would lead to lost kingdoms, secret worlds, and magical objects. It was a treasure that would lead to more treasure. "These maps will keep L.O.S.T. busy for decades," he mumbled.

"Half of the maps," Lorelei corrected. "Half of the maps will keep L.O.S.T. busy for decades. Remember, we are splitting it fifty-fifty."

"Right," Homer said. "I remember." It tormented him to think that Lorelei would take six of these maps and sell them to the highest bidder. Or worse, she'd go on six quests and the discoveries would end up on the black market for someone's private collection.

"Too bad Lord Mockingbird didn't live to see this," Hercules said. Homer nodded sadly. Lord Mockingbird had been a renowned mapmaker, and only a mapmaker could truly appreciate this trove, not only for what they led to but for the craftsmanship, the instruments used, the measurements taken, long before satellites and GPS units, some even before longitude and latitude had been figured out.

For the rest of the trip, with the autopilot in control, Homer studied the maps, Hercules wrote in the notebook, and Lorelei read Rumpold's diary. Dog ate the last of the energy bars and stretched out on the floor, his legs kicking as he drifted in and out of dreams.

Maybe he was dreaming about being swallowed by a whale shark. Or falling out of a hot air balloon. Or running from a berserk seaplane. Or maybe it was a happy dream of chasing rabbits across the goat-strewn pastures of Milkydale. Whatever the case, he was safe, his belly was full, and he was on his way back home.

PART SEVEN

HOME

34

Another Gentleman's Agreement

Homer awoke to the sound of the seaweed-
powered engine kicking into gear. He was
lying on the floor, the maps scattered around
him like wrapping paper on Christmas morning. He
raised his head. The view through the observation window showed half water, half air.

"Oh, good, you're awake," Hercules said from the
pilot's seat. He gripped the steering wheel. "Autopilot
shut off when we surfaced. City Lake is just ahead."

They'd made it. They'd finished their quest in one piece. Homer pulled a treasure map off his chest and rubbed his eyes. Sunlight streamed in through the upper half of the window. Dog lay at his side, another map covering him like a blanket. Homer pressed his nose into the back of Dog's neck, inhaling the stinky scent of basset hound. He smiled. Nothing smelled better. It was the scent of loyalty. The scent of courage. The scent of friendship. "You're a good dog," Homer whispered. Dog opened one eye, groaned, then went back to sleep.

"He's a very good dog," Lorelei said. She sat against the captain's chest, the diary propped on her knees. Dark circles clung beneath her eyes. "We wouldn't have found this diary without him. I just finished it."

"You read the whole thing?" Homer pushed the maps aside and sat up.

"Yep. I didn't sleep at all. You snore, by the way."

"Entering City Lake," Hercules announced as he turned the wheel. The water grew murky. Some fast-food containers floated by the window. A pair of mallard ducks pecked on the glass, then swam away.

"Is the diary good?" Homer asked. He wanted it to be good. He wanted it to be brilliant. But not all diaries are brilliant. Not everyone knows how to tell a story.

What if Rumpold turned out to be a terribly boring

writer? What if all her entries were like, *Dear Diary, Today I got some treasure, and then I went to bed.*

"Is it a good story?" he asked.

Lorelei smiled. "It's the best story ever!" She closed the diary and hugged it to her chest. "She lived the life I dream about. She made her own rules. No one told her what to do. Every day she faced danger and adventure. I would give anything to live that kind of life."

"But it sounds like your life," Homer pointed out.

"My life?"

"Sure." He began to fold the maps into a tidy pile. "You make your own rules. You live where you want. You eat what you want. You have no parents or teachers to tell you what to do. And you just rode a seaweed-powered submarine at hyper-speed. If that's not an adventure, I don't know what is."

"Don't forget about the hot air balloon," Hercules said. "That was definitely dangerous."

"You're right," Lorelei said. "I'm kinda like Rumpold." She squeezed the diary tighter. "I want to keep it."

Homer stopped folding. "Huh?"

"I want it. I want this diary. I want to keep it. You can have the maps."

"*Huh?*" Both Homer and Hercules did a double take.

Dog groaned, then rolled onto his back for a belly

scratch. But Homer was too stunned to notice. "You don't want the treasure maps?" he asked, his mouth falling open.

"I want to trade my six maps for the diary," Lorelei said. She stuck the diary inside the captain's chest, then got to her feet. With her hands folded behind her back, she stared out the observation window. "I think it's a fair trade. You can take all the maps and give them to L.O.S.T."

Homer got to his feet. Was she up to something? Was this another one of her plans? "Why?" he asked, scratching his matted hair. "Why would you give up the maps?"

"I want to write a book about Rumpold." She spun around and smiled. "I want the whole world to know that she was a girl who did all these amazing things. She was a girl like me."

"A book?"

"Sure. I can do it. And then I'll turn it into a movie. Maybe I'll give myself the starring role!" She laughed. "Why not? I can dress like a boy and wave a sword."

"But the treasure maps..." Homer couldn't believe what he was hearing. "I thought you wanted to be rich."

"I still have a bag of harmonic crystals. I don't need money." She held out her hand. "So, do we have a new deal? A new gentleman's agreement?"

"You sure about this?" Homer asked.

"Yep."

"Okay, but there's one more thing I want you to add to this agreement." He could hear The Unpolluter's voice in his head. *If there's a way you can keep her from blabbing, you'll save me some work.* "You can't ever tell the world about L.O.S.T. Even though you're not a member, you must agree to secrecy. If you make that part of our gentleman's agreement, then I'll agree to the trade."

"You got it," she said. "I'll never tell."

And so they shook. Hercules slid out of the pilot's seat, grabbed his notebook, and wrote, "And with a handshake, they sealed the deal that would change history." The submarine bumped into a paddleboat. "Oops," Hercules said as he rushed back to the pilot's seat and steered the sub around the paddleboat and its wide-eyed passengers.

"Does this mean you're giving up treasure hunting?" Homer asked. The question troubled him because he could never imagine making such a drastic decision. That would be like cutting out his heart.

"Give it up? No way." She flared her nostrils. "I can be a writer *and* a treasure hunter. I expect you to include me on your next quest. I mean, let's face it, you need my help. Without me, your map would still be in Milkydale and Rumpold's treasure would still be in that dragon's neck. You may not always like the way I do things, Homer, but at least I *do* things." She smiled. "I'm the yin to your yang."

Homer furrowed his brow. "The what to my what?"

"Yin and yang are polar opposites," Hercules explained as he pulled the submarine up to the lair's gate. "Even though they are different, they complement each other. Even though they are opposites, they work together."

Homer slowly nodded. There was much truth to what Lorelei had said. She was a doer; he was a dreamer. She twisted the truth to get what she wanted; he preferred honesty. And without her stealing the map, he'd be back home, waiting to grow up. Waiting to set out on the quest.

"Urrrr," Dog complained, his legs up in the air, his white belly still waiting for its morning scratch. Homer obliged.

"I promised to hold another press conference when I got back," Lorelei said. "But don't worry. I won't tell the world about the maps. I will only tell them about the diary." She pushed the button on her remote control, and the gate rose. Hercules drove them through the tunnel and into the lair's pool. Soon, they were gathered on the deck, the captain's chest at their feet, the treasure bundle in Homer's arms.

Lorelei stood frozen, her joyous mood gone as she stared into the lair. At first, Homer thought she was upset because Madame had made such a huge mess. But then, as tears pooled on her lower lids, she whispered, "Daisy."

Homer couldn't imagine what it would feel like if he went home and Dog wasn't at his side. No Dog sitting on his feet, keeping them warm while he ate breakfast. No Dog lounging beside him, chewing on straw while he milked the goats. No Dog hogging the bed, snoring and breathing dog breath all over his face. That would be very sad indeed. His gaze darted to the garbage can. Madame had dumped Daisy's body into that can. He didn't want Lorelei to look inside. Somehow, he and Hercules would move the can and—

"Daisy!" Lorelei suddenly belted, the word echoing off the stone ceiling. She leaped from the deck and ran into the lair. "Daisy!" A gray rat scurried across the floor, then clawed its way up Lorelei's jumpsuit. Lorelei hugged so hard that the rat squeaked. "Daisy, you're alive. I love you. I missed you."

"But…" Homer stepped off the submarine. "Are you sure that's Daisy? That rat looks skinny. Daisy had a big belly."

"Of course I'm sure." Lorelei hugged the rat again. The rat climbed onto Lorelei's shoulder and twitched its nose and whiskers. "But you're right. She has lost weight."

Hercules stepped close and pointed. "I'm no doctor, but I think that rat is nursing," he said. "Look at all those nipples."

"What?" Lorelei lifted the rat, revealing her underside.

Sure enough, six nipples poked out from the rat's belly. "Daisy? Are you a mommy?"

"That would explain the weight loss," Hercules said.

Daisy wiggled out of Lorelei's hands and scurried over to the vending machines. She climbed into the coin return bin. Homer, Hercules, and Lorelei gathered in front and watched as Daisy climbed into tray A3. There, in a nest of gum and candy-bar wrappers, lay five tiny, squirming pink things. Dog stood on his hind legs, trying to get a better view. "Oh, they're sooooo cute," Lorelei cooed.

Homer and Hercules raised their eyebrows. *Cute?*

"Hey!" Lorelei's cooing turned angry, and she punched Homer's shoulder. "You told me Daisy was dead. Why'd you do that? Were you trying to hurt me so I'd give up the quest?"

"No. I wouldn't do that. I wouldn't lie to you about your rat dying. I really thought she was dead." He rubbed the sore spot. Lorelei sure could throw a punch. "I saw Madame put a rat into that garbage can. I thought it was Daisy."

Lorelei narrowed her eyes in disbelief, so Homer walked over to the garbage can and opened the lid. "Oh, how sad," she said as she looked inside. "That must be the daddy rat."

Hercules peered in. "That does look like Daisy. It was an honest mistake." Then he plugged his nose and stepped away.

Lorelei gently touched Homer's shoulder. "I'm sorry I hit you. And I'm sorry I thought you'd lied to me. I'll bury him out in the museum garden. Daisy would want her babies' daddy to be buried in a nice place." It wasn't a fake apology. There was no wicked smile or snicker. Homer could tell that she meant it.

"Yeah, okay," he said. As he closed the lid, a buzzer sounded.

"Who could that be?" Lorelei asked. Homer grabbed Dog, and he and Hercules stepped into the corner, so that whoever was calling wouldn't be able to see them. Lorelei sat in her red throne and turned on the screen. "Hello?" she said. Torch's image came into focus, her hawk balanced on her shoulder, chewing on a piece of fake map. Torch had a piece of fake map stuck to her cheek and another stuck to her fingers.

"Oh, it's you," Torch said. "What's going on? Where's Madame?"

"She's not here," Lorelei said sweetly. "She's gone back to jail."

"Jail?" Torch's snake tattoo flinched. "Jail?"

"That's right," Lorelei said, folding her hands on her lap. "Is there something I can do for you?"

Torch picked the map piece from her face, but it stuck to her fingers. A glue stick fell out of her hair. "Something you can do for me? Yes, there's *something you can do for me!*"

Her face turned flaming red. "You can get over here and help me with this map, you little—" The hawk shrieked, leaped onto the table, and flew off with one of the pieces.

"What did you say?" Lorelei asked, cupping a hand around her ear. "There's some sort of problem with the connection."

"Get over here and help me put this map together!" Torch got so close to the camera, Homer could see that wobbly thing in the back of her throat.

"That's called a uvula," Hercules whispered in Homer's ear. "It looks inflamed. That's what happens when you yell too much."

"Sorry," Lorelei said, cupping a hand around the other ear. "I can't hear you. I don't know what you're saying."

Torch's face pulsed red. She pointed a glue stick at the camera and opened her mouth to shout something else, but Lorelei interrupted. "Uh-oh, you seem to be breaking up." Lorelei made buzzing sounds as she spoke. "Too… *bzzzz*…much…*bzzzz*…interference. I'm…*bzzzz*…losing…*bzzzz*…you." She pressed the button, and the screen went blank. Then she reached under the screen and unplugged it from the wall. She turned to look at the boys and broke into laughter. Homer laughed, too. So did Hercules. Dog, who didn't laugh in the way of humans, but who appreciated joviality as much as any dog, turned in a circle and barked.

Hercules laughed so hard he started coughing. After finding his first-aid kit, which was floating at the side of the pool, he helped himself to a lozenge. Then they all took drinks from the soda fountain. Homer held two cups under the green stream. Dog slurped the lime-flavored beverage, then whined for more.

After the laughter and thirst had passed, Lorelei sat on the side of the fountain and yawned. "I haven't slept in forever," she said. "I'm really tired."

"We should get going." Homer's watch indicated that it was noon in The City and that it was Friday. "I need to get back for my sister's sweet sixteen."

"Yes, and I've got to register for the World's Spelling Bee." Hercules gripped his first-aid kit.

Silence fell over the lair as the intrepid adventurers looked at one another. Was this the end? Was it time to pack up and leave? Homer wasn't sure what to say to Lorelei. Although he was eternally grateful that she'd saved his life, he still had some doubts about her. She'd been his friend. She'd been his competitor. She'd been his rescuer, his copilot, the yin to his yang. He held out his hand. "Thanks," he said, "for the great adventure."

"Anytime," she said, her cheeks dimpling. And then she hugged him, real quick. And then she hugged Hercules.

After gathering his backpack and tucking the bundle

of maps under his arm, Homer pushed Dog's rump up the lair's staircase. "Do we have to go through that spider-filled tunnel again?" Hercules complained.

"Once you exit the tortoise statue, you can use the museum elevator," Lorelei called from the bottom of the stairs. "It will take you to the museum lobby. It's the easiest way out. My security code is D-A-I-S-Y."

"Thanks," Homer called. It didn't matter if security cameras recorded his movements now. Or if a museum guide told him that dogs aren't allowed inside. He'd completed his mission, and he was on his way home.

"Hey, Homer," Lorelei called as he reached the balcony.

"What?" He peered over the railing.

She stood next to the captain's chest, the diary in her hand. "Which quest do you think you'll go on first? It would be really fun to go find that warrior queen's belt. Don't you think that would be fun?"

"Yeah. Definitely."

Twice before, he'd said good-bye to Lorelei, wondering if he'd ever see her again. But she'd managed to keep popping back into his life. Good-bye seemed unnecessary. As long as there was treasure waiting to be found, they would keep bumping into each other.

At least, that's what he hoped.

35

And the New
President Is...

When Homer, Hercules, and Dog arrived at the Mockingbird Hotel, Hercules carried Dog through the revolving door. Homer appreciated the help, though he was amazed that Hercules had any strength left, considering what they'd just been through. Even with success flowing in his veins, Homer felt as if he could sleep for a month. Tucking the treasure bundle under his arm and adjusting his backpack straps, he darted between the glass doors.

"We've got your belongings right here," the bellhop told Hercules, pointing to a suitcase, a briefcase, and a dictionary, all left behind when Hercules had followed Homer to Lorelei's lair. Hercules set Dog on the ground, then swept his beloved dictionary into his arms—a happy reunion evidenced by his wide grin. "Your friends are in the tearoom." The bellhop pointed down the hall.

Even though the tearoom's doors were closed, Ajitabh's voice roared down the hallway. "He is not a traitor! Why the devil would you spew such blasted nonsense?"

Traitor? Homer and Hercules shared a confused look. Dog, who must have recognized Ajitabh's voice, bounded down the hall, his folds of skin undulating. Homer and Hercules hurried after, stopping outside the doors to eavesdrop.

The next voice was low and rumbly, tempered by its ever-present notes of sadness. "You will never convince me that Homer has abandoned our cause."

"Nor will you convince me. There's no bloomin' proof Homer joined FOUND," Ajitabh said. A thud followed, as if he'd smacked his fist on a piece of furniture. "I won't listen to such rubbish."

Dog whined and pressed his nose against the door. Hercules and Homer leaned in closer.

"But it doesn't loo…loo…look good." Professor Thaddius Thick was the only member of the society who stuttered.

"Dang right it doesn't look good," Jeremiah Carson said with his western twang. "Those two whippersnappers went straight to that girl and joined her team. Angus saw them. What more proof do you need?"

"We need to talk to the boys," Zelda said. "But if they don't return today, we'll have to call the authorities and report them missing."

"Don't do that!" Homer cried. He grabbed the door handle and pushed. "We're here. And we're not traitors!" Dog barked, as if in agreement. Or perhaps he was happy to see all the familiar faces, because that meant there'd be some petting and some rump scratching.

The heavy scent of flowers filled Homer's nostrils as he barged into the tearoom. The room itself was a small atrium. Tropical vines climbed the walls, and potted plants hung from the ceiling. Mismatched chairs and overstuffed davenports were strewn about. A tea cart stood off to the side, its teapot steaming, its trays filled with miniature sandwiches and iced cakes.

"Homer!" Zelda strode toward him, her cape billowing. She pulled him into a hug. For a moment, he couldn't see anything but black fabric.

"You're going to suffocate the boy," Ajitabh said.

Zelda released her grip, and Homer found himself looking up into a pair of dark, serious eyes. Ajitabh folded his arms. "Well?" he said. "Where the blazes have you been? And where's Hercules?"

"I'm here," Hercules said as he dumped his belongings onto the floor.

"My dear boys." Zelda hugged Hercules, then pressed a giant hand to his cheek. "Why are both your faces covered in scratches? What terrible things have you been up to?"

"We fell out of a hot air balloon," Hercules said. "And then we…" He bit his lower lip. "Uh, maybe Homer should tell the story."

Homer looked around the room. Jeremiah Carson and Professor Thick were seated, plates of sandwiches at their sides. Zelda, who'd been stooping so she wouldn't hit the ceiling, slowly lowered herself onto a red love seat. Wisps of silver hair hung over her eyes. "Go ahead, Homer. We're listening." Ajitabh tapped his boot, his dark eyebrows raised in a this-better-be-good expression.

Homer opened his mouth, but no words came. How do you begin to tell one of the greatest stories ever?

"Go on. Tell yir story so ah can git outta here."

"Mr. MacDoodle?" Homer hadn't noticed Angus, who sat in a corner chair, half hidden by afternoon shadows.

"Aye, it's me." He held out a plate and whistled. "Come here, wee beastie, and have some vittles." Dog pranced over to Angus and inhaled the crustless assortment of cucumber, radish, and cream cheese sandwiches.

"Gosh, those look good. Can I have some?" Hercules asked. He grabbed a platter off the tea cart and shoved sandwiches into his mouth three at a time, as if he'd taken eating lessons from Dog himself. "I'm starving!" he said through stuffed cheeks. He held out the platter to Homer. When had they last eaten? Homer grabbed two, then two more.

"What are you waiting for, boy?" Jeremiah Carson stretched out his legs and rested his cowboy boots on a coffee table. "Get on with your story."

And so, after swallowing and wiping his mouth on his sleeve, Homer told them what had happened. How he'd gone to find Lorelei and get his map back. "I can't tell you where she lives, because I made a gentleman's agreement with her," he added. Everyone nodded, because among honorable treasure hunters, a gentleman's agreement is as good as law.

He told them how Lorelei had outwitted Torch and Gertrude. How the team of L.O.S.T. and FOUND had put the map together, and how Hercules had translated the riddle. How they went to the Office of Celestial Navigation, where Angus calculated the coordinates.

Then he told them how they used Ajitabh's submarine to travel to the southernmost tip of Greenland.

"You found my submarine?" Ajitabh clapped his hands. "Blimey, that's good news. I was worried Madame had sold it on the black market."

"Lorelei might let you have it," Homer said. He wasn't sure about this. Now that she was going to be a writer, she might not care about the submarine. "But then again, she might claim finders keepers."

"Finders keepers," Ajitabh mumbled. "Well, if that's the case, I can always build another one."

Homer told them how Dog found Rumpold's diary in the captain's chest, but of course he left out the smelling-treasure bit. And then he told them that Rumpold was actually a *she*.

"What a delightful surprise," Zelda said with a rare smile. "We need more girls in the treasure-hunting world."

Then Homer reached the part about how they solved the riddle and how Madame la Directeur tried to squash them with a seaplane. How they narrowly escaped and how he wore Ajitabh's diving suit and walked along the seafloor. He described the removal of the amber eyeball and the thrill of reaching into the dragon's neck and finding the treasure. But that was followed by the horror of being caught in a net. "If the whale shark hadn't crushed one of the pontoons, I probably wouldn't be here," Homer said. "And if Lorelei hadn't used the robotic arms to pull me back to the submarine, I definitely wouldn't be here. She saved my life."

"She did," Hercules said after eating another sandwich. "I saw it all happen. Lorelei saved Homer's life."

"How did Madame find you?" Jeremiah Carson asked.

"Tha's my fault," Angus MacDoodle said, sliding out of the chair. His kilt flapped against his hairy knees as he strode up to the tea cart to help himself to a cup. "Ah gave Madame the coordinates. She held me favorite telescope for ransom. And then, after she left, ah got worried tha' she might hurt the wee beastie. So ah came back here tae tell the membership what had happened." He dropped three lumps of sugar into his cup.

Homer looked over at Hercules and smiled at the realization that Lorelei had been telling the truth. She hadn't given Madame the coordinates. She hadn't been working for Madame after all.

"If you care about the wee beastie, then how come you locked us on the topmost floor?" Hercules asked. "We might have starved to death up there."

"Ah left a note for the cleaning woman," Angus said. "She would have set you free in the morning."

Homer nearly laughed. If they'd waited a few more hours, they could have avoided the death-defying balloon ride.

"Forgive me for saying, but Homer's story sounds a bit far...far...far-fetched," Professor Thick said.

"His story is true," Hercules said. "I took notes during the quest. I'm going to write up an official questing report and make each of you a copy." He opened his briefcase and shuffled through the contents. "I've got the form in here somewhere."

Ajitabh ran his hand over his beard. "Let me get this straight, Homer old chap. Are you saying that you currently possess the treasure of Rumpold Smeller the Pirate?"

"Yep." Homer held out the bundle.

Jeremiah Carson leaped out of his chair, rushed to the doors, and locked them. Professor Thick hurried around the room, pulling the curtains closed, while Zelda cleared off the coffee table. Then everyone grabbed a chair and gathered around. Wide-eyed and openmouthed, they waited, perched at the edge of their seats. Homer knew they'd each spent countless hours imagining the treasure, but nothing they'd imagined could be as good as the real thing.

As Homer unwrapped the Jolly Roger flag, the strange little creature fell onto the table. "Be careful with that thing," Hercules warned. "It could be poisonous."

"What is it?" Professor Thick asked.

"We don't know," Homer said. "It came with the treasure."

"I'm the fossil expert," Jeremiah Carson said. "Let me take a look." He poked at the dead creature with the end of a spoon. "Hmmmm. Eight barbed tentacles, black as a moonless night..."

"It looks like a squid," Zelda said.

"Why, I'll be hog-tied." Jeremiah Carson carefully turned the creature over. "You bet it's a squid, but not just any old squid. It's a vampire squid."

"Vampire?" Hercules stepped away. "It sucks blood?"

"No." Jeremiah Carson chuckled. "It got its name because of its bloodred eyes. Don't worry. The critter's not poisonous."

"Is that all ya found?" Angus asked. "A wee squiddy?"

"No," Homer said. "The squid's not the treasure. Here's the treasure." He opened the layers of waterproof wrapping and spread the pieces of parchment on the table. Gasps filled the air, followed by sighs of wonder and delight as the L.O.S.T. membership passed around the maps. Whispers of astonishment arose. Shivers darted down spines. Homer and Hercules smiled. It was a moment to be savored, more delicious than birthday cake.

"Congratulations are in...in....in order," Professor

Thick said once all the maps had been viewed. "It does appear that you boys found Rumpold's treasure."

"Dog found it, too," Hercules said.

"And Lorelei," Homer added. "Don't forget about Lorelei. She also found it."

"Then L.O.S.T. must share the booty with Lorelei and her FOUND organization," Zelda said. "But do you think we can trust her?"

"Trust her?" Jeremiah Carson spat. "Of course we can't trust her. That girl's as wily as a chicken-loving fox with a pair of wire cutters."

"She does have a cunning mind," Ajitabh said as he stroked his pointy beard. "Most impressive."

"We don't have to worry about Lorelei," Homer explained. "She made a trade. She kept the diary and we get the maps. The diary belongs to FOUND and the maps belong to L.O.S.T."

There was much discussion among the adults at this point. Homer took the opportunity to grab some of the petite iced cakes. He dropped a few onto the ground so that Dog could enjoy some vanilla buttercream and lemon sprinkles. Finally, the conversation died down and Zelda cleared her throat.

"Homer, since you claimed the treasure in the name of L.O.S.T., it will be your responsibility to keep it safe until the membership has decided exactly what to do with it." She pressed her large fingertips together. "Do you have a safe hiding place?"

Now that his sister, Gwendolyn, knew about the loose floorboard under his bed, he had no idea where to hide the treasure. He shook his head.

"L.O.S.T. has a safe-deposit box at the university's bank. We can store the treasure there," Ajitabh said.

"But the safe-deposit-box key is always kep…kep… kept by the current president," Professor Thick pointed out. "We have no current president."

Jeremiah Carson stomped his cowboy boot. "Then let's get on with it and elect a new president. I'm sick and tired of sitting around this dang hotel. I wanna get back to Montana and unearth me a mastodon tusk."

"Agreed," Zelda said. "There's no use trying to delay what needs to be done. Lord Mockingbird is gone, and we must choose his replacement. Records keeper, will you call the meeting to order?"

As Angus poured himself another cup of tea, Hercules pulled a gavel from his briefcase and cleared his throat. "I hereby call to order the eightieth meeting of the Society of Legends, Objects, Secrets, and Treasures." He tapped the gavel three times, then pulled an attendance book from his briefcase. "With the recent loss of three of our members, Lord Mockingbird the Eighteenth, Gertrude Magnum, and Torch, we currently have a membership total of nine. In attendance are Ajitabh, Zelda Wallow, Angus MacDoodle, Jeremiah Carson, Professor Thaddius Thick, myself, and Homer Pudding. Not in attendance are Sir Titus Edmund, whose whereabouts are still unknown, and The Unpolluter, who never attends meetings."

"Seven in attendance gives us a quorum," Zelda said. "So we can take a vote."

"Would someone please make a motion for the first agenda item," Hercules said.

Ajitabh rapped his knuckles on the table. "I motion that we vote for our new president."

"Here, here," Professor Thick said as he picked crumbs from his bushy mustache.

"Giddyup," Jermiah Carson said. "Let's do this thing."

"Do we have any candidates?" Hercules asked, pen in hand.

Everyone looked around. Angus's slurping and the *thwapp*ing of Dog's tail were the only sounds. Homer raised his hand and was about to say that he thought Ajitabh would make an excellent president when Hercules blurted out, "I move we vote for Homer."

All eyes rested on Homer. His cheeks felt as if someone had rubbed spicy peppers all over them. Certainly they'd all laugh and move on. But no one laughed. No one chuckled. They looked at him as if seeing him for the first time.

"It's what His Lordship wanted," Zelda said with a slow nod.

Ajitabh narrowed his eyes and stared hard at Homer. His long dark hair fell over the shoulders of his embroidered shirt. His fingertips, stained with oil and ink, marked him as an inventor. He was the most brilliant man Homer had ever met. Surely he'd volunteer himself for the job. But after a long pause, he spoke. "I believed that you were too young to be our next president. But after seeing you today, victoriously delivering a treasure the whole world has waited for, I've changed my mind."

Changed his mind? Homer's stomach clenched. Dog sneezed, spraying buttercream frosting across the floor. "You've lived up to the Pudding name, old chap. Your uncle would be bloomin' proud. Mockingbird saw your potential. He was no fool." Ajitabh stood and said, with utmost sincerity, "I nominate Homer W. Pudding to be the next president of L.O.S.T."

"I second the nomination," Zelda said.

Jeremiah Carson mumbled something, then scratched beneath his cowboy hat. "Well, I guess we could give him a try. How 'bout we do it on a temporary basis. Say, one year, just to test him out."

"That's a goo…goo…excellent idea," Professor Thick said.

Angus, who'd been quiet this whole time, grunted. "Git on with it. Ah want tae catch the next train outta here."

Homer sank against the back of the chair. Was this really happening?

Hercules picked up the gavel and tapped it three times. "A motion has been made to make Homer Winslow Pudding the next president of L.O.S.T. on a one-year trial basis. All those in favor?"

Everyone but Homer and Dog said, "Aye."

"All those opposed?" Hercules waited. Then he burst into a smile. "The motion is carried. Homer Winslow Pudding is elected by majority vote to be the next president of L.O.S.T."

Homer didn't know what to say. He felt kinda giddy, as if he'd eaten too much sugar. Dog had definitely eaten too much sugar because he was walking in a circle for no apparent reason.

"So, Mr. President, what will your first agenda item be?" Ajitabh asked with a wink.

Homer didn't need any time to think about his answer. He'd been trying to figure out a way to bring this up since the moment he returned to the Mockingbird Hotel. "I think we should let Lorelei join." He scooted to the edge of his chair and took a long breath. Then, as he spoke, he looked each member in the eyes so they'd understand that he was dead serious. "I know she's made lots of mistakes, but she's a great treasure hunter. She's one of the best. Without her, we wouldn't have Rumpold's treasure. She made a gentleman's agreement to never tell the world about L.O.S.T., and I believe she will keep her word. I think she'd make a good new member."

"Now that we've lost Torch and Gertrude, I'm the only female at the meetings," Zelda said. She pushed a silver lock from her eyes. "That doesn't seem fair. Even Dog is male." Dog stopped turning in circles, wobbled a bit, then lay on his belly and groaned. Was he overfed or simply bored? L.O.S.T. meetings aren't as exciting for dogs as they are for people.

And so, another vote was taken, and it was agreed that if Lorelei accepted, she'd be given membership.

"Oh, she'll accept," Homer said with utmost certainty. "She'll accept."

Angus grabbed his plaid suitcase and telescope. "Dinna anyone try tae follow me. Ah'm going north tae find mysel' a nice wee cave and a nice bright sky." And with that, after a quick pat to Dog's head, he hurried from the room.

"Thanks for your help," Homer called after him.

Zelda filled everyone's teacups, even Dog's. "Let us

raise our glasses and welcome our new president," she said.

"Here, here," everyone said.

As teacups clinked, Dog pawed at Homer's leg, then rolled over and stuck his own stubby legs in the air. Homer slid to the carpet. After all, just because he was the president of a secret organization didn't make him too important to scratch his best friend's belly.

"We'll share the job," he whispered in Dog's soft ear.

"Urrrr."

36

The Best Birthday Present Ever

Because the Pudding driveway was blocked by an enormous inflatable bouncy castle, the limousine stopped next to the mailbox. The engine idled as the driver waited for good-byes to be said. Homer didn't like good-byes. In the treasure-hunting business, you never know when a good-bye might be permanent.

"When will I see you again?" Homer asked.

Ajitabh smiled, though no twinkle lit in his eyes. "Only time knows the answer." He reached into his pocket and pulled out a key. Then he attached it to the chain that hung around Homer's neck, right next to his membership coin. "This key will open the L.O.S.T. safe-deposit box. You are the sole owner. Keep it close at all times."

Homer gripped the chain. "I'll never take this off. Not even when I'm in the shower."

Ajitabh set his hand on Homer's shoulder. "When I first saw you, I wasn't convinced you'd be able to follow in your uncle's footsteps. You didn't look like a treasure hunter."

"That's because when you first saw me you were hanging upside down from your cloudcopter," Homer said, remembering that spring day in the orchard. "Everyone looks weird upside down."

"Quite right," Ajitabh said. The familiar twinkle appeared in his eyes, like a star waking in the night sky. "If Drake were here, he'd burst with pride. You've done him credit and more. Perhaps I should keep calling you Mr. President."

Was he joking? Homer cringed. "That sounds strange. Please don't call me that. I'm still Homer."

Ajitabh chuckled. Then he rapped on the glass partition. The driver walked around and opened the passenger door. Ajitabh stepped out, followed by Homer and

Dog. "Your uncle used to talk about how much he missed country air—the scent of grass and goats, the fresh breeze." He inhaled. "I think it's even nicer than the scent of cloud cover."

Homer took his own deep breath. The air filled his lungs in a refreshing way, cleaning out the last remnants of The City.

Ajitabh reached down and patted Dog's head. Then he ducked back into the limousine. "Enjoy the rest of the summer," he said. "School will be starting soon enough."

"When will we—?"

"All in good time," Ajitabh interrupted. "All in good time." The driver closed the door, then settled into the driver's seat. Ajitabh's window rolled down just enough for his voice to escape. "Cheerio, Mr. President." The limousine pulled away and headed back down Grinning Goat Road. Homer watched until the license plate, MBIRD18, disappeared from view.

He sighed. *All in good time.* What kind of answer was that? A week? A month? Twenty years? Maybe it wouldn't be too long. One thing he'd learned about this whole treasure-hunting thing—it always popped up when he least expected it.

Homer had spent one last night at the Mockingbird

Hotel. He collapsed right after the election meeting and didn't stir until morning, enjoying the deep sleep of victory. And now he and Dog were back home.

A pink balloon floated past, as did a stray streamer. The farm dogs, Max, Gus, and Lulu, bounded down the driveway, their shiny coats rippling with their graceful steps. They sniffed Homer's legs and Dog's rump, then circled as herding dogs do. "Hey, there," Homer said, giving each a long pet.

The goats stuck their noses between fence boards, ever curious about the happenings on the other side. Homer stopped and scratched a few noses. One goat nibbled on his shirtsleeve; another bit off a piece of shoelace. The rest stared at him with inquiring eyes. "I'll tell you all about it later," he told them. Goats are the snoopiest of farm animals. The chickens, on the other hand, couldn't have cared less about where Homer had been or what he'd been up to. They scratched at the dirt, searching for potato bugs and worms.

When Homer and Dog reached the top of the driveway, the bouncy castle was tipping from side to side. "Hello?" Homer called.

"Hi, Homer!" Squeak slid out and landed on the gravel, his cheeks bright red, his hair matted with sweat. "I've been bouncing all day. It's really fun. I threw up two pieces of birthday cake!" Dog licked Squeak's face, then farted when Squeak squeezed him around the middle.

"Where is everyone?" Homer asked.

"The party's over. All the girls went home." Squeak scrambled to his feet. "I'm going to bounce some more. Want to bounce with me?"

"Sure, but first I'm going to tell Mom and Dad I'm home."

"Okay." Squeak climbed up the inflated drawbridge. "Whoopee!" he cried as the castle tipped from side to side.

The picnic table was covered with a pink tablecloth. Bouquets of pink balloons floated above the porch railing. Plastic spoons and cups lay strewn about the yard, along with paper crowns. Gwendolyn sat alone at the table, slumped in a chair that had been decorated to look like a throne. "Hi," Homer said.

She glared at him from beneath her brown bangs. Piles of crumpled wrapping paper circled her throne. A paper crown hung off the side of her head. "You missed it," she grumbled, her arms tightly folded.

"Sorry," he said. "Did mom give you a...a princess party?"

"Can you believe it?" Gwendolyn slumped lower. "She thinks I'm still eight years old. I wanted a roadkill theme and she chose princess."

Homer sat on the bench next to his sister. A ring of pink frosting and sprinkles was all that remained of the birthday cake. He ran his finger through and tasted strawberry. It was pretty good, but Gwendolyn wasn't a strawberry-flavored, princess-themed kind of girl. "Where's Mom and Dad?"

"Mom said she needed a nap, and Dad is driving my friends home."

Homer pulled wrapping paper from Dog's mouth. "I'm sorry I missed your party." Then he reached into his backpack. "I got you something." He pushed aside some paper plates, then set a small bundle on the table. He'd used the Jolly Roger flag to conceal the present.

The crown tumbled off Gwendolyn's head as she sat upright. "You got me something?" She carefully unfolded the flag and gasped. "What is it?"

"It's a vampire squid. It's really old." Homer waited for her reaction.

She scrunched up her face and poked at the little dried creature. "Vampire?"

"You said you wanted roadkill." Homer shrugged. "It isn't technically *road*kill. It was killed by a pirate, so I guess it's pirate-kill. Does that count?"

"Cool." Gwendolyn pinched the creature between her fingers and held it up for inspection. A huge grin broke across her face. "Really cool. This is the best present ever." And then she did something she hadn't done for a very long time. She hugged her brother. "Thank you."

"You're welcome. Thanks for doing my chores while I was gone." He hoped she'd tell him that he didn't have to do her chores for one month, as he'd promised, but she didn't. Oh well. That was Gwendolyn.

She grabbed her lab coat off the back of the throne. As she buttoned it over her party dress, she looked sheepishly at Homer. "Uh, I did something that maybe I shouldn't have done." She flipped her braids behind her shoulders. "I gave one of your weird books to a girl with pink hair. It was a book about reptiles, and it was under your bed with all your other weird stuff. You're not mad, are you? It didn't look like an important book."

"I'm not mad," Homer said, holding back a smile. *If you hadn't given her the book*, he thought, *then Rumpold's treasure might still be at the bottom of the sea.*

"Okay, then. No harm done." Gwendolyn grabbed the vampire squid and hurried off to her laboratory. "Thanks again!" she called before disappearing inside.

Homer sat at the picnic table amid the remains of the princess party. He gazed around. A few months ago, this had been his whole world—the rolling green hills, the barn with the sagging roof, the goats, chickens, and farm dogs. But now he'd traveled across the sky and beneath the ocean. He'd amassed secrets and treasures with more waiting to be found. The future was brighter than ever for this farm boy.

"Urrrr."

And the future was brighter than ever for this basset hound.

Homer knelt on the ground and pulled another piece of wrapping paper from Dog's mouth. "Come on. Let's go inside and get you some real food." Dog wagged his tail.

Homer took another long breath. Ajitabh and Uncle Drake were right. There was something special about country air. The sweet notes of mowed grass, the earthiness of dirt, the tanginess of buttercups warmed by the sun. He buried his face in Dog's fur. And the sour and saltiness of basset hound.

In other words, the beautiful scents of home.

37

The Return of Prisoner #90

No one seemed happy to see her. The prison didn't hold a welcome-back party or anything like that. They just gave her a new pair of pajamas and showed her to the old cell she'd had before.

"You're going to be in here a long time," the warden said with smug satisfaction. And then he attached a chain around her ankles so she couldn't run, couldn't climb, couldn't escape. "A *very* long time."

She wasn't allowed to work in the prison kitchen. She

wasn't allowed in the exercise yard or the TV room. The only room she could enter was the visiting room, but who would come to see her? She'd made plenty of enemies on the outside, but no friends.

That's why it was most surprising that on the sixteenth day of her incarceration, someone came calling.

Prisoner #90 sat in the chair, tapping her slippered feet. Who had the nerve to keep her waiting? Didn't anyone have any respect? She was and would always be Madame la Directeur.

She leaned forward, peering through the thick glass window, as the door on the other side opened. An old woman shuffled through. Her stained gray dress and white apron flapped against her shins; her rubber boots squeaked along the concrete floor. She adjusted her plastic shower cap, then sat.

A sour taste filled Madame's mouth. "Come to gloat?"

The Unpolluter said nothing. She scratched her blueberry-sized mole.

"Or maybe you wanted to make sure I was comfortable," Madame said sarcastically. "Maybe you were worried about me."

The Unpolluter's voice drifted through the speaker. "I came to tell you about the kids."

"The kids?" Madame snorted. "Why would I care

about the kids? I despise both of them, and I wish they'd never been born!"

"I thought you might like to know that Homer W. Pudding is the new president of L.O.S.T." A smile, ever so slight, formed on the old woman's lips. "I thought you might like to celebrate his good fortune."

Madame's body temperature rose five degrees, turning her face and neck crimson red. Hot breath shot from her nostrils, as if she were part dragon. "President?" she hissed. *"President?"* She shot to her feet. The ankle chain tightened as she lunged at the glass partition.

"Sit down," the guard hollered.

Madame's body shook with fury as she lowered herself back onto the chair. "President," she whispered. "A twelve-year-old boy will lead L.O.S.T. What is the world coming to?"

"That's not all," The Unpolluter said cheerfully. "There's something about the girl I thought you should know."

"That girl is a menace. I took her off the street, gave her a job, and she turned against me. She stole my..." Madame hesitated.

"She stole your lair," The Unpolluter said. Madame's eyebrows darted upward. "Don't be so surprised. Of course I know about the lair. It's my job to keep my eyes open. Besides, I've been watching over the girl ever since she was left at the orphanage."

"What do you mean, watching over her?" Madame asked. "You've been protecting her?"

"No, not protecting. My job is to protect L.O.S.T. The girl needs no protection. She has to be strong and make her own way. I've simply been keeping track of her."

"Why would you do that? She's a street urchin, nothing more."

"But she is more. Much more." The Unpolluter stood. She pulled up her kneesocks and smoothed out her apron. "I'm so happy I didn't have to get rid of her. I'm so happy she'll be joining L.O.S.T. The organization could use her talents. Her blood runs true."

Once again, Madame's face burst with color. She took a ragged breath. "Her... *blood*?"

"Yes, her blood." The Unpolluter headed toward the exit but turned just long enough to deliver the information she'd come to deliver. The thing that would haunt Madame la Directeur for the rest of her days.

"Lorelei's last name is Smeller."

Madame clenched her hands in her lap and tried, with all her might, to control the surprise that hit her like a piano dropped right onto her head. The pink-haired street urchin was a Smeller.

"A Pudding and a Smeller working together. Imagine that," The Unpolluter said with a smile. "There's no telling what amazing things those two will accomplish." Then, with a little wave, she left.

The visiting room door closed with a thud.

Prisoner #90's scream echoed throughout Soupwater Prison.

Dear Reader,

Because Drake H. Pudding was a very important part of Homer's life, and because his advice was more valuable to Homer than any material treasure, I've decided to include some of his quaint sayings in this addendum. Feel free to quote him. It will make you sound wise beyond your years.

"It is a sad truth of human history that those who dare to be different are often judged to be not quite right in the head."

"Only the curious have something to find."

"A treasure hunter must always cover his tracks and night provides the best cover of all."

"Solitude is the treasure hunter's destiny.... You will face the final test of endurance and intellect on your own."

"All that sparkles is not splendid."

"Sometimes a map doesn't take you where you want to go."

"Never ignore lunch or a hunch. One can fuel the body while the other can fuel a discovery."

"If we had one-tenth of an ant's determination, we could do anything. With determination, anything is possible."

Acknowledgments

I've written quite a few books thus far, and what I've learned is this: Writing can be gosh-darn lonely, and unless you want to be like Angus MacDoodle and live like a hermit, you must close the laptop and go out into the world for guidance and the occasional pat on the back.

For many pats on the back, I offer my thanks to my family—Isabelle, Walker, and Bob.

For priceless guidance, for reading my first drafts, and for helping me through my competing bouts of self-doubt and delusions of grandeur, I offer my thanks to Carol Cassella, Claire Dederer, Elsa Watson, and the newest editor on the team, Pam Garfinkel. Christine Ma copyedited the manuscript, and she's the best copy editor I've ever worked with! Thank you, Christine.

I couldn't have translated the Latin without Elsa Watson, Susan Fidelman, and Anna Backer. As for the Scottish lilt, I relied on Margaret Trent, who hails from that glorious country. Thank you, thank you!

Michael Bourret and Julie Scheina, well, really, do I need to keep thanking you in every single book I write? For Pete's sake, don't you know by now that I think you're both wonderful?

To my readers, thank you for continuing this adventure with me. Without you, I would be all alone in my imaginary worlds. I love getting your letters, and I hope you'll keep visiting me at www.suzanneselfors.com.